John Niven

Kill 'Em All

WILLIAM HEINEMANN: LONDON

1 3 5 7 9 10 8 6 4 2

William Heinemann
20 Vauxhall Bridge Road
London SW1V 2SA

William Heinemann is part of the Penguin Random House group of companies
whose addresses can be found at global.penguinrandomhouse.com.

Penguin
Random House
UK

First published by William Heinemann in 2018

www.penguin.co.uk

A CIP catalogue record for this book is available from the British Library.

ISBN 9781785151576 (Hardback)
ISBN 9781785151583 (Trade Paperback)

Typeset in 13.5/15.5pt Perpetua
by Integra Software Services Pvt. Ltd, Pondicherry

Printed and bound in Great Britain by Clays Ltd, Elcograf S.p.A.

Penguin Random House is committed to a sustainable future for
our business, our readers and our planet. This book is made
from Forest Stewardship Council® certified paper.

MIX
Paper from
responsible sources
FSC® C018179

Kill 'Em All

John Niven was born in Irvine, Ayrshire. He is the author of the novella *Music from Big Pink* and the novels *Kill Your Friends, The Amateurs, The Second Coming, Cold Hands, Straight White Male, The Sunshine Cruise Company* and *No Good Deed*.

For Keith

'All empires are built of fire and blood.'

(Pablo Escobar)

January

ONE

Hertfordshire, England. Friday 20 January 2017, 6.40 a.m.

It is too cold in the Maybach.

I tell Grahame to turn the A/C off. Cold outside too, winter fog in the black night, a light sleet tipping against the smoked glass as the fields slide silently by, the headlights picking out the words 'Luton Airport, 3 miles' and then the sign vanishing behind us as we come off the M1. I'm in the back, reading the newspapers (the inauguration, later today) and the trades – *Billboard*, *Variety*, *Music Week* – on my phone. I note with neither joy nor rancour that on the singles chart it has been a good week for the Chainsmokers, Ariana Grande and Bruno Mars. Bad week (again) for Unigram, whose share price has (somehow) managed to drop even further. The lead story on the cover of *Billboard* is about Unigram's biggest artist, Lucius Du Pre, who is beginning rehearsals for his comeback shows this summer – twenty nights at

Madison Square Garden in New York, then twenty at London's O2 Arena.

There was a time, a very long time ago, when reading the trades was a weekly source of anxiety. Colleagues and competitors rising (traumatic) and falling (pleasurable). Firings and hirings. Now? Today? It's almost like reading reports on a battle whose front lines are far away from me. In another country. On another planet.

A quick recap, in case you're in the Taliban or something, living in a cave, making nail bombs and inserting yourself into goats. This is from my Wikipedia entry: '*Following a successful career in the music industry as an A&R manager, in 2003 Stelfox created the ABN television talent show* American Pop Star, *on which he initially acted as one of the judges.*' Yeah, and it was all good too, until this kid who thought he was Jesus took the whole brand down the shitter in the US. You saw the show. Trailer-park fucks performed Mariah Carey songs for the pleasure of other trailer-park fucks who used up their welfare cheques phoning in to vote for them. We licensed the rights like crazy – at one point we were running in thirty-two countries – until we sold the format in late 2011 and I cashed out to the tune of two hundred million dollars. That was six years ago. Semi-retirement at forty-two. What's it been like? you ask. What do I get up to? How am I living? Well, take the past month . . .

In mid-December I left the house in freezing London (7,500 square feet in Holland Park) to the staff (Roberta my London housekeeper, Grahame who is driving right now) and we (we being me, a couple of girls I know and my mates Hedge Fund Paul and Investment Banking Mel) took a private jet to Barbados, where we boarded the yacht *Mistrial*. It's the second time I've rented it and it's really something. You should see it. Just under two hundred feet long, seven bedrooms, including (for me) the huge master suite, space for up to fifteen crew, gymnasium, jacuzzi, 5,000-mile range, max speed of sixteen knots – perfect for touring the Med or the Caribbean.

In Barbados we larged it in the usual spots with the usual suspects – in and out of Sandy Lane, the Cliff, Cin Cin, the Tides and Daphne's with Tod, Wayne, Philip, Simon, Lev, Vlad, Roman and a revolving, interchangeable cast of TIBs (Top International Boilers) – the Kellys and Meghans and Svetlanas and Brooks and Whatevers. (The girls all share some common characteristics: none of them over thirty, all with giant racks, tiny waists and the ability to laugh long and hard at our jokes. The guys all have something in common too. Can you guess what it is? That's right – no one is fucking poor.)

After a week or so of this utter nonsense we upped anchor and cruised to Grand Cayman – via St Lucia, Montserrat and Turks and Caicos – where I had some business to take care of. Your procedure on all of these islands you visit will be much the same. Drop anchor and then speedboat (the *Mistrial* has a VanDutch. Ten-seater, it can do 60 mph easy) into town for a long, boozy lunch at the hottest spot available. While doing this you will attract the eye of many of the girls who haunt the cool restaurants around the harbour and who have watched you anchor and come ashore. Back to the boat for an afternoon nap and then maybe some swimming over the side, some board games, bugger about on the jet skis, before the cocktails start on deck at 7 p.m. A few of those and we're into the VanDutch again and over to town for dinner at another local sex pit. After that there'll be a nightclub where we'll pick up a few of the superyacht groupies who've been eyeing us all night and then back to the yacht where we'll pump the tunes on deck and party until 3 or 4 a.m. when you slope off downstairs with whoever. You'll wake up in the early afternoon, one of the crew will take the TIBs back to shore and you'll do the whole thing all over again.

After a solid fortnight of this I actually quite enjoyed getting to the Caymans and taking care of business for a couple of days. Edgar, head of the team who look after my accounting, had flown out from London with some forms that needed signing in connection with the several companies I have in Grand Cayman. Of course Cayman isn't a tax shelter any more. How dare you. They've taken to calling themselves an 'international finance centre'. Which is great. It's like Ian Huntley calling himself a 'bathing coordinator'. Sometimes, when I think of the schools, the hospitals and the roads that aren't getting their piece of my cash, I swear to God, it's all I can do not to get my cock out and start wanking. Do you pay tax? I'm guessing you do. You're probably paying somewhere between 25 and 45 per cent of the disgraceful pittance you call an income. In fiscal 2015–2016 I paid tax at a rate of roughly 12 per cent. It's too much of course. Every January I find myself screaming at Edgar, '*The cunts want how fucking much?*'

But there is no tax here in Grand Cayman. None. You get to keep all your money and pass it down as you see fit. It is the ultimate expression of trickle-down. How's that working out for the indigenous population you ask? Well,

40 per cent of the toerags live in poverty and a packet of fish fingers will cost you eight and a half quid. What a fucking result.

Take a look at your life. Go on. Your gaff. The clothes you wear. The restaurants you eat in. The holidays you take. Pretty good, eh? You're not doing too badly.

Mate, you're *nothing.*

In the world of pure money, your life is a urinal. A human toilet. Your very existence a suicide job. The average UK salary is twenty-eight grand a year. I made twenty times this betting against the pound before Brexit. I made even more than that with a single bet on the US election. Why? How did I know to do this? How did I pull these rabbits out the hat while you're sat there scratching your horrific balls on your pleather sofa, ringing Domino's for an American Paedophile with hot-dog crust while your monstrous beastwife lumbers around in her jeggings, her feet creaking and cracking on your millimetre-thick laminate wood floor, her IMAX-sized fucking chobble getting in the way of the single most valuable asset you own: your massive plasma-screen TV? (Doubtless bought on credit from some high street den called TolerHouse! at an interest rate of 3,000 per cent per annum.) I pulled this off because I learned one very important thing in the music industry, something gleaned from two decades of pushing reeking musical log after reeking musical log down the throats of idiots, something that has stood me in very good stead in the past year. It is this:

Never overestimate the taste of the general public.

Music, TV, movies, furniture, food, architecture, politics – there is absolutely no depth to which those cunts will not sink. They will willingly vote themselves into living in an extreme, real-life version of *The Road* for eternity for the chance to say 'fuck all Pakis' once. Where there's that kind of thinking going on, there's *always* cash to be made.

Anyway, we spent a few days in the Caymans before boarding the jet back to Heathrow, where the plan was to hang out in London before the traditional end-of-January skiing trip to Courchevel with a few of the guys I used to work with in the music industry. (The successful ones of course: not the ones who went mad, or broke, or into rehab.) But then this plan was interrupted by what can only be described as a distress call. From Trellick.

You'll remember James Trellick. Lawyer.

We came up together, back in the nineties. Trellick is now managing director of Unigram in Los Angeles. We stay in touch, celebratory emails when a mutual adversary is publicly destroyed, the odd lunch or dinner when he's in London or I'm out there. We lived near each other in Beverly Hills for a while, back in the noughties, when I was still doing the show. Now you'd always have used one word to describe Trellick, that product of Eton and Oxford: 'unflappable'. Not last night. Last night Trellick was distinctly ... flapped. He couldn't go into it on the phone, couldn't put anything in writing, but it was urgent enough that he wanted me in LA this morning. Urgent enough that he agreed to my enormous consultancy fee just to take a look at his problem. Urgent enough that it awakened something within me that very rarely gets an outing these days: genuine curiosity.

'Here we go, boss,' Grahame says from the driver's seat.

I look up to see the lights of Luton Airport coming up ahead. I picture what will be happening inside it. Tattooed mums and dads punching their screaming kids around KFC. Fights and rows in the two-mile-long queues. Crazed Arsenal fans smashing back pints of Tits in the Great British Boozer at seven o'clock in the morning, all of them stunned that their quid now gets them about half a euro, none of them having seen that coming when they proudly ticked the box marked 'LEAVE'. Right at the last moment, when I've had just enough time to convince myself of an alternative life fantasy where we actually drive up to Luton Airport and I have to walk into the terminal and witness first hand all the horrors I've just been picturing, Grahame makes a left at the roundabout, the minty-green signage of the Holiday Inn Express on our right now, and we are turning into the familiar entrance for the RSS Private Jet Centre. Over behind the small VIP building I can see the plane, a Gulfstream G550, and on its tail the Unigram logo.

Imagine it. Imagine flying commercial.

But more than all this, more than wanting to help an old mate out (yeah, right), I have to admit, great though life is at the moment, there is the odd day when I worry that a lifestyle like the one I've been outlining here could be described as a tiny bit … vacuous. So I'm retired, but I'm not. Because you have to do something, don't you? You'd go fucking mad otherwise. So I work occasionally as a 'consultant'. If the project is interesting enough, and the fee large enough, I'll get on a plane. Like a few years back, when Warner Music bought EMI. I helped put that together, behind the scenes. A few months' work for seven figures that, pleasingly, provided a bonus opportunity: engineering the firing of a few clowns who'd had the temerity to offend me back in the nineties. (Like the great man says in *Think Big*: '*I love getting even when I get screwed by someone. Always get even. When you are in business you need to get even with people who screw you. You need to screw them back 15 times harder. You do it not only to get the person who messed with you but also to show the others who are watching what will happen to them if they mess with you. If someone attacks you, do not hesitate. Go for the jugular.*') There's also, and I hate to admit this, been the slight niggle recently that I might have got out of the music industry at the wrong time ...

The music industry. What do you think happened to it? If you ask the man on the street, the average mongoloid shuffling his hump from the boozer to the bookies, you'll get something like the following: '*Oh yeah. It's over. The Internet destroyed the music business. You don't need record companies now. My mate Glen put his own album out online and sold eight hundred copies. The gatekeepers are gone, man.*'

I pick up my phone and open my Twitter account. I find a tweet I favourited last week, from one Roger McGuinn, the former guitar player in 1960s proto-indielosers the Byrds. Roger says: 'Pandora played 'Eight Miles High' 228086 times in the second quarter of 2016 and paid me $1.79.'

A quid and a half for a quarter of a million plays.

After a moment, and even at this ungodly hour of the morning, I am laughing so hard that Grahame has to ask me if I'm OK. Now, granted, it got a bit scary for a while, back there in the early noughties, what with Napster and everything, but in the end it worked out fine. We did it again. Can you believe it? From sheet music, to the 78 rpm shellac disc, to singles and albums, to cassettes, to CDs, to now, today, the Internet: the music industry has once again managed to insert a ten-foot dildo made of broken glass into the anus of an entire generation of musicians. That royalty break clause, the one that covers 'all technologies yet to be discovered', the one that we've been putting into contracts for the last thirty-odd years, that was a fucking doozy. I'd like to go back in time and shake the hand of the scumbag animal lawyer who came up with that beauty. Back in the day, in the late eighties and early nineties, it meant that for a while we got away with paying artists the same royalty on a CD single we sold for four quid as we did on vinyl that sold for half that. Today it means some songwriter looks at Spotify and sees his one million plays have earned him a fiver. Where's the rest of that money going? *Where do you fucking think?* The gatekeepers are gone? That's right, mate – they're in your house, eating everything in the fridge and doing your wife.

I send a couple of pro-Trump tweets from my troll accounts ('#godonald! #MAGA #inauguration') to take my mind off my pre-flight anxiety while Grahame deals with the luggage and the whole check-in palaver, out there in the chill January dawn. Passport and security take all of two minutes. ('Hi, sir! Nice to see you again.') When I do this, I spare a thought for you out there – the dear, the gentle – taking your belt and shoes off, furiously scrabbling through your bag for that laptop or iPad, wearily walking back through the scanner, then extending your arms skywards as the guy with the wand does his stuff, the whole thing taking an eternity because, in the queue ahead of you, there are people who, today, in 2017, seemingly haven't been on a plane since Mohamed Atta and his lads did their thing back in 2001. Who don't understand about the whole laptop, belt and shoes deal. Who are utterly *astonished* when they are asked to take these things off/put them in a tray/whatever. By the time you stumble out of security two hours later you're needing that pint of Tits in the Dog and Lettuce. You're suicidal and you haven't even left the fucking airport yet.

I stride briskly across the tarmac, jog up the gangplank – to more effusive hellos from the pilots – and settle into my favoured seat on a Gulfstream G550 – front right window facing forward. A stewardess appears with a silver jug of steaming coffee and plates of fruit, freshly baked croissants, pastries and smoked salmon. Enough to feed the eighteen seats in the jet even though I am the only passenger. The stewardess is blonde, in her late thirties, and a definite DB, although she is good-looking enough to have possibly once been an RB. (The Three Categories of Boiler: Romancing Boilers: singers or actresses or models who have found a certain level of fame. Here you know you are in for the long-haul job, for a fair few dinners and drinks and movies and going to awards ceremonies together and fuck knows what else before you can fair and square get your cock out. Then there are Doable Boilers: aspiring singers, actresses and models on the way up, or very attractive girls working in the industry or a related field – fashion, film, whatever. These are the type you take out for a few drinks, dinner, then at the end of that first date, you get them back to your place where, of course, you get your cock out and it's all good. Then there are Bogs

Boilers – the kind of skanks who hang out on the fringes of any creative industry who are basically a notch above groupie. A Bogs Boiler you can drag into a toilet cubicle and smash her back door in within fifteen minutes of meeting her. As with any class system under late-period capitalism there is some fluidity between the ranks. A Doable Boiler can, with enough success, become a Romancing Boiler. A Bogs Boiler can, with a little maturing and self-respect, become a Doable Boiler. Conversely, a Romancing Boiler, with enough failure and passing years, can fall to become a Doable Boiler. Almost never will a Romancing Boiler suffer a fall so complete as to become a Bogs Boiler. Courtney Love, say, would be a notable exception here.)

I ignore the food as I settle back into the cream leather and light a cigarette. (Again, I think of you, out there in seat 44F, with your two foot of seat space, the remains of a microwaved tray of eyelids and anuses in front of you, the three-hundred-pound housewife with screaming infant to your left, the Somali marathon runner who has come straight from his latest triumph without showering to your right, your every pore screaming for nicotine as you gaze without hope at a 'No Smoking' sign that will remain resolutely illuminated even in the event of nuclear war. I feel for you, I truly do.) About that pre-flight anxiety. It never used to bother me, getting on a plane. Weirdly I've become more nervous about it in the last few years. It's two things, I think. Obviously there's the Russian roulette factor: the more you fly, and I fly a lot, the more bullets you put in the chamber. But it's also this: I have so much to lose these days. Looking for a distraction, I pick up the inflight magazine (called something like *High Flyer* or *True Player* or *Just Rape the Poor*) and flip through pages of adverts for private islands, walk-in humidors and yachts with helipads, stuff aimed solely at people like me. I stop at a lifestyle feature, the ageing wife of some Hollywood studio boss – she's very much like a sixty-year-old version of the stewardess on this flight, old now, but surely a hard-gobbling miracle sometime around the late seventies – is giving a tour of her Pacific Palisades home. Accompanying the article is a photograph, clearly taken many years ago, of her cradling her son (now a famous actor, in and out of rehab. Remember: if you *have* to stop drinking you're a fucking loser) when he was a baby. I find myself staring at the baby for a long time: the huge limpid pools of his eyes, the softness of his skin almost palpable even in this two-dimensional form. Unsettled for reasons I cannot name, I toss the magazine aside and focus my gaze on a more reassuring sight – the buttocks of the stewardess, bending over in the galley kitchen up ahead as she gets something out of a low cupboard.

Ok, I confess. There's something I've not been telling you. Another reason I'm bothering to do all this …

I had a moment this winter, down in the Caribbean. We were docked in the Tobago Quays for a day or two, fucking around on the deck, when suddenly, a shadow fell over me. I looked up and saw Geffen's boat, the *Rising Sun*, coming in to dock beside us, all 453 feet, five floors and eighty-two rooms of it, blocking out the rising sun, looming over us like the Death Star above a Fiat 500. And, in that instant, I realised just how fucking poor I was. *You think you're a player?* I might as well have been downing that pint at Luton

Airport myself. I tried to repeat the lulling mantra I find calms me in moments of stress – *I am Steven Stelfox. I am worth three hundred million dollars* – but it wasn't working.

I stood there with one thought.

I need to earn some proper money.

Because three hundred mil is *nothing* these days. I need to sort this out. Go big or go home.

So I am going on a journey. Jesus Christ, not that kind of 'journey'. Not the kind of journey the simpering slags, skanks and bumboys think they undertake on the kind of TV programmes you watch. Not the kind of journey that celebrities claim to have been on when they're flogging their book or their movie or whatever. These kinds of journeys are all lies designed to get you to part with your cash. These kinds of journeys imply that the people involved have learned something. That they have grown in some way.

I will learn nothing.

I will not grow.

I am fully formed.

Come on now.

Come with me.

TWO

Malibu, California. Thursday 19 January, 10.50 p.m.

The party was beginning to wind down.

Lucius propped himself up on his raft of pillows and surveyed the room. Some of his guests were still laughing and chatting in the corner by the picture windows overlooking the five thousand acres of grounds, the Pacific Ocean visible in the distance in the daytime. A few were still engaged with the movie showing on the cinema-sized screen on the wall opposite his bed (an advance screener of Universal's *Despicable Me 3*). And three, including Jerry and Connor, were stretched out on his bed, Jerry's head pleasingly close to Lucius's hand. Opened bottles of Pinot Noir and Skyy vodka were scattered around the room. He ruffled the straw-blond mop close to him, its texture feeling amazingly thick and lustrous under his touch. Everything felt good, looked good. Man, Dr Ali had really come through tonight. He might have to have

another shot of candy ... just one more before bed?
Before his milk? Maybe that would be too much? Then
again – who was anyone to tell him what was too much?
He was Lucius Du Pre. The Emperor of Pop. He'd sold
over five hundred million albums. He was adored by
millions as a living god. He'd agreed to do this fucking
comeback tour – at fifty years old! – to make everyone
else happy. He could have a little more candy if he
wanted, right?

He picked up the phone next to the bed and rang Dr
Ali, who lived just ten minutes away, in the Malibu hills,
overlooking the PCH1. Lucius wished Ali would take up
his offer of a cottage within the Narnia grounds, but the
doctor valued his independence. Ali seemed surprised to
be getting another call so soon, but he brooked no complaint
(he had no cause to on his retainer) and said he'd be right
over. Lucius hung up and smiled, picturing the black bag
glistening on the passenger seat of the doctor's Porsche
(leased by Lucius of course) making its way towards him.
He stretched out and looked at his body – still thin, after
all these years. (No surprise, for many years he only ate
one small meal every other day.) The skin on his stomach
though, that didn't look good. Mottled, brownish-grey
patches. The last operation. He'd have to go back in. Thank
God it hadn't affected his face yet. Though down there,
around what his daddy used to call your 'peanuts' ('*oh yeah,
get my peanuts in there too, get 'em in your mouth*') was starting
to look pretty bad. He was surprised some of them didn't
scream.

Talking of screaming, he became aware of a noise,
breaking in on his consciousness, rupturing his buzz. Two

of his guests were having an argument that seemed to be ending in tears.

'Hey, Jonah, what's up?' Lucius called over to the window bay in his unusually high, piping voice.

'Nothing,' Jonah, a relative newcomer, said sulkily.

Lucius looked at the Disney clock on the wall. It *was* getting late.

They'd had a grand afternoon around the ranch, visiting all the artistic garden statues featuring children in various poses, going to his petting zoo, riding on his railroad – on the little steam locomotive named *Betsy* after his mother. They'd gone on his Ferris wheel, his carousel, the zip wires, the octopus, the roller coaster, the bumper cars and, finally, they'd spent a good hour in the amusement arcade, playing the slots and the video games. But now it was nearly eleven o'clock, and there'd been a fair bit of liquor in the mix once they'd got back here. Not a crazy amount. Just enough Jesus Juice and Holy Spirit to get the party going. Yes, a grand day out. But still, tempers could get frayed around this time of night.

Especially when your average guest was aged twelve.

The Emperor would soon have to start making decisions. He looked at the two mops of hair on the bed close to him. Jerry and Connor. Connor had been his 'special' friend for the last few years, the one who would be invited to stay overnight when the other guests were being corralled down the hallway, to be collected by parents, or driven back to their homes in LA by Marcus or Jay in the customised Hummer. Connor was beautiful. But Connor was nearly fourteen now. He was starting to get a little bit ... hairy. His voice was deepening. And – there was no getting away from this – he'd been putting on a few pounds recently. Those bags of cookies and tubs of Ben & Jerry's late at night, while they watched movies, until the milk kicked in and Lucius could finally sleep. More recently Connor had been given to tantrums and outbursts too. Ah, the teenage years. It must be hard, Lucius thought. (Lucius hadn't really had any. By the time he was twelve he was on the road. Holiday Inns and soundchecks. Concrete arenas and tour buses. Airline food and interviews. And his father. Always his father. Saying it hadn't been good enough. That he'd missed a vocal cue. Fluffed a dance step. Not sucked hard enough. There had always been something. His belt buckle whipping down through the rented light of some hotel room.)

Whereas Jerry. Jerry was just about to turn twelve. The ideal age. He was so sweet and innocent. But not too innocent. The ideal combination. Yes, Lucius decided. It would be Jerry tonight. The heart wants what it wants.

He thumbed one of the speed dials on the phone and got Marcus. He whispered as he used his code word. 'Platypus. Jerry.'

'S'cuse me, guys. Nature calls,' Lucius said, slipping off the huge bed and heading down the small, narrow corridor that connected his 'entertaining' bedroom from his 'sleeping' bedroom. This second bedroom he was entering was much smaller – around twenty feet by fifteen – than the enormous one he had just left, which was on the proportions of a grand drawing room at Versailles. He went into the little bathroom off this bedroom and rummaged through the pharmacy of pills in the medicine cabinet: as well as the harder stuff doled out by Dr Ali –

the Percodan, Demerol and Dilaudid – Lucius was on a bewildering regime of mood-stabilising drugs: Xanax, Klonopin, Ativan, Serax and Librium. They had also experimented with beta blockers like Inderal and Tenormin and more exotic antidepressants like Norpramin, Elavil, Sinequan and Desyrel. The pills, sometimes dozens of them, were brought to Lucius in a champagne glass every morning and he washed them down with a beaker of orange juice. They helped to still the voices in his head. The voices that sometimes told him odd things. He sat on the toilet and popped a Valium to hold him over until Ali got here, crunching it as he played with himself and read the Bible.

'Platypus, Jerry' meant that the following would now be happening. Marcus and Jay would come into the master bedroom and tell the kids the party was over, but that they'd all be back out real soon. Some of them would ask where Lucius was and they'd be told he had to attend to some important business. The kids would be walked out to the waiting cars, except for Jerry, who would be taken aside and told – breathlessly, excitedly – that Lucius had asked if he'd like to sleep over for the night and Jerry's parents would be informed. (No one ever said no. No one.) It was the perfect arrangement – one that prevented Lucius from having to deal with the single thing he hated most in life: confrontation. He hated confrontation. He just wanted everything to be beautiful.

Being constantly surrounded by beauty did not come without its attendant costs. In order to keep Narnia running to Lucius's satisfaction, the estate required the following: thirty gardeners, a staff of fourteen who maintained and ran the twenty-four / seven amusement park (Lucius never knew when the urge for a visit might take him), and an eight-man security team, including Marcus and Jay, his praetorian guard. Within the 13,000-square-foot main house there was a team of four cooks on constant rotation. There was his butler Teddy and four permanent cleaning staff. His drivers.

A full-time staff of this size did not come cheap at the best of times. And, given Lucius's idea of what constituted 'the best of times', there were also regular, considerable 'thank you' payments to be made on top of the salaries. Payments his lawyers (and those lawyers also added up) took to be necessary for keeping everyone happy, harmonious, loyal and – above all – *quiet* about what went on at Narnia. Add it all up, whistles and bells, and you soon understood how it cost Lucius a little over two million dollars a month to live the way he wanted to live. (Lucius of course could no more have told you this figure than he could have embarked on a conversation about politics or Renaissance art. He just wanted whatever he wanted whenever he wanted it. But even Lucius could dimly see that the way he liked to live was somehow linked to the fact that he was having to do these dreaded comeback shows.) And how did he live, one of the bestselling recording artists of all time, a man with a record-breaking fifteen Grammys, a man rich beyond imagining? With the insomnia, the sleeping through the afternoon, rarely out of his pyjamas, the watching movies all night, the eating ice cream and never leaving the estate, sometimes not leaving his bedroom for days on end ...

From a distance, to the impartial observer, Lucius's lifestyle resembled nothing more than a study in terminal depression.

He looked up from Revelation (*'Yet you have a few people in Sardis who have not soiled their clothes. They will walk with me, dressed in white, for they are worthy'*) as he heard the squelch of the alarm sound and saw the red light above the sink flashing. He'd had sensor pads implanted in the floor of the corridor that led to his private chambers. They let you know when someone was fifty yards away. Even at a brisk pace it took someone the best part of a minute to cover fifty metres. A minute was long enough to, you know …

Lucius sat and read the Bible some more and thought about white. White. It could be so beautiful, for the shows. Everyone, all the backing singers, the musicians, robed in white, walking with him, for they were worthy. There were other things in Revelation that made Lucius anxious (*'the cowardly, the unbelieving, the vile, the murderers, the sexually immoral, those who practise magic arts, the idolaters and all liars – they will be consigned to the fiery lake of burning sulphur'* – he didn't like the sound of that one bit) but this, this could be so … beautiful. His favourite word. He'd talk to Lance about it in the morning. Lance Schitzbaul. His manager. The man who dealt with all the confrontation Lucius spent his life avoiding.

After a moment of contemplation (about the only thing he did on the toilet these days, his bowels having been almost completely seized up by the daily, colossal doses of uppers and downers) he got up and looked at himself in the mirror. That skin, around his ears, was it reddish? Peeling? Revealing pale skin beneath the lustrous brown?

Lucius, they'd told him since he could walk, walked like a black man. He danced like a black man. He sang like a black man. Unfortunately, and to his never-ending rage, he'd been born white. The last two decades had seen a series of costly, ambitious and, in some cases, strongly ill-advised operations to correct this situation. He'd experimented with skin dyes and injections. With pigmentation drugs, creams and elixirs. Ten years ago he'd travelled to Japan for a procedure that had resulted in him looking like a Hiroshima victim who'd been spattered with brown paint and had left him unable to go out in public for six months. Right now Lucius looked about the best he ever did – like a white man who has spent months alternating between hundred-degree direct sunshine (he loved the heat, he always felt cold) and a tanning bed. Which is to say, just the right side of crazy. To Lucius the movie *Soul Man* was a tragedy far sadder than anything wrought by Shakespeare.

There was a gentle knock at the bedroom door. Lucius tiptoed out of the bathroom and opened it. There stood little Jerry, already in a pair of the guest pyjamas (Disney ones of course – Lucius bought them by the crate) and clutching his toothbrush. 'Jerry!' Lucius said. 'You gonna stay over? Wanna watch another movie?'

'Yeah!' Jerry said. 'Can we have ice cream again?'

'You bet! Look ...' Lucius gestured to his bed, where a tub of Caramel Chew Chew and two spoons was already on the nightstand. An advance screener of *Smurfs: The Lost Village* (admittedly a movie too young for Jerry's tastes, but exactly right for Lucius's) was already paused on the TV. 'Go on and scoot into bed. I'll be right back.'

Lucius went off down the hall back to the entertaining bedroom, which had already been straightened up by the staff. He took a seat by the window and, presently, heard the squelch of the approach alarm and then the soft knock at the door.

'Come,' Lucius said.

Dr Ali entered. 'Good evening, Lucius,' he said. Always formal. The doctor was Iranian, in his sixties, with a thick beard and moustache. He'd got out in '79, when the Shah got in.

'Hi!' Lucius said.

'Would you like your milk now?'

'Not yet. I want another bit of candy first!' Lucius was beaming, excited as a ten-year-old.

'Hmmm.' The doctor hesistated. As a physician Dr Ali knew the risks involved. 'Candy' was the code they used for what was basically a high-end pharmaceutical speedball: part morphine, part methamphetamine. Lucius had already had two shots of this today. 'Milk' was more serious and was what Lucius used at bedtime every night: propofol. A drug used in procedural sedation. So, yes, Dr Ali definitely had his reservations about alternately shooting Lucius up with speed and then general anaesthetic. But more than this it was the tedium that it would entail: it was already after eleven o'clock. A shot of candy at this time would mean Du Pre would be up for several hours – taking his pleasures in what the staff called the 'romper room' – before Ali had to return to administer the milk sometime around 3 a.m. Infuriatingly, the good doctor had a twenty-two-year-old honey waiting for him at home. A gorgeous, but decidedly simple, Du Pre fan he'd been introduced to at a club in Hollywood last week. (Another undoubted perk of the job.)

'Hmmm?' Lucius said. 'Uh, what's with the hmmm?' Lucius didn't sound like an excited ten-year-old any more. He sounded like Joel Silver with a hangover.

'Not a thing,' Ali said, suddenly beaming. Lucius Du Pre was his client after all. (And it helped, Ali found, if you thought in terms of clients rather than patients.) His only client. One who paid him a retainer of a million dollars a year. Who leased him a Porsche and provided a home, and access to beautiful girls and the countless other perks that come with being physician on call to one of the most famous men in the world. 'Let's proceed, shall we?' Lucius had already rolled up his sleeve.

A moment or two with the cotton swab, the two tiny brown bottles, the tourniquet and the syringe, Ali saying, as he always did, 'Tiny sharp scratch now', and then – *ohhh-hhhhhhhhhhh. Jesus. Sweet Jesus. Come kiss my face.*

Lucius vaguely dismissed Ali and then wandered off through his large rooms. Smiling. Touching things. Lamps, books, tapestries. Everything felt nice. *White*, Lucius thought. *They will walk in white. By my side. For they are worthy.*

By the time he reached the small bedroom he didn't even bother to hide it. Just walked straight in with it hanging out, already half hard, massaging it. Jerry gasped, there on the bed in his Disney pyjamas, his lips stained with ice cream, bathed in the blue light of the cartoon film.

'I hope you've saved some room,' Lucius said, giggling.

THREE

'I hate him!' Connor Murphy screamed, lashing out a kick at the back of the driver's seat of his father's Mercedes.

'HEY!' his dad yelled. Glen sniffed hard, pulling a tangy rope of cocaine back down his throat, concentrating on the twists and turns of Sunset as it snaked through Brentwood. It was late. He'd had to do something to cope with the nearly two-hour round trip out to Malibu and back to Echo Park. 'Mind the fucking seat!' He pulled his thick mane of grey-blond hair out of his face, hiked the sleeve of his biker's jacket up over the Celtic cross tattoo on his forearm. In his early forties now, Glen still dressed like a rock star. Or Kiefer Sutherland circa *The Lost Boys*.

'He's a fucking asshole!' Connor continued. 'This Jerry kid. It's all "Jerry this" and "Jerry that" now.' The pain was still fresh for Connor. Being led out of the bedroom like that, with all the others. Realising that Jerry wasn't with them, that Jay had taken Jerry off to one side as they filed down the hallway. That Jerry had received the Golden Ticket that, until very recently, had been Connor's own invite to the Chocolate Factory.

'Easy, sweetheart,' Connor's mother Bridget said, turning round to look at her son in the back seat, trying to smile, finding it difficult through a combination of Botox and the same rough cocaine she'd snorted with Glen before they left the house. Turning forty this year, Bridget was displaying a good deal more cleavage than might be thought necessary for a night-time drive across the city. But old habits died hard. Fifteen, twenty years ago, had Bridget been making a midnight run across LA it would have been for entirely different reasons than picking her child up.

Bridget and Glen found themselves in a difficult position. They were trying to sympathise with their son's hurt, with the fact that he had been slighted by someone he loved. But, and even as emotionally insulated with cocaine as they were, it was impossible for the couple not to understand that their integrity was compromised here by the fact that for months they had been allowing their teenage son to be routinely buggered by a fifty-year-old paedophile. Still, the end was in sight. Bridget reached back and patted her son's leg. 'It's nearly over, Connor. We've got him. We've got him now.'

'Damn right we've got him,' Glen said.

The Murphys' story followed a curve familiar to anyone within Lucius Du Pre's inner circle. They were a poor family, Bridget and Glen having both followed the archetypal LA trajectory: she had got off the bus from Toledo back in 1996 at the age of nineteen. She tried to become an actress, succeeded in becoming a hooker, then took to waitressing when her looks began to go. He too tried to become an actor, failed at becoming an agent, then turned to dealing cocaine. Somewhere along the way Bridget got pregnant and Connor was born shortly after George W. stood on the deck of that aircraft carrier and said, 'Mission accomplished.' Connor was a beautiful boy. Everyone said so. So they got him an agent. Just like his parents before him, Connor failed to get a single part, until four years ago, when, just shy of his tenth birthday, he was cast as an extra in the video for Lucius Du Pre's Christmas single 'Love All the Children'. (Yes, a title that caused untold hilarity for those in the know. Not so much hiding-in-plain-sight as frantically-masturbating-in-plain-sight.)

Connor and his parents met Lucius on the set. Lucius was very taken with Connor. They were invited to occasional gatherings at Narnia. After a while, once he was twelve, Connor started getting the invitations on his own. After about a year of this, Bridget found a pair of her son's bloodstained underpants stuffed under his bed. Go straight to the police? This was their initial thought. But Glen had a friend. A lawyer friend, Art. And Art had a slightly different take, a way to exact a far greater revenge. Like the true LA players they were, Glen and Bridget began to ask – *What's the angle? Where does my leverage lie?* They bided their time and enjoyed the fruits of the Du Pre patronage for a while. Their credit card debts paid off in full. The Mercedes they were sitting in. Lavish gifts at Christmas and birthdays. And, gradually, they came up with a plan. Glen invested the last few hundred dollars available on one of their Visa cards in some technology, at a place over in the valley. The camera fitted inside a baseball cap. You couldn't even see it.

'Yeah,' Glen Murphy said, accelerating as the lights changed, crossing out of Beverly Hills and into West Hollywood now, remembering the look on Lance Schitzbaul's face in their meeting the day before yesterday, his jaw dropping, the way the arrogant, high-handed old Jewish fuck was finally lost for words, 'we got him over a fucking barrel.'

After a moment he realised this might have been an unfortunate turn of phrase given his son's recent experiences.

FOUR

So you go from the air-conditioned chill of the car, to the air-conditioned chill of the jet, to (via a brief walkthrough of the LAXVIP arrivals) the air-conditioned chill of another car, the car taking me from the airport to the Unigram building in West Hollywood. I don't bother going to my apartment, having slept a good five or six hours on the flight and showered and changed on the plane. As we get snared in traffic on La Cienega, I turn on the TV in the back of the limo and there it is on CNN – the camera showing a blank stretch of space in cold, wet Washington. The empty bleachers, the preparations. 'And we're now moments away,' the CNN chick says, 'from something many people thought was impossible, something that would never come to pass ...'

The inauguration of the Donald.

It's a blinder, isn't it? A twenty-four-carat belter. I mean, a year or so back, most people wouldn't have dared imagine he would ... that he could. 'What if he gets the nomination?'

I asked my liberal Californian friends, after he'd bowled down the escalator and called all the fucking beaners rapists and muggers and whatnot. '*Oh, Steven,*' they laughed. '*You don't understand American politics. He'll never get the Republican nomination because the GOP establishment / the moon's in Uranus / fucking whatever.*'

Well, as you know, after a few months of the Donald literally Sieg Heiling to arenas packed with salivating rednecks, he got the nomination. 'What if he wins the fucker?' I asked. '*Oh, Steven,*' they laughed, all the queer fools you're forced to hang out with in the entertainment industry, '*you don't understand. The numbers don't work for him. Given the Hispanic vote / the electoral college / the number of Latino shirtlifters in fucking Miami he can't possibly blah blah blah ...*'

You know what? These cunts aren't laughing now.

The GOP establishment? The electoral college picture? The voting block of People of Colour? Turned out no one gave a fuck about all that bollocks. They just wanted to hear all the words. It reminded me of back in the day, when you'd sign the most appalling dance record imaginable. There'd always be a moment where you'd think – 'Hang on. This is too much. Even the fucking cheap seats aren't going to be having this.' And then there you'd be – larging it at number one for a couple of months. This is why the liberals are all going so crazy. The Vengabus is coming? Mate, the Vengabus is going to be number one for the next eight years and you're all Belle and Sebastian fans.

'Yeah!' I shout delightedly at the TV. 'Suck it up, bitches! MAGA!'

'How's that, Mr Stelfox?' Mike, my usual LA driver, says, turning half around.

'The inauguration,' I say, gesturing at the TV. 'Your new president.' Mike is black, in his thirties, shaved head, athletic-looking, and I realise we might be about to have a disagreement here. Which I wouldn't totally mind. Something to get the blood pumping, the faculties sharpened before I go in to meet Trellick.

'Yes, sir,' Mike says. He's smiling and shaking his head slowly, revealing his glittering mouth of crocodile teeth. 'Hell of a day. Between you and me, and it ain't a popular view out here ...' he gestures out of the window, at the burger joints, car parks, palm fronds, tanning salons and bumper-to-bumper traffic of southern California, 'I voted for the man.'

'Fantastic,' I say. And then add, genuinely curious, 'Why?'

'Ah, you know ...' he thinks, punctuating this process with a blast on the horn when the car in front of us fails to notice the lights have changed, '... we been pushed around enough.'

Brilliant. Mike must make, what? Fifty grand a year max? It's like ... you're at Treblinka, or Sobibor, or Belsen, in '43 or '44, and you're there huddled by the smokestacks in your striped pyjamas, weighing forty kilos, watching your kids floating up into the sky in ash form, and instead of voting for more soup or, say, something mental like an actual end to concentration camps, you're voting to *increase* the production of Zyklon B like you've got shares in the stuff. You're voting for more guards and a faster turnaround time in the fucking showers. You want to know what happened? Two vectors in history intersected: 'everyone reckons they're a player' met 'overwhelming fear of sand negroes' and – bosh – here we are. It's too fucking good.

'Amen,' I say, raising my glass of Evian to the mad darkie.

And then, on-screen, it's happening. The great man is coming out, walking along with Obama. Obama is trying to smile, put a brave face on it, but he knows it's over. His liberal dream gone, wiped on the arses of the millions of patriots who voted for the huge black shape lumbering along beside him. I turn the sound up as Trump begins his address. It's all business as usual until he gets to a line that makes me sit bolt upright in my seat.

'*This American carnage*,' he thunders, '*stops right here and stops right now.*'

American carnage. I fucking like the sound of this.

The elevator takes me up. Samantha, Trellick's PA (packed into an insanely tight woollen wrap dress), meets me in reception and walks me through the main offices (heads turning at the desks of the juniors. I am, I'll thank you to remember, something of a legend in this business) with the usual enquiries about my flight and how long I'm in town for. I pass young guys in T-shirts, boilers, beasts and doables, gold and platinum discs and water coolers. It is all very familiar from the offices I spent my youth in, with one major change – there is almost total silence apart from the tapping of keyboards. No phones ringing, no screamed conversations. No blaring music. Everyone is locked in the private atmosphere of their own desk. And then we're approaching the double doors to the office at the very end, Samantha opens them and ...

'Oi oi,' James Trellick is saying as he comes across his office to greet me. As everyone who lives out here does after a while, Trellick has a certain California health glow about him – tanned, complexion fresh and healthy from hours of hiking and the gym and parties where you nurse one drink for an hour and a half. Trellick turned fifty last year, but he'd easily pass for ten years younger. He's wearing a crisp white shirt and jeans. No tie. However, beneath all of this, he looks tired, like he hasn't slept much in the last couple of days. The eyes are red and I can almost feel the stress radiating from him as he hurries Sam out of the office, saying, 'We're not to be disturbed. Oh – and can you tell Lance and Brandon we'll meet them in the board-room in –' he looks at his watch, a Piguet, a fiftieth birthday gift from yours truly – 'fifteen minutes?'

'Of course,' Sam says. 'Steven, can I get you anything?'

'Just coffee,' I say, 'Bl—'

'Black. I remember.'

She closes the doors behind her. Trellick and I walk over to his desk. His office is vast, with huge windows giving onto a terrace that looks towards the Hollywood Hills. 'Right,' I say as soon as the doors close. 'Out with it.'

'Just a sec. Wait till Sam brings the coffee.'

'I'm assuming this is properly mental if you couldn't even go into it on the phone?'

'Off. The. Fucking. Scale,' Trellick says, slumping down behind his desk. I pick up one of the framed photos on it. Trellick's wife Pandora and his two sons, James Jr and Alex, now aged eleven and nine. He had another one too, recently – a year or two ago. That's right, even Trellick did it. Did the decent thing. Straightened up and flew right. Can you imagine it?

'How's Pan and the boys?' I ask.

'All good.'

'You behaving yourself?'

'Mmmm ...' he says, grinning, meaning that there will be stories worth hearing at lunch later. A soft knock at the door, and a girl's head pops round. 'James,' she says, 'sorry to disturb you. Have you got a second?'

'Christ, literally a second, Chrissy,' Trellick says, beckoning her in. 'Steven, Chrissy Price, one of our A&R people, Chrissy, Steven Stel—'

'Hi,' I say, extending a hand as she comes over.

'Oh, I know who you are,' she says, cutting Trellick off. 'Really pleased to meet you. Sorry for interrupting.' There's a slight Texan twang in her accent, her reddish hair cut in a longish bob that covers much of her face, a freckled face that is undeniably sensational. She's also been given one of those jackpot body deals: tiny, slender waist with a huge rack and cheeks, her jeans straining to keep the arse in check, the vintage tee (Black Flag) similarly not quite up to the job of keeping the jugs tethered. 'I just thought you should know that it looks like Capitol have upped their offer on NDC to half a mil.'

'For fuck's sake,' Trellick says.

'We're still in the frame, but I think we're going to have to go there, or near there, if we want to stay in the frame.'

'Do we want to?' Trellick says.

'I think we do,' she says. 'Their new track is blowing up.'

I've been reading about this. I've heard a couple of tracks. NDC means Norwegian Dance Crew: a bunch of no-mark rave chancers from Oslo who couldn't have got arrested in Britain twenty years ago but who have now become – since America suddenly decided it 'got' rave a few years ago, or 'EDM' as the half-witted colonial spunkers insist

on calling it – the hottest unsigned dance act in the business. 'What do you reckon?' Trellick says to me, leaning
back in his chair, smiling, relishing this trip down memory
lane, when this was how I used to earn a living.

What do I reckon? I reckon these Nordic bastards
couldn't write an actual song if you had their immediate
families tied up in front of them with knives at their throats.
I reckon their 'live' set consists of them jumping up and
down in matching boiler suits while they play a CD labelled
GENERIC RAVE IDIOCY. I reckon they probably have as
much longevity as the kind of plastic toy the fucking gyppos
give you at the fair when you shoot down five ducks in a
row. But I also reckon that this is exactly the kind of thing
that the millions of sunburned redneck fuck-faced inbred
Yank ravers who pack the clubs at Vegas week after week
to lose their minds to DJ Rectal Cancer or MC I've Actually
Shat Myself are after. I also reckon stranger things have
happened. I also reckon that this Chrissy boiler smiling at
me now, begging for my approval, is completely fucking
doable and would likely suck your cock like she was trapped
underwater and the only source of oxygen was your fucking
urethra. So . . .

'Yeah,' I say. 'Half a mil? Worth a punt.'

'Okey-dokey,' Trellick says. 'Tell business affairs we'll
match it.'

'Fantastic,' Chrissy says. 'They're spinning in Vegas in a
couple of weeks. I'm going to go up.'

'Sure.'

'Great, thanks, James. Nice to meet you, Steven. How
long you in town for?'

I look at Trellick. 'I'm not sure,' I say.

'Well, see you around.' She leaves as Sam comes in with the coffee, Trellick and I both watching that fine Texan backside sashay away across the room. We exchange a look that says 'very doable'.

'Thanks, Sam,' Trellick says. 'No calls, OK?'

She leaves.

'OK,' he says finally, 'outside of the people who made it, the existence of what I am about to show you is known to three people.'

'For fuck's sake,' I say. 'Let's crack on …'

'All right, boys and girls,' he says, turning his laptop towards me. 'Eyes down for a full house …'

Do you know much about pornography? Are you well versed? The footage Trellick shows me belongs to the genre known as 'amateur POV': low grade, shot in a domestic setting with poor lighting and zero production values. The thrill of this particular substratum is its extreme reality, the fact that while you're frantically tugging at your crazed baton you can easily picture this being real, almost filmed without one party's consent, as the clip Trellick is showing me almost certainly was. The camera seemed to have been placed squarely in the centre of what you'd normally take to be the woman's head. Except, in this case, judging by the genitalia, the woman's role is being played by a young boy. So, for a bit, we get a shot of a man's head, a thick tangle of black curly hair, as he enthusiastically works away between the kid's legs. (Apart from the fact that we are watching gay porn, the experience of sitting in a darkened office during the day watching disgraceful filth with Trellick is reassuringly familiar, reminding me of when we used to work together in the nineties.) Then there's a rushed, jerky, change of positions, banging and blurring, and then some pixelated, shot-much-too-close footage of the man's stomach, the camera rushing in towards it and then back out, in and back out ... The guy's stomach, you notice, is mottled, very tanned but with pink, reddish patches, like bad sunburn. Some more frantic changing of positions and now the kid is facing a large mirror so we can see his face perfectly. He is very good-looking, maybe twelve or thirteen, and he is wearing a baseball cap. And ... Jesus.

Right behind him in the mirror, banging and thrusting like a madman, pumping away as though the very act of sodomy itself were about to be banned or rationed, is ...

Lucius. Fucking. Du Pre.

My jaw drops.

On-screen Du Pre's does too as he starts unleashing an urgent, primal howl, as he starts shouting in the high-pitched voice I know so well from countless hit records, countless interviews, 'THE EMPEROR IS COMING! THE EMPEROR IS COMING! THE EMP ... OHHHHHHUURRRRRRR!'

Du Pre collapses on the kid's back, panting, and the screen goes black. Trellick stops it. It, and Du Pre, has lasted all of one minute and fifty-two seconds. I take a deep breath, exhale, and say the only thing I can say.

'Fuck. Me.'

'Exactly,' Trellick says.

I mean, I'd heard rumours – who hadn't? But industry rumours are one thing. Actual footage of one of the biggest pop stars in the world viciously buggering a child, that's a whole other kettle of prison.

'So where are you at?' I ask.

'Come on,' Trellick says. 'We'll go meet the others.'

Down a long hallway and then he's opening the doors to a boardroom where two men sit at the head of the dark wood conference table, the matt-black pyramid of the speakerphone in the middle of it. I know one of them. 'Lance ...' I say, extending a hand. I haven't seen Lance Schitzbaul, Du Pre's manager, in five or six years. He's gained weight, an impressive feat considering he was starting from about 250 pounds. He must be in his early sixties now and looks like he's aged twenty years in the last five. Broken blood vessels on his cheeks, the eyes rheumy. It's a Brian Clough pus. A drinker's coupon.

'Hey, Steve,' Lance says, getting up, already sweating, from the breakfast smorgasbord he has spread in front of him. 'Some fucken deal, huh?'

He embraces me into his hefty German-Jewish-American mass, his silk shirt damp, his bearded face scratching my cheek.

'Yeah,' I say. 'I just saw the, um, show.'

'And this is Brandon Krell,' Trellick says, gesturing to the other guy in the room, a bearded thirty-something in suit and tie. 'Our CFO. He's the only other guy at the company who knows what's going on.'

'Brandon,' I say, shaking his hand.

'Steven. Heard so much about you. A real honour.'

We all settle around the table. 'Right,' I say, shooting my cuffs. 'Just let me ask all the obvious questions first so we can get through it. Lance, I'm assuming you've been here or hereabouts before, why not just pay the cunts off?'

'They want fifty million dollars,' Lance says.

'So? Your client's a billionaire.'

A pause as the three of them look at each other.

'Lance?' Trellick says.

Lance sighs as he slides a manila folder towards me. 'Take your time ...' he says, his mouth full of bear claw.

A master at reading balance sheets, it takes me ten minutes – flipping back and forth, my eyes going over the columns, down and up, turning to the appendix and back again – to fully come to grips with things.

Lucius Du Pre is broke.

Not broke like you're broke, you, you idiot, sitting there in your flat *reading a fucking book like a cunt*.

It's not like he can't afford to go on holiday or go out for a big night with his mates or buy a new sofa. But in real terms, in rich person's terms, another three months of living like he does and he's fucked. I look at some of the expenses – millions of dollars a year on plane charters, clothes and paintings. Trips to London and New York with an entourage of fifteen to twenty people, hairdressers, stylists, bodyguards, chefs and so on and so on. The costs of running his Narnia ranch alone seem to come in at over two million dollars a month. Among larger expenses are things like the thirty-minute short film called *Mirage* which Du Pre scripted and self-funded and which he had directed by the late Tony Scott (*Top Gun*, *Black Rain*) at a cost of twenty-five million dollars. It went straight in the bin when he decided he didn't like his hair. Some years back he spent ten million dollars buying the Elephant Man John Merrick's skeleton.

I look at some 'miscellaneous' expenses: 46,000 dollars in architect fees for a house Du Pre was going to buy in

Pacific Palisades. (He changed his mind.) A million-dollar fee to the actor Charlie Sheen for appearing at a party Du Pre threw. 380,000 dollars on a convertible Bentley, 210,000 on a customised Lincoln Navigator sports utility vehicle. 250,000 on an antiques shopping spree in Beverly Hills. There are also some smaller incidental items: a few Tiffany lamps, a vintage IWC watch, a dinner for twenty-two people at Nobu. It comes out at about a million and change.

And that was how August 2015 went.

I mean, don't get me wrong, I like spending fucking money, but this . . .

There are also, starting a few years ago, large, regular and ominous payments listed in the 'legal services' column: ranging from ten thousand dollars to a few million. Payments, Lance explains, made 'without prejudice' (i.e. we admit nothing but here have some cash and fuck off and shut up) to the guardians of various children who enjoyed especially close relationships with his client.

'OK,' I say. 'James, Unigram gives them the money. Advance it against royalties, buy a bit of his publishing off him or something.'

'Brandon?' Trellick says.

Krell slides another manila folder towards me. 'Again, take your time,' he says.

This file takes longer to digest. It details Unigram's dealings with Du Pre over the last fifteen or so years. Fifteen years ago things were fine. Du Pre was laughing. All the way to the bank. Happily buggering infants along the way. And then a couple of things coincided: he bought Narnia and he pretty much stopped recording and touring. Well, after five years of this things got understandably shaky on the cash flow front. So Du Pre sold half of his publishing company to Unigram for just over 100 million dollars. I remember the deal going down at the time, thinking they'd got a bit of a bargain there. This cash injection obviously shored things up a bit. Then, after another few years of shopping like a cracked-up Eva Perón on *Supermarket Sweep* and buggering kids like it was the Walton Hop Christmas party, and this part I don't know because it was obviously kept very quiet, Du Pre sold the *remaining 50 per cent of his publishing* (his only real asset) off for another hundred-plus million.

Getting more recent now, 2013, Schitzbaul came to the company and begged for their help. Du Pre was promising a new record, promising to tour again. Trellick was in charge by this point and he authorised a hundred-million-dollar loan against future royalties as well as helping Du Pre arrange lines of credit, to get him through the rough patch, until his monster comeback record came out. These are listed in an appendix – 120 million from Bank of America, for which Unigram stood guarantor, 25 million from Citigroup and another 30 million from something called Crystal Finance, a private 'wealth management group' (a kind of TolerHouse! for the incredibly rich), both collateralised against Narnia. I look at Trellick and shake my head. He looks suitably shamefaced.

In short, not only is Du Pre broke, he owes the label a hundred million plus interest. He owes private lenders nearly twice that. His monthly debt payments are almost five million dollars.

'Fuck,' I say. I look at Schitzbaul. 'How did you let it get to th—'

He's been on edge since we sat down. Now he explodes, banging the table.

'THE FUCK IT'S MY FAULT, YOU FUCKING LIMEY COCKSUCKERS! You try managing that guy for five fucken minutes. Don't listen to no one! I fucken told him – "Lucius, if you keep spending like this and you ain't earning, then –" I GAVE THAT SONOFABITCH THE BEST GODDAMN YEARS OF MY LIFE AND THIS IS HOW IT PANS OUT! MOTHERFUCKER!'

Big managers have to rant now and then and we let Schitzbaul get it out. But really, he's got nothing in his hand. After a minute or so I raise my left index finger and say, softly, 'Uh, Schitzbull?'

'IT'S SCHITZ*BAWL*!'

'Lance, shut the fuck up, OK?' To my surprise he immediately does so, pushing back his chair and walking over to the bar, where he begins fixing himself a Stoli on the rocks at ten o'clock in the morning. 'Of course,' I say to Trellick and Brandon, 'even if there was fifty million sloshing around to pay them off there's the question of . . .'

'Good faith,' Brandon says.

'Exactly,' Trellick says.

Which is to say, the kind of people who'd arrange to videotape their own child being anally raped by a madman and then *not* go to the police but instead use the tape for blackmail purposes aren't going to be at the top of a list headed 'people you'd trust to keep their end of a fifty-million-dollar deal'.

'There's also the question of Unigram being a publicly traded company . . .' Trellick says.

'Meaning that if it got out that you'd helped with this in any way you're finished,' I say.

'Correctos,' Trellick says.

This is bleak. I think for a moment then ask, 'Who's met with them?'

Trellick and Brandon both look at Schitzbaul.

'Glen and Bridget Murphy. They're scumbags,' he sighs, draining his glass, the fight gone out of him now, 'just a pair of fucking scumbags.'

'Have we considered . . . ?' I don't finish.

'Whacking the pair of them?' Schitzbaul says. 'Sure. I'd happily do it my fucking self. But it's the usual: their lawyer, one Art Hinkley of Pasadena – and this guy's another piece of work, believe me – has a "letter to be opened in the event of our deaths". It . . . it's a nightmare.' Schitzbaul wanders off, looking out of the windows, presumably picking one to jump from.

'How long do we have?' I ask.

'A week and then the tape gets mailed to *Good Morning America*,' Trellick says. 'Stupid fucking hicks probably think you can go and get fifty million out of the ATM.' He shakes his head. And then puts it in his hands. 'If this goes public . . .' I have never seen Trellick so stressed.

I follow his train of thought. If 'Lucius Does Little Boys' goes public . . .

Unigram is out a hundred million immediately.

Plus another 120 million when Bank of America comes calling and says 'fuck you, pay us'.

Du Pre's comeback tour? Gone. Overnight the cunt will become the most toxic brand since American Airlines said 'we beat our customers'.

As for Unigram? They're done too. They're the label that funds paedophilia.

There is silence for a long time, broken only by the tinkling of ice in Schitzbaul's glass as he stands up at the windows, looking out at sunny LA, pursuing the only course open to him at this point – drinking himself senseless – until I say, 'OK, guys. You're going to have to give me some time with this. Lance, how much does Du Pre know?'

'About the tape? Jackshit.'

'Keep it that way for now. How about his financial situation, how clued up is he there?'

'Well, he ain't doing these comeback shows for fun. I'll tell you that for fucken nothing. Had to be dragged into it kicking and screaming. He knows it ain't great, but as to how bad it really is? Nah, with the drugs, the injections and whatnot? He's pretty much got his head in the fucken sand.'

'You need to get it out. Make him understand how bad it is. Now.' Schitzbaul nods. 'Trellick, let's have dinner tonight when I've got my head around all this a bit. It ... it's a fucking belter. Brandon? Nice to meet you. Can you get all these files over to my place?'

'Sure,' he says as we shake.

'Steven?' Schitzbaul extends his hand. This old, broken alky clown, overseeing this as the last act in a management career that has spanned four decades. 'Thanks for trying to help us out here. Sorry I lost my temper for a minute back there. It's just ... the fucken pressure, you know?'

'You call that losing your temper?' I say, smiling.

'You know what's really painful?' Schitzbaul says. 'And I say this with all due respect, because I love the kid. I mean, he's got problems like you wouldn't believe' (no shit) 'but, you know, he's been like a fucken son to me. But, it has to be said, I can't even see him living much longer. The amount of shit he's putting into his veins. Never eats. Weighs about a hundred pounds. I think he last took a fucken shit around Thanksgiving. It's, you know, now this could be the end of him. His legacy. Fucking shame.'

'Lance,' I say, 'I'll call you later.'

The meeting breaks up and something occurs to me that the average person might find odd. That you out there might find strange and unsettling. It is this: at no point in the hour plus we spent discussing the matter did one of us express any interest in, or sympathy for, the buggered child.

Hey, this is the music industry. You must be looking for the door marked 'Social Work'.

I have Mike swing by Book Soup on Sunset on the way back to the apartment. I want to pick up some reading.

FIVE

Lucius was crying. This was not unusual. He cried most days, at everything from a stray memory – usually to do with his father: punching his tooth out backstage in Cleveland, unexpectedly telling him he'd done a good job when he came out of the vocal booth one time, jerking him off roughly in the back of the tour bus when he was seven or eight – to an insurance commercial to not being able to get the cap off the toothpaste. But these were real tears. Barking, howling, uncontrollable sobbing. After a couple of minutes Jay panicked and did the only thing he could think of, the only thing he knew *always* put Lucius in a good mood – he sent for Dr Ali. Roman Klorovsky – choreographer to the stars – looked down at his client, gnashing and wailing on the floor, and said, 'Lucius, darling, please, what is wrong, baby?'

'I CAN'T DO IT!' Lucius screamed, lying on his back, kicking his heels on the sprung wood floor, yelling over the hard, pounding backing track.

'Sure you can!' Roman leaned down and patted his shoulder comfortingly. He looked around the huge gymnasium (one of three at Narnia), looking for the MD to kill the music. Roman made the throat-cutting gesture and blessed silence reigned. 'Come. Come now. Is easy. We get this.' It was a fairly simple step after all, just a sort of turn, pivot, kick thing. And Lucius was renowned as one of the greatest dancers in the business. (Although, from what he'd seen in the past couple of days, Roman sensed he might fast be entering his twilight in that respect. Well, the guy had to be fifty at least.) Roman had taken the gig partly out of curiosity and partly because – the usual reason people worked with Lucius Du Pre – the cheque was eye-watering. The NDA he'd had to sign was like the phone book.

'NO! NO! NO! I MEAN – I CAN'T DO *IT*! ANY OF IT!'

Lucius took a dance shoe off and threw it across the room – at the room, at Narnia, at everything – and Roman realised what this was about. He'd come up in the Moscow Ballet (Lucius was nothing compared to a prima ballerina who hasn't eaten in three days) and gone on to work with everyone from Spielberg to Spike Jonze to Kanye and there was one thing he'd learned along the way – the tantrum was almost never about what it was about. It wasn't the dance step Lucius didn't want to do.

'Uh, Lucius,' a voice said, off to the side. Roman turned to see Jay poking his head back in the door, 'Lance is here, in the conservatory. You want me to tell him you busy?'

With a deep breath, Lucius pulled himself together. Actually, this was good. Good timing. They'd have it out. Put paid to this ridiculous idea once and for all.

Lance saw Lucius coming towards him across the conservatory – more like the atrium of a grand hotel than something a middle-class homeowner would tack onto the back of their semi – and, drunk as he was, he couldn't help the ache that fluttered through his heart. He'd managed Lucius for thirty years, since he left the band and went out on his own. Lance had borne witness to the blossoming of his talent and now, he realised, he was witnessing its decline. He took a tug on his drink and tried to clear his head. Now was no time for sentimental trips down memory lane. Now was a time for tough, clear talk.

After they'd listened to each other lie about how well the other looked, Lance had to listen to Lucius witter on about Jesus for a long time. This was difficult to take – Lucius's pious talk being somewhat undercut by the image burned in Lance's mind of his client screaming 'THE EMPEROR IS COMING!' – but Lance bore it the same way he bore most things these days: with a lot of vodka, repeatedly refilling his glass from the bottle in the silver ice bucket beside him. Lance didn't bother trying to interject or cut Lucius off. He just kept drinking and let it run its course. Finally, when he'd run out of steam, Lance began gently, with a long speech about how great Lucius was, how talented, how successful and so on and so on. Finally, he got around to it. 'But, Lucius? All that said, you know we've been having some cash flow issues lately?'

'Mmmmm ...'

'Well, I think we're gonna have to cut back the expenses some. I mean, the tour's gonna help, no question, but if we just –'

Lucius said something, soft and indistinct.

'What?' Lance said.

Lucius repeated it with more force. 'I don't want to do the tour.'

Lance took this in for a moment. Then he hurled his vodka tumbler across the room, hearing it splinter somewhere far away on the marble floor as he let it all out. 'YOU AIN'T DOING THE TOUR? YOU AIN'T DOING THE FEKOKTAH TOUR, YOU LITTLE PISCHER?! LEMME TELL YOU SOMETHING – YOU DON'T DO THE TOUR WE'RE OUT TWO HUNDRED MILLION FUCKEN DOLLARS! TWO HUNDRED MILLION WE DON'T FUCKEN HAVE! YOU'RE FINISHED! OVER! KISS GOODBYE TO ALL THIS!' He gestured around, at the glass ceiling thirty feet above them, the mature trees, the jungly interior. 'YOU'RE GONNA BE LIVING IN AN APARTMENT IN FUCKEN PASADENA LIKE A FUCKEN SCHMUCK! YOU DON'T DO THE TOUR YOU ARE FUCKED WITH A FUCKEN ELEPHANT DICK AND YOU'RE GONNA BE LOOKING FOR A NEW FUCKEN MANAGER 'CAUSE WE'RE DONE! GOOD LUCK FINDING SOMEONE ELSE WHO'LL DEAL WITH ALL YOUR … YOUR …' He tailed off, unable to verbalise it, unable to admit to what he knew about Lucius's 'problem'. (And even now, outside the windows, a couple of the Hummers were pulling up, disgorging a bunch of pre-teen boys for the afternoon's tour of the amusement park.)

Lucius looked at his manager, his bottom lip a couple of inches below the top one, his bottom row of perfect teeth visible. Lance looked at the floor. He'd surprised himself. He hadn't talked to Lucius like this in a long, long time.

Since the early nineties, since after *Monster* landed, since Lucius had inhabited that holy stratosphere of stardom occupied by only a handful in every generation, a rarefied band of humans who had only one thing in common: they never heard the monosyllable 'no'. For a second Lance thought Lucius was going to go berserk. Fire him? Attack him? Have Marcus or Jay attack him? (Lance could see the two bruisers peering anxiously through the glass at the far end of the conservatory.) Eventually, however, for the second time in an hour, Lucius broke down in tears. 'I ... can't ... do ...' the words coming between the racking sobs, like a child crying, '... it ... any ... more.'

'Jesus, kid, easy. Come on now ...' Lance moved in, sat down next to Lucius on the overstuffed sofa covered in ostrich hide, and put an arm around his charge. Lance was sixty-two. When he'd met Lucius he'd been thirty-two and Lucius had been nineteen. Calling a fifty-year-old man 'kid' still came naturally to him. 'You can't do what any more?'

'All of it. None of it.' Meaning the singing, the dancing. Everything.

'Listen, Lucius, kid, you're fi—' Lance realised he was about to say the actual age out loud. 'You're fine. You're just not twenty-one any more. Everyone gets that. No one's expecting this to be like the old days. They just wanna see you. It's been so long since you were out there. You could get up and stand like a statue and sing the fucken Yellow Pages and they'd still go crazy.'

'That's not good enough,' Lucius said. Strangely, weirdly, given his current life of utter squander and debauchery, somewhere deep inside him, Lucius still wanted to be the best. The guy who could sing and dance and write songs like no other. The idea of getting up there again and not being able to cut it ... not for the first time in recent years he started thinking about how easy it would be. That cabinet full of Demerol and Dilaudid. Or convince (or pay) Dr Ali to give him an extra-big shot of milk one night at bedtime. He sometimes felt that, like Jesus, his time on earth was done. He had given the humans all the help he could. Everything would be so beautiful. White.

'Lucius, help me,' Lance said. 'Help me to help you. What is it you want?'

'I want ...'

What did Lucius want? He just wanted to be left alone. He wanted his little playmates and his milk and his candy and that was about it. Why did that have to be so difficult? 'I want ... I just want everything to be *beautiful*,' Lucius said as he collapsed, crying again.

Lance cradled him. He sighed and looked out of the windows, down towards the amusement park, where the Ferris wheel was now turning. Lance thought about the only time he had ever tried to confront Lucius about things, a few years back, when he began to grasp the full extent of what was going on at the 'slumber parties'. The conversation had taken place during a walk around the Narnia grounds, just a few hundred yards from where they were sitting now. 'Lucius,' he'd said, 'you're going to wind up in a lot of trouble. Why don't you just stop all this stuff with the young boys?'

Lucius's reply had been bracing in its simplicity. 'I don't want to,' he'd shrugged. Then he'd wandered off towards his petting zoo.

Lance had watched him go, feeling like he'd at least tried, like he'd done his bit for decency and humanity.

SIX

My apartment, a corner penthouse, is on Doheny, the street that marks the border between West Hollywood and Beverly Hills. The writer Bret Easton Ellis has a place here too. You see him around a bit, in the lobby, in the garage. Proper chunky old bumboy.

I had a house just along the road, on Alpine, back in the noughties, when I was doing the show. Now that I only spend two or three months a year out here it was too much space – when you have vast properties you don't live in you're just turning money into problems – and so I downgraded. Although you would feel 'downgraded' an utterly inappropriate word if you were to be reclining where I am now, in the original Eames chair by the window in the 1,300-square-foot living room, looking out at the views south, towards downtown LA, and west, towards Santa Monica and the Pacific. I yawn and turn on the lamp next to me. Dusk is falling and far below me lights are starting to twinkle amid the greenery of Beverly Hills. I sip my drink – sparkling water and fresh lime juice – and reread a passage that has caught my eye.

> By all accounts Jordan Du Pre was a violent man who would routinely beat his wife and son. There were frequent rumors that his abuse of the young Lucius extended into the sexual. This has never been confirmed by Du Pre himself, although he seemed to allude to it on his infamous 1998 appearance on The Oprah Winfrey Show ...

I slip the book back onto the top of the tower of Du Pre biographies on the low table beside me and pick up a sheaf of papers I've printed off of the Internet, turning to a page I have marked in yellow highlighter.

> None of Du Pre's superfans comes close in obsession to Abdullah bin Rahman, son of the Sultan of Quatain. Bin Rahman (born 1995) recently paid in excess of 15 million dollars at auction for the Bally dance shoes worn by Du Pre in the video for 'Sexx Jacking'.

There is the easy way to do this. The obvious way. As Old Joe Stalin said: 'Where there is a man there is a problem. No man – no problem.' And then ... there might be another way. A two bites at the cherry way. Something that's never been done before. It's not without risk, but the potential rewards could be ... Off. The. Fucking. Scale.

By the way, about that sparkling water and lime, you're probably wondering at this point ...

Of course I still drink (if you *have* to stop drinking you're a fucking loser), but I don't *drink* drink any more. I haven't taken cocaine since my early thirties, around the time the Twin Towers came down. No NA, no programme, no sitting around in church halls having coffee and biscuits with a bunch of crying, whining fucking disgraces. I just stopped. You know why? *It's not player.* Go to a party. The people nursing a single beer or a glass of water and out the door at 10 p.m.? I guarantee you they're in the office at 8 a.m. *ruling.* What, you think David Geffen was smashing that fourth pint on a Tuesday night? Racking them out in the early hours of Sunday morning with some fucking bass player, talking about how they were going to conquer the world? Fuck that. I see them around now and then, the guys I knew in the nineties. Going into the Groucho. In the lounge at Terminal 5. Coming out of Soho House. The guy who ran some dance label. The guy who was some minor league A&R at Sony. The loser agent. They fall into two categories – the clowns who are still doing the coke and the shots, looking like red-faced walking corpses as they stumble towards that first heart attack at fifty. Or, even worse, the ones who can't do *anything* any more. Who exist on yoga, mineral water, Red Bull and fifteen espressos a day. They grin insanely and tap their feet as they talk to you, urgently telling you about how great their fucking kids are, about how long it is since they put a drink to their lips. Who fucking cares, you utter spastic? The only thing you could put to your lips that would raise a flicker of interest in me would be the barrel of a fucking shotgun as you decorate the walls of your toilet gaff in Willesden (that you just managed to buy with the very last of your ill-gotten nineties gains) with the remnants of your 'brains'. And these are the *successful* ones. There are the others that you only hear about, the ones who shat the bed so comprehensively, whose lives are so terrible, that they now live in the Lake District, or Scotland, or Somerset or someplace, going for runs and writing a blog or trying to become writers or lawyers or some fucking thing, all the while all of them thinking much the same thing – '*Why the fuck didn't I sign more hits and buy a house in W11?*'

Tired though I am (not jet-lagged. Only tourists get jet lag), I pick up the phone and dial Trellick.

'I've got an idea. Two in fact.'

'Thank fuck.'

'You're not going to like them.'

'I think at this point we're looking at anything,' he says.

'Tick-tock, Clarice.'

'Right, I'll be over in twenty.'

'We can order in,' I say, hanging up.

I call Terry on his encrypted phone. I need to check his availability. If Terry can't do this then I'm sure he'll recommend someone, one of his elite band of colleagues (in my experience Terry doesn't really have peers), but I'm not sure the whole thing's a goer if Terry's unavailable. I leave the usual coded message ('Are you guys still delivering?') and he calls me back ninety seconds later, from Bogotá. We exchange pleasantries (we haven't spoken in three years) and, very pleasingly, Terry tells me that he's just finishing up a job down there and will be free in a couple of days. Terry's rates are insane but that's Trellick's problem. If he doesn't want to go forward with it, then it's hello public disgrace, goodbye Unigram, and yours truly flies back to London a million quid up for having taken a gander. It is, as we used to say back in the day, a no-risk disc for me.

I call Urasawa and order sushi. I pick up another Du Pre biography to kill time before Trellick gets here. A thought keeps running around in my head — what if the *Enquirer* and all those crazy supermarket tabloids were right after Elvis died?

What if, a few months later, it turned out Elvis *was* still alive?

And what if you were RCA? If you were Colonel Tom Parker?

How might that have gone?

Trellick's initial reaction is exactly what I expected: 'Are you out of your fucking mind?'

But, after a couple of hours, the dining table littered with sushi cartons, CNN flickering in the background with the sound down, by the time I've gone through the whole thing for a third time, while he's not quite at the 'it might just work!' stage, he's stopped with the 'you're nuts' stuff and is now asking questions about practicalities.

In my experience, when this happens, you're getting close to a sale. As the great man said in *The Art of the Deal*, 'My style of deal-making is quite simple and straightforward: I aim very high and then I just keep pushing and pushing and pushing to get what I'm after.'

'It's just,' Trellick says, leaning back in his chair, 'if this goes tits, the fucking blowback ...' Behind him, on CNN, the anchors are almost crying as they analyse the inauguration speech over and over.

I like Trellick, I really do. But he's a lawyer. If you listened to lawyers you'd never release a single record. I sit forward and help myself to a bite of fifteen-dollar sashimi. 'Look,'

I say, 'it might not even be doable. I'll need a few days just to try and put the principal elements together.'

'And then we have to sell it to Du Pre.'

'I think that'll be the easy part. Don't you get it? He's begging for something like this. Screaming for it.'

'What would you need?'

'For now? Just give me the jet for seventy-two hours. And I'll need to meet with the Murphys and this lawyer of theirs. Art whatever. Right away, like tomorrow.'

'And tell them what?'

'That we're paying them. It's just going to take a while. Buy us a couple of weeks. We'll need to give them a deposit. Cash. Say a mil. And I'll need it tomorrow too.'

He whistles through his teeth.

'Listen, James, if it looks like we can't follow through on plan A for whatever reason then we fall back on plan B. My guy could do that in his sleep. And you'll only be out the mil. Maybe not even that depending on how it goes. If all this comes off it's nothing compared to what you'll make on back catalogue.'

He's thinking. He's really thinking. 'It's just,' he says, 'the amount of bullshit we'll have to spin. The scale of the fucking lies, the amount of balls you'll have to keep in the air ...' I say nothing while he talks, I just keep my eyes fixed on the TV screen behind Trellick: a rerun of this afternoon's inauguration speech, Trump's face, filling the screen, gigantic and mad, his white panda eyes screaming out from the orange panstick, thumb and index finger of his right hand doing that 'O' thing where it looks like he's wanking the cock of a tiny invisible air spirit.

'Fuck it,' Trellick says finally. 'See if you can line it up. Take the jet. Watch the expenses.' He smiles at this reference to our old life, when expenses used to mean drinks and dinner for some indie band, not . . . this. 'What will we tell Schitzbaul?' he asks, getting up.

'A bit. Not the whole thing, obvs. But we'll need him onside for at least the first part of it. I'll meet him tomorrow, after I see this pair of cunts . . .' I hold up the file Schitzbaul's PI has prepared on the Murphys.

'Thanks, Steven. I appreciate all this.'

'Hey, what are friends for?' I say before continuing, 'Well, friendship aside, there is something we need to talk about . . .'

'I thought there might be.'

I outline what my fee will be on this.

I will take no cash upfront. It is all in the form of back end. Inevitably, Trellick baulks. We look each other in the eye. 'Don't be stupid,' I say. 'If it doesn't work you're out nothing. If it does, we're all getting crazy rich.' I hold his gaze a moment longer. He blinks first.

'OK,' he says, extending his hand.

We shake on it.

'Oh, by the way,' I say as he slips his jacket on, 'how's it going on your Norwegian Dance Crew deal? The one what's-her-name —'

'Chrissy.'

'— Chrissy's chasing.'

'Fucking hell,' he grins. 'You'll never guess who the manager is.'

'Who?'

'Remember old Danny Rent?'

'Fuck me.'

'Indeed. See you tomorrow.'

Trellick lets himself out and I wander onto the terrace. Pitch dark now, after midnight, red tail lights all along Santa Monica Boulevard, heading west. I am very tired.

Danny Rent, like all two-bob managers, the proverbial bad penny. We had great success together twenty years back with a girl band, a cobbled-together Spice Girls knock-off called Songbirds. (I have intermittently monitored the decline of its four members with great pleasure over the last two decades. They're all in their late thirties now, two of them constantly in and out of rehab, one of them nearly got lynched by her fellow contestants a few years ago on *I'm a Barely Remembered D Lister Please Shoot Me in the Fucking Head*, the other one married that footballer who turned out to be an enthusiastic and talented wife-beater – forever turning up with a face like a tenderised steak in the kind of magazines monstrous housewives pick up when they're paying for their frozen chips and fizzy drinks. Hi, girls, I hope you enjoyed your trip around the fair.) Danny pops up every five years or so, signs a band to a major label for a ton of money and then disappears into his hole until the next one comes along. I put a note on my phone to give him a call. I lean on the railing and look west, along that line of tail lights, towards Santa Monica and, somewhere in the blackness north of it, Malibu, where Lucius Du Pre will now be doing whatever it is he does instead of sleeping. I yawn and dial the mobile number Lance gave me for Bridget Murphy.

SEVEN

'We're getting the fucking money!'

'Please don't talk to me about this on the telephone.'

'Are you talking to Artie? Ask him if he wants to come to Palm Springs this weekend!'

The first interlocutor, Mrs Bridget Murphy, excited, giddy. The second her lawyer, Art Hinckley, and the third her husband, Glen. 'Shut up, Glen,' Bridget said, stepping out onto the porch and lighting a cigarette in the late-morning sunshine.

At the other end of the phone, somewhere in Pasadena, Artie clamped a hand to his forehead and reminded himself to stay calm. 'Let's not get ahead of ourselves here, OK? Now, without going into too much detail, who did you speak to?'

'Some English fruit. Steven something.'

'Not Schitzbaul? Why weren't you speaking to Schitzbaul?'

'This guy said he was acting on Lance's behalf from here on in. What's the difference?' Bridget threw a couple of thin cotton dresses into the case splayed open on the bed.

She could hear Glen, in the shower now, singing the same words over and over – '*Going loco down in Acapulco*'.

'The difference, Bridget, is that we told Lance to keep this to himself. Clearly that's not the case if you're already talking to some fucking Brit.'

'What are you worried about, Artie? The guy said everything was cool.'

He said everything was cool.

It did sometimes wake Art Hinckley, attorney-at-law, in the middle of the night with icy, panting terror that he'd chosen to embark on a fifty-million-dollar blackmail plot with a pair this stupid. He'd met Glen Murphy nearly a year ago, after his regular cocaine supplier got pulled over on Ventura Boulevard with half a key and a loaded handgun in the trunk. Glen's product was a little like Glen himself – weak and unreliable, but Artie still rang him now and then. One night Glen had hung out longer than usual with Artie and the two hookers he was with. After the girls went home, they stayed up, chasing the sun, chopping lines and drinking Canadian Club, and Glen had started to tell Artie the story of his son's strange friendship with Lucius Du Pre. Artie had heard the rumours about the guy of course. He'd made a point of inviting Glen and Bridget out to dinner shortly after that. She'd broken down crying at the table when she revealed the full extent of young Connor's friendship with the Emperor of Pop. He remembered Glen, the fucking idiot, actually saying, 'I'm going to kill him. I'm going to go up there and kill him.'

'Hey,' Artie had said, 'don't get mad. Get even. In my experience there's only one way you really hurt these people ...'

'You wanna come with us?' Bridget was saying. 'Meet him?'

'No. No I do not. But do me a favour – record the conversation on your phone. Just in case there's any ... ambiguity later about what gets said.'

'OK. Relax, Artie. He sounded totally genuine. I can read people.'

'Bridget, I fu— Artie got a hold of himself. 'Just call me as soon as it's over and tell me what happened, OK?'

'Sure, Artie, later.'

She hung up. He was twitchy, their partner. A full partner too. Bridget wasn't quite sure he'd merited that. Yeah, he'd come up with the plan. But it was *her* son who had been, who was getting ... Bridget tried not to think about that. The way she looked at it, yes, an awful thing had happened to Connor, but if they'd gone to the cops, then what? Like Artie said, with all the money he had, the representation he could afford, Du Pre would most likely walk. Look at Jackson. Look at OJ. They didn't even have any definitive proof. Then, once they got the proof, Artie had said, 'Well, wait a minute, There might be another way to go here ...' They'd get Connor therapy and stuff down the line, when it was safer for him to talk about what had happened. And they could afford it. Besides, the ancient Greeks and stuff, they used to do this stuff with boys Connor's age all the time. It was, like, culturally accepted in some civilisations. Bridget had read up on all of this shit, online.

She looked around the cramped bedroom of their two-bed one-and-a-half-bath Echo Park bungalow – you could barely see the floor for all the crap, clothes and dishes and magazines. The damp patch working its way up the wall of the hallway. The chipped Formica countertop of the breakfast bar that separated the living room from the kitchen. That brownish stain on the carpet. A few jewels shone amid this dreary clutter: the top-of-the-line sixty-inch LCD with the PlayStation 4. The his-n-hers Rolexes on their dresser. The Mercedes parked out front. All gifts from Du Pre. But, like they say — what have you done for me lately? A car, a TV and a couple of watches in return for sticking his ... for ... no. Not enough. Not by a long chalk. They were going to get theirs. Big time. Satisfied with her packing for Palm Springs, Bridget turned her attention to what she was going to wear for lunch with this Limey fag. At some Mexican place over in the valley. (She'd been disappointed, hoping for somewhere glamorous — Chateau Marmont or Soho House. Somewhere like she used to go back in her twenties, when it had all seemed possible.) She wanted an outfit that said, 'Player. Don't fuck with me.'

'*Going loco down in Acapulco ...*' Glen came dancing out of the bathroom, wet, a towel around his waist. 'What time is it?'

'Eleven thirty? Shit, just nearly twelve. We'd better get a move on. Artie says one of us should record the conversation, by the way.'

'Smart.'

'What you gonna wear?' Bridget asked.

'Shit, I don't know.'

'Glen, it's important. He needs to take us seriously. Wear a suit.'

'A suit?' He slid the wardrobe door back and examined his meagre selection. 'Seriously?'

'Seriously. Wear the dark grey. The Calvin Klein. It's not too bad.' Most of Glen's suits had seen better days, had been acquired back in the late nineties, when he was moving mad volume. He took it off the hanger, sniffing, singing again. '*Going loco* ...'

'Have you ...?'

'Just a bump. Sharpen me up to deal with this Eurotrash fuck.'

'Jesus, Glen.'

'Don't make a big deal of it. Everything'll be fine. We're holding all the cards here, baby. There's one in there for you.'

'Maybe after. Oh, fuck it ...'

Bridget did the – admittedly small – line and started fixing her make-up in the mirror. She found herself singing too. '... *down in Acapulco.*' Everything would be fine. Like he said, they were holding all the cards.

EIGHT

The fucking state of this pair. It is all I can do when they walk in the door not to openly piss myself laughing. They're both wearing sunglasses, even though it is dark in this place, some beaner cave off Ventura, and they're dressed like extras from a Mexican remake of *Miami Vice*. I wave to them across the near empty restaurant and they walk over and sit down. I get up and extend my hand.

'Glen. Bridget. I'm Steven.'

It takes a moment for her as we shake hands, the wheels slowly turning. 'Aren't you that guy? You used to be a judge on that show a few years back? *American Pop Star?*'

'Very good, Bridget.'

'Wow. How —'

A waiter appears. 'Sir, madam, something to drink?'

'Two margaritas,' Glen says, sliding into the booth.

But she's already spotted my glass of ice water and says, 'No, just some water for me.'

He looks at her oddly, then back to the waiter. 'I'll drink hers. Bring two.' The waiter nods and fucks off. She sniffs, fiddling with her napkin. A coked-up pair of broken alkies. *Oh, this is excellent news*, I think to myself.

'How come you're handling this instead of Schitzbaul?' she continues. 'You know he was told not t—'

'I'm working as a consultant for the record company. They have an interest in seeing this happily resolved too.'

'Yeah,' this Glen says. 'I bet they fucking do.'

'So, what have you been up to since the show?' this idiotic prostitute says, trying to keep it pleasant, conversational, thinking we're going to do a bit of Hollywood-style chit-chat before we get down to the pitch.

'About the money,' I say, ignoring her. 'Let's get serious.'

A beat.

'The fucking video of that animal raping our kid isn't serious enough for you?' Glen growls.

'You should know that no one's judging you here. Me? I'd have done the same thing. You go to the police, what happens? You're in a long, expensive legal battle with a man with nearly unlimited resources.' (Little do they know, etc.) 'You go to the press, yeah you might get a few mil for the tape, but your life as you know it is over. You're in every tabloid in the world every week for the rest of your days. I'd have done exactly what you're doing. It's the only way you'll really hurt him and get to walk away.' They look surprised at this.

'Fucking A,' Glen says. 'That's what we figured.'

'But fifty million? Come on.'

They both look at me for a long beat. I sip my water, pretending this is actually a negotiation. Really we could be talking about two hundred million or fifty pence. It's just important to let them think that this is real. That this is actually happening. They look at each other. It is Bridget who speaks first. 'Forty million.'

'Ten,' I say.

'Fuck you,' Glen says. 'Thirty. Thirty fucking million.'

I wait a moment, shaking my head, kind of enjoying this fiasco. 'Twenty,' I say finally.

They look at each other. 'We'll need to talk to Art –' Glen begins, before she cuts him off.

'No, we don't. Twenty,' she says. 'But I swear to God, if you –'

'You'll need to give us some time of course.'

'What?' Glen says, leaning in. I notice that his suit, some aged Calvin Klein piece-of-shit, has hash burns all over it. 'How much ti—'

'Guys,' I say, 'it's *twenty million dollars* we're talking about here. That takes some planning.'

'Bullshit,' she says. 'Private bank can wire that in sixty seconds.'

'They can,' I say. 'But there's the question of where the money came from. Traceability. Our mutual friend doesn't just have an account labelled "blackmail funds", you know.'

'How long?' she asks as their, his, drinks arrive. He attacks the first one greedily. Oh man, this is actually going to be fun. I wait a beat until the waiter retreats again.

'A week. Maybe two.'

'Listen to me –' Glen says, about to get assertive.

'But,' I say, looking at her, cutting him off completely, 'as a gesture of good faith, I have personally arranged for a cash deposit of one million dollars to be paid to you today.' I put some car keys on the table. 'There's a brand-new black Mustang in the car park out back. It's in the boot.'

'The what?'

'The trunk.' Fucking colonials. 'You get to keep the car too. Call it a bonus. We want you to know we're serious about paying you. I'll be in touch about the balance in a few days. At which point I'll need to speak with your lawyer, Mr . . . ?'

'Hinkley. Art Hinkley,' she says.

'. . . Mr Hinkley, to get his assurance that all copies of the recording will be destroyed.' The idiots look at each other, not sure whether they've lost a pound or found a fiver. I stand up, smoothing down my sweater.

'Hey,' Glen says. 'How do we know this ain't a set-up? We open that trunk and, like, a fucking bomb goes off or something?'

'Glen,' I say. 'Sober up. Catch a fucking grip.' I lean down on the edge of the table, standing over them, quite close. 'You're going to like it, you know. It's good. I highly recommend it.'

'Like what?' she says.

'The Mustang?' Glen says.

'Being rich,' I say, grinning. 'Speak to you in a few days. Have some lunch. The fish tacos are excellent.'

I leave, whistling.

With just over two hours before I have to catch the jet out at Van Nuys, I head back over the hills to Soho House for lunch with Schitzbaul. (Picturing, with some pleasure, the Murphys chomping down on some semen-infested taco in the khazi I've just left.) As the limo crosses Mulholland I call Trellick to tell him how it went. He's still nervous despite my incredibly upbeat tone. 'James,' I say soothingly, 'you worry too much.'

Schitzbaul is already there when I arrive, sat at a table on the south terrace of the bar. You can see my apartment building. He's smoking his tits off and, by the way he stands to greet me, is already working on his second martini. 'Tell me something good,' he says as we embrace. I lower my voice, needlessly, it's after three o'clock and the place is very quiet. 'Lance,' I say, doing my best Michael Caine, 'I've got a lovely little idea ...'

Fifteen minutes later, after I've finished speaking, after he's ordered and drained another martini, after he's tried to interrupt three times, each time silenced by me raising my index finger warningly, he finally gets to speak.

'You're fucking nuts,' he says.

Wearyingly, I go through a rehash of the exact same conversation I had with Trellick the night before. But my pitch is better now, second time around. Faster. Sharper. Foreseeing any objections before they arise.

'I don't know,' he says. 'I just don't know ...'

I go for the close. 'Lance,' I say. 'Look at me.' He looks at me. His thinning silver hair, his great, straining belly, his old eyes, eyes that have seen everything, every combination humans can do to each other to elicit pleasure and pain. I feel sympathy for this ancient manager, once a legend in this business, now shackled to a maniac, praying for someone to put him out of his misery. (Remember – every executive career eventually ends in ignominy. No one goes quietly.) 'I need you to help me sell this to him. Understand me – this is it for you. This is as good as it gets. Get the fuck on board, you fat, useless old bastard, or me and

Trellick will personally ensure you go down with the rapist cunt for aiding and abetting. You'll spend your retirement in San Quentin, bent over in the laundry room, looking over your shoulder at a queue of spearchuckers with ten-inch cocks in their hands, waiting their turn. Are you with me?'

He looks at me, broken. 'I think we can sell it.'

'That's the spirit,' I say.

We talk a little longer — mostly about practicalities involving Dr Ali — before I leave him, staring into his empty glass, wondering about the living hell he has just signed up for. As I'm striding through the main club, a girl, twenty-something, walks by and, very clearly, very deliberately, smiles coquettishly at me. (Well, as coquettishly as this type of West Hollywood spunk devotee can.) Total Bogs Boiler. The upsides of fame. You just grab 'em by the pussy. You don't even wait ...

When it happened last year, when it came out, the amount of arse I had to listen to, at dinner parties, in restaurants, in meetings. 'Oh, he's finished. Over. That's the end.' Really? Really, cunt? You know what? It turned out he was only finished in the tiny oatmeal-eating, *Guardian*-reading corner of the world you live in. It turned out that this was just 'locker-room talk', and that the locker room was basically the rest of the fucking planet, the place where the real people live, the people who live on the *Daily Mail* website, the people who want to hear all the fucking words, the people who buy Ed Sheeran's records. *And there are fucking billions of the cunts.* You got women speaking up for Trump. I saw them, on Fox, even on CNN. Getting interviewed in the streets of Idaho,

Nebraska and Wisconsin. It turned out that, far from the dinner tables of Manhattan, Silver Lake and Hampstead, there were boilers who actually *wanted* their pussy grabbed. Who didn't want to be asked. Who wanted the right to be dragged into the bogs and have their back door kicked in. It turned out that this was part of the American dream too: the right to be used as a flesh lavatory by some player just because he'd been on TV for ten minutes. 'The struggle', it turned out, still had some way to go. The resistance still had warm work to do. And I feel for you girls. I feel your pain. It must be exhausting, a century of feminism and there you are – still struggling, still resisting, as some madman pins you up against the wall of the hotel room, pins you down in the back of the cab, and says, 'Suck this, you horrible fucking cow'. Meanwhile, there's a few million of your sisters out there, all saying, 'Fuck that bitch. Grab *this* pussy.'

Thinking these fine thoughts, I hear a voice calling out 'Steven! Hey! Steven!' I turn warily, not breaking stride, and see a girl with red hair waving to me from one of the banquettes opposite the bar. It takes me a moment to realise it is Chrissy Price, A&R woman. Now here is a DB clearly on her way up to being an RB. I break stride.

'Hi there,' I say, walking over, 'how's tricks?'

She has it all laid out in front of her – notepad, iPad, trades, coffee pot, the remains of a salad. 'Just catching up on some work before a meeting,' she explains, 'saves me going all the way back to the office.'

'I see . . .' I say. And I do. She really is genuinely working.

Kids today, they do this. Back in my day, it was a little different. I look around the fairly quiet Soho House. There's a gaggle of models over there, several hot waitresses floating around, the writer Kennedy Marr and a few friends pissed in the corner. Right across the street are the Hollywood Hills – packed with coke dealers – and, behind me, a long, fully stocked bar. Yeah, suffice to say, back in the day, at four o'clock in the afternoon we'd have been fucking *ruling* this place: smashing cocktails, bugling up, and doing secretaries in the bogs like it was going out of fashion. (Which, of course, it was.) But this was the nineties – you could actually be a convicted paedophile who'd signed one dance single that charted at number 72 (in Holland) and *still* find someone willing to pay you a hundred grand a year plus car and expenses. 'What's funny?' she says off my expression.

'Nothing, just reminiscing. Do you mind ...?' I gesture to the banquette next to her.

'Please ...' she says, scooting over as I slide in, then adding, 'How's the jet lag?' She's nervous, looking for conversation.

'I don't get jet lag,' I say. 'It's vulgar. Listen, Trellick tells me that Danny Rent's managing this house act you're after, Norwegian Dance Crew?'

'Yeah, you know him?'

'Back in the day and all that. How's it going?'

'It's a fucking nightmare. Danny's a friend of yours?'

'Define friend,' I say in a tone that leaves her plenty of leeway.

'Well, excuse me, but he's a fucking lowlife cocksucker who should get AIDS and die.' I'm beginning to like this girl. 'Two weeks ago this was our deal and then suddenly Capitol get let back in the door and now he's taking meetings with XL too? Fuck me.' She sweeps red hair out of her face and leans forward to sip her coffee, allowing me an eyeful of vast, milky cleavage in the scoop-neck T-shirt.

'Where are you at?' I ask.

'Money-wise? Six fifty now.'

'Mmmm,' I say, thinking. 'Is it worth it?'

'You've heard them. It's nothing. Just standard-issue, David Guetta, Calvin Harris-type shit.'

'But ...' I say.

'But the kids fucking love it and we need some hits, right?'

'Good girl,' I say. I wonder if she's quite turned thirty yet. 'Well, if I can do anything to help, let me know.'

'They're spinning in Vegas this weekend. If you fancy slumming it and flying commercial ...'

I stifle the usual burst of murderous rage I experience when Americans use the phrase 'spinning'. What the fuck was wrong with 'DJing', you Sherman cunts? We managed fine with it for the twenty years before any of you thought to even bosh a fucking pill. Obviously the list of things I'd rather do than go to Vegas to watch some dance cretins 'spinning' is fairly exhaustive, but then I look at this mane of red hair, that rack, those clear blue eyes. 'Might be difficult,' I say. 'I've got my hands fairly full at the minute ...'

'Yeah,' she grins, 'what's going on with you guys? All feels very ... cloak and dagger.'

'Oh, nothing. Just helping James out with a couple of things. Anyway,' I change the subject, 'what else are you looking at these days? Who's happening?' I ask. She starts talking about bands, singers, DJs, tapping away at her iPad to show me things, numbers of hits on websites, the number of streaming plays on Spotify and Pandora.

I drift off, remembering a meeting we had at the label, back in '94, over twenty years ago, in another lifetime, when I was a junior A&R guy, back in the days of dial-up, the screeching, squeaking modem, taking four hours to download your nude photograph of Pamela Anderson. There was me and Trellick and Waters, Derek, Ross and a couple of other guys from marketing. A pair of American fruits came in to show us how the Internet was going to affect our business in the future. They were looking for an investment, something like fifty grand for some new business they were setting up. 'So, the kid will download the track onto his computer,' this guy said. 'And he'll be able to do this anywhere, in a cafe, on a train, in the street ...'

'Eh?' Ross said. 'How ... where will he plug it in?'

'Excuse me?'

'The wires, the computer. What, there'll be sockets you can plug into all over the place?'

The American guys looked at each other. 'No,' they said. 'In, like, ten years or so there won't be any wires any more. Everything will be wireless.'

We all exchanged looks at this point.

'And the CD will be burned straight onto your computer?' Derek asked.

'No, no. There won't be any CDs then.'

'What? Where will the music be?'

'Just ... on your computer.'

Now we were all wondering about the guy's sanity. 'And the artwork?' Ross asked. 'Will that print off from your computer and you'll be able to —'

'Guys,' this Yank said, taking his glasses off, 'you need to get it – there won't be any CDs. Or any artwork. Or albums as you know them. No one's going to care about that stuff any more. Listen to me – people just want to hear that song they like.'

Well, we looked at each other one more time and then we burst out laughing. We sent that pair of bumlords out of our building with a fucking boot ringing on their backsides.

The company they were setting up was called Yahoo!

Later, much later, over redundancy drinks, some of the accounting staff worked out that if we'd invested fifty grand in Yahoo! in 1994, rather than making, say, the second Rage album, we'd all have been worth ...

Well, you win some, you lose some. I tune back into Chrissy, who is saying '... you know, that whole Upper West Side Soweto thing –'

'Shit,' I say, looking at my watch, 'I gotta run, sorry ...'

'Where you headed?

'Van Nuys.'

'Oh yeah, I heard you have the jet right now,' she smiles. 'You wouldn't believe how pissed a couple of people are about that. You headed somewhere nice?'

'Just a quick business trip,' I say.

'Have fun,' Chrissy says.

'Oh yeah,' I say with absolutely no enthusiasm whatsoever.

NINE

I wake up and pull the blind up, to see we are over a glittering expanse of sea. I check the inflight monitor on the TV screen, yawning, calling for coffee and water, and see the little aeroplane icon is over the Red Sea. We've just passed Egypt. I breakfast, shower and change into fresh clothes: my navy linen Huntsman suit and a crisp white shirt. I reset my Pepsi-Cola GMT to the new time zone. We are twelve hours ahead of LA now.

When I disembark the Gulfstream the heat is so great that your nostrils burn when you inhale. I take my first few breaths with a hand over my mouth and nose, trying to diffuse the heat before it enters. I've been over this way a couple of times before (to Dubai recently, a shopping mall built on slave blood – capitalism at its finest) and, even by Gulf standards, the heat is deranged. Fortunately, I don't have to endure it for very long. As soon as I'm on the tarmac a tall, bearded Arab is introducing himself, saying how pleased he is to meet me, and walking me towards

the inevitable Maybach. There are two others flanking it. I
ride alone in the back seat, stretched out on cool leather,
gazing numbly at the endless desert that slides by through
the tinted glass as I work on my pitch.

I wonder idly how much of my adult life has been spent
doing what I'm doing now: gazing through smoked glass
as I try to figure out what I'm going to say when I get
there. Many, many hours. (I can hear you saying, *You don't
need to work, Steven. How much money can you need?* I'll assume
if you're asking that last question you are actually dirt poor.
Poor people will often ask – 'What's the difference between
220 million and 230 million dollars?' The answer, of course,
is *ten million dollars, you fucking clown.*) I'm pulled out of a
half-nap by the lurching feeling of the car slowing down.
The drive from the private airfield has taken just twenty
minutes. I look up to see the palace rising in front of me
out of the desert, at the end of the two-mile driveway lined
with mature trees. (The irrigation costs alone . . .)

This . . . to call it a 'family home' would be a savage
understatement, like calling Peter Sutcliffe 'unreasonable'.
It is immense, in pale stone. I know from my reading that it
covers 250,000 square feet and contains three swimming
pools, an ice-skating rink and its own mosque. It is the
only structure as far as the eye can see. The car comes to
a stop in front of a two-hundred-foot artificial lake studded
with fountains spraying water high into the air. More func-
tionaries appear and I am ushered into the hall – a cool
expanse of pink marble the size of a football pitch. And
then the Sultan of Quatain is walking towards me, smiling,
extending his hand.

Game on.

*

The Sultan is shaking his head gravely and repeating 'this poor man'. The Sultan's son? He's actually *crying*. We're drinking mint tea and eating dates in a vast lounge, sitting below a huge Rothko. 'Abdullah,' the father eventually says, patting his son's shoulder, 'please. Stop.' (Remember, family is a big deal for these guys.) With a sniff, the kid pulls himself together. I say 'kid' – he's twenty-two and, I strongly suspect, a raving fucking iron. 'Mr Stelfox,' he gestures to me, 'I apologise. My son is an ... emotional boy.' Yep, Dad knows son's an iron. 'Please, continue.'

'He's ... he's very sick. What he needs most now is total rest. Utter seclusion. The way things are in our country, in the West, with the press, the tabloids, social media, he'll never get that. If this story, these lies, come out ... well, I don't think he could live through it. It ... it would kill him.' Young Abdullah has to stifle a scream, or a sob, or a bit of both at this. He stuffs his fist in his mouth. 'I've been trying to find a solution. Somewhere he can recuperate, somewhere journalists would never find him. Somewhere ...'

'Like here!' Abdullah exclaims, beyond himself with excitement.

'Well, exactly,' I say.

The Sultan just nods, having figured out long before his son where this was all headed.

'Father,' the kid says, 'we must help him.'

'Of course we'd pay for all the living expenses. Mr Du Pre has his personal physician who would be with him, so all his medical needs would be catered to. We'd just need access to a pharmacy. His medications, for his disease, are

... extensive. It's just, the most important thing is – *no one could ever know he was here.*'

'Mr Stelfox,' the Sultan says, 'you arrived here today. You landed at my private airfield and travelled over my estate to this house. We are hundreds of miles from anyone. Privacy is not an issue.'

'Of course. I meant more in terms of your staff. Of loose tongues.'

'He could be installed in his own wing, with his own staff, whose loyalty to me is unquestioning.' I believe this. You do not fuck with these guys. They'll chop your fucking cock off for looking at their wife funny. Your hands off for stealing a chocolate bar. 'But ...' I can see the dad still has some reservations ...

'Father,' Abdullah says, 'what is there to think about? Lucius Du Pre is asking for our help!'

'Abdullah,' the Sultan says, 'leave us.'

The kid stands up and goes to leave. He turns back. 'If we do not help Lucius then *I* will kill myself!'

The Sultan doesn't reply, just dismisses his son with a wave of his hand. It takes a good thirty seconds for Abdullah's heels to click across the marble and out of the door. 'I apologise for the impudence, Mr Stelfox. As you can see I am a soft father who indulges his children too much.'

'He seems a fine boy,' I lie.

He ignores this. 'Tell me, Mr Stelfox, these crimes he is accused of. Your Du Pre. Are the accusations real?' Yeah, he's done his homework, this old clit-chopper.

We look at each other.

'He is a complex man,' I offer.

'Please, let's not be coy with each other. Understand – I make no moral judgement. Sheep, goats, women, boys, whatever a man wishes to loose his seed into is no concern of mine.'

I like this guy. I lean forward. 'Excellency, I understand you have been trying for some time to invest a more significant part of your income in the United States.' I've done my homework too. The tsunami of dirty money flowing through the Middle East these days. 'But, as you know, this can be difficult. The *abeed* Obama and his regulations.'

'Well ... that might all be changing soon.'

'Indeed. But for now, the company I represent, Unigram, their share price is very weak. Something occurred to me. An opportunity for you ...'

We talk for a long time about financial instruments. Shell companies. Cypriot banks. Junk bonds. The long bond curve. The talk of pure money. I admit, he's way ahead of me. I don't quite follow all of it. But I get the gist. You bet I get the fucking gist. After a while I say, 'Sir, I will speak with my bankers in New York. They are very ... creative.' (This is an understatement. Stern, Hammler & Gersh? They'd channel the profits from blood diamonds to fund human trafficking.) 'I am certain we can find a solution that may help us both. And I can assure you of my utmost discretion. As I will have to depend upon yours.'

He pours more tea. 'There was one other matter.' Here we fucking go. You scratch my back, I'll do you up the coalhole with no lube. 'You are an A&R man, are you not? A finder of talent?' I nod. 'I have nine children. My eldest daughter, Aesha, she yearns to be singer. She has made a recording . . .' Nothing fucking changes. Whether it's a cab driver, or the TV repair guy, or some cunt at a wedding, or the Sultan of fucking Quatain, as soon as they find out what you do it's 'my brother/son/girl-friend/whatever has a fucking demo you need to listen to'.

'I think,' I say, sensing the close drawing near, 'Mr Du Pre's label would be very interested in hearing your daughter's music.'

The cunt grins for the first time, expensive, capped teeth showing in his mahogany face. 'She is most talented.'

'I'm sure.'

'Besides,' the Sultan sighs, 'I fear if I refused your request Abdullah really might kill himself.' We both laugh, making light of it, but I feel his pain. Imagine your son *was* an iron? How might that go? You're sitting there, happily picturing his first girlfriends, the immense amount of pumping you're going to get to see him doing, then the grandkids, the continuation of the line. You're thinking about succession, about passing on assets, the family name growing and strengthening into future generations, long after you are gone, and then the kid says 'Dad, this is Sebastian . . .' and there's some brick shithouse of a bender standing there, massive cockduster moustache, leather cap, aviators, white vest, the lot. And your actual son is standing there holding his hand, asking you to be pleased for him, *proud* of him, for telling you that he is sodomising – or being sodomised by – a man. That he has chosen to sow his seed (your seed) in the barren wilderness of the male anus, where nothing will ever grow or blossom. Fucking *imagine it*. Speaking of which . . .

'I too have one last request, Excellency,' I say. 'As we touched on earlier, Mr Du Pre ... his needs are not limited to the purely medical, if you understand me ...'

He smiles again. 'Mr Stelfox. We have some of the finest boys in the world. Twelve, thirteen years old. Virgins. Whatever he requires. We will make him most comfortable. And, please, I do not want to hear any talk of payment. Mr Du Pre will be my honoured guest and will be treated accordingly.'

'Sir, I am in your debt.'

'Now, I will tell Abdullah. You will undoubtedly hear his shriek of delight from here.' He rolls his eyes. 'You will be spending the night of course? I have prepared a suite of rooms for you.'

'Forgive my rudeness, Excellency, but I must return immediately to Los Angeles. The matters I am dealing with here, they are extremely time-sensitive.'

'I understand.' He rises and we shake hands. 'Do you have children, Mr Stelfox?'

'Allah has not given me that blessing yet.'

'One day, when he has, you will understand the decisions fathers must make.'

He leaves. I quietly high-five myself. Phase one is done. Phase two is up next. Lots of hurdles yet to cross. One thing though – I'm kind of looking forward to telling Trellick he's going to have to give some crazed Arab boiler a record deal. But first things first. I make the call from the car on the way back to the jet.

TEN

Terry Rawlings, in first class, in seat 4B of an American Airlines flight from Bogotá to LAX. Terry chose the smoked salmon and then the beef, thanking the steward and handing the menu back before putting his screen up for privacy. He sipped his Bloody Mary and returned to his work – a notepad, a stack of papers and a ballpoint pen on the little table in front of him, his feet up on the footstool, stretching his six-two frame out. Terry was sketching plans, outlines, contingencies. He was thinking about possible sites, somewhere that met exacting specifications: remoteness, plausibility, ground exit routes, the availability of nearby airstrips and so forth. Helicopter though, Terry was definitely thinking helicopter.

It amazed him that so many high-net-worth individuals still chose to use them. They were so much more vulnerable than planes in bad weather. They flew lower to the ground, a chopper's max ceiling without pressurisation was about 12,000 feet (also, conveniently, ideal height for a jump without oxygen), making you far more likely to encounter buildings or hills that suddenly appeared out of fog. They also had a lot more moving parts than aeroplanes, a lot more things to potentially malfunction: main rotor, tail rotor, gearbox, and the drive shaft running the entire length of the aircraft, all these things in constant motion, the parts wearing out more quickly. Terry had a couple of hundred hours under his belt – Apaches, Lynxes – and knew how much trickier they were to handle than aeroplanes: the cyclic control, the collective control, the anti-torque pedals, the throttle, all happening at once. The rate of accidents during instructional flights was twice as high for helicopters as for aeroplanes. (Terry had seen a couple of nasty spills during advanced training, at Middle Wallop, down in Hampshire, back in the nineties.) Yeah, on grounds of plausibility alone, it was definitely helicopters. He took a map of southern California out of his stack of papers and began thinking about flight paths. Oh, this right here, this mountain range, this could be good ...

Terry had been introduced to his current employer at a party, a little over ten years ago, on a yacht in Cannes, by Lev Kalonsky, the Russian energy billionaire whom Terry had done a few jobs for – boom times workwise in Russia over the last decade. It surprised Terry that his career trajectory was the stuff of novels and movies, because for him it was so boringly obvious it almost defied belief. From public school to Sandhurst – where he excelled in everything – straight on to SAS training, and then eight years of ops before entering the private sector. There were a tedious couple of years of bodyguard stuff before some more interesting jobs started to come his way. He was forty-two now though, and the aches and pains were starting to become increasingly real. For the first time, thoughts of retirement were beginning to cross Terry's mind. This job, insanely well paid by anyone's standards, would definitely help.

After an hour or so, the remains of his lunch cleared away, sipping a second cup of coffee to clear his head of the rich burgundy he'd had with his beef, Terry closed his notepad, satisfied he had the rudiments of a plan he could take to the boss. Terry thought of some of the things he'd seen and done in his career – the polonium swirling gently in a teapot in the kitchen of an Israeli hotel, Terry in waiter's uniform. The Ukrainian politician he'd killed with a syringe in a lift. That perfect shot in the Gulf, a little under two thousand metres in a high wind – with the CheyTac, the .408 calibre, a wonderful American weapon that had cost him 12,000 dollars, how he wished he still had it – the guy's head just evaporating in a red mist. Indulging a rare moment of introspection – as we are all given to with a little alcohol at high altitude – Terry saw himself in various poses over the years: behind a door clutching piano wire, crouched in a bedroom closet with chloroform and hunting knife, in the freezing cold on moorland with his eye pressed to the telescopic sight for hours on end, and, just the other day, in Bogotá, on his back in the parking structure, underneath the embassy car with pliers and a pan to catch the brake fluid. Yes, it would be fair to say that morality hadn't featured much in Terry's professional life. Indeed, the only time he felt he was in the presence of a force less indebted to morality was when he did what he would be doing tomorrow.

When he met the gaze of Steven Stelfox.

ELEVEN

'You're kidding, right?'

Dr Ali was stretched out on the sofa of his house, fresh from the golf course in chinos and Lacoste polo shirt, the Pacific crashing just the other side of the highway. Schitzbaul sat across from him, uncomfortable, sweating, in rumpled suit and stained shirt. He was, of course, drinking, a bourbon on the rocks to Ali's tumbler of pineapple juice. He reckoned he'd averaged about two hours' sleep a night for the past week.

'I'm not. Trust me. This is the only way out of this.'

'No, I mean you're kidding about the money.'

Ah. Schitzbaul relaxed a little. So the hard part was over. This was now a negotiation. What he did best. 'What were you thinking, Ali?'

'You said "a few months", right? You're asking me to uproot my life, not see my kids –'

'You never see your kids.'

Ali – four kids, three wives – let this slide. 'I don't know. Two seems low.' Tossing off 'two' as though he were talking about bagels, or toffees, rather than *two million dollars*. The lack of respect for money irritated Schitzbaul, an old Jew who had started out the lowest of the low in the William Morris mailroom, back in the seventies. 'Five would be more in the ballpark ...'

'You know, Ali,' Schitzbaul said, getting up and crossing over to the wet bar in the corner, 'if this goes down, who knows where it'll end.' The fresh ice clanged like bells as he dropped it into the heavy crystal. 'I mean, I'd think, given the allegations involved, the man's personal physician would very likely be subpoenaed. There could be a court-ordered physical. A search of the property. Who knows what they'd find in his medicine cabinet. In his system ...'

'DON'T TALK BULLSHIT, SCHITZBAUL!' Ali exploded.

'I mean,' the manager continued, staying calm, listening to the styrofoam creaking of the ice as it splintered under bourbon, 'where does the buck stop with all that? Whose name are they finding on all those prescriptions?' He sipped his drink. The rich old Arab and the rich old Jew regarded each other.

'Are you fucking threatening me, Lance?'

'Not at all. Just pointing out that we both have a dog in this fight. My interests are best served by staying here. Yours by being with your patient.' Schitzbaul watched Ali's shoulders slump. 'Three,' he said, going in for the kill. 'I can get you three, Ali.'

Ali grinned. A three-million-dollar bonus for a few months' vacation. There were worse ways to earn a living. 'Do they have golf there?'

'They sure do,' Schitzbaul said, his tone brightening, putting his briefcase on the table, popping the catches. 'Matter of fact – I think the Sultan has a personal course, so you're guaranteed a good tee time, right?'

'And when is this going to happen?'

'Not one hundred per cent on that yet. But soon, maybe next week. So pack a go bag. Here, survival kit …' Schitzbaul started laying things out on the coffee table: a passport with Du Pre's face on it, but bearing the name of his new identity, Mr Fergal McCann, a Platinum Amex in the name of Mr Fergal McCann and several banded stacks of hundred-dollar bills. 'Just in case. Otherwise keep track of your expenses and you'll be reimbursed. Just think – you'll be with your own people! Back in the old country!'

'Ha ha – very fucking funny.'

'We'll bring you home in a few months and this'll all be over.'

'When you say "this" – what exactly is going to happen?'

'That's on a need-to-know. And, trust me, pal, you do not need, or want, to know.'

TWELVE

Another day, another endless ride up the long driveway of a madman. It's just Trellick and me in the back of the limo (Schitzbaul will already be there, hopefully having 'warmed up' the room) as acre after acre of Malibu scrubland slides past.

Have you ever done an eleven-hour and two sixteen-hour flights across a dozen time zones in the space of a few days? Even given the extreme comfort of the Gulfstream, it's a shocker. You don't need drugs, sex or music to have an out-of-body experience, *everything* is an out-of-body experience. Opening a can of soda. Crossing your legs. Yawning, which you're obviously doing a lot of. Here in LA it's 10 a.m. In my body it's three o'clock in the morning somewhere over the Atlantic. Of course, back in the old days, I'd have dealt with this via the simple method of snorkelling a ton of Vim up my fucking hooter. Given all the travel – London/LA, LA/Quatain, Quatain/LA – I'm actually in pretty good shape. Not boozing or doing class

A's any more definitely helps. Back in the day a trip across the Atlantic was basically a ten-hour drinking session, starting in the bar at Heathrow and finishing just before the 'Fasten seat belts' light came on for landing. But we were in our twenties then. It was all doable. Instead I take a draught of coffee. 'What time is it?' I ask.

'Just after ten,' Trellick says.

'Actually, fuck that, what *day* is it?'

'Friday,' Trellick says. 'Racking up the air miles, eh?'

'Christ.'

'Do you think he'll go for it?' Trellick asks, again.

'James,' I say, knackered, 'if he doesn't then it's plan B. It'll be a lot less profitable and a lot more boring, but it'll work.'

'And you reckon you can trust this what's-his-name?'

'The Sultan? It's a gamble,' I say. 'But at this point ...'

'Everything's a fucking gamble?'

'Correctos.'

'When does your guy get in?'

'Right about now. I'm meeting him after this.'

'Is ... is he –'

'Mate,' I say, 'you really don't want to know any more. Trust me.' He nods. 'I just want to get through this fucking meeting, go home and sleep for ten hours.'

'Remember, we've got James's birthday party tomorrow.'

'Who the fuck is James?'

'Ah, my son?'

'Oh yeah, shit. Sorry.'

'From three. At the house. Bring a date if you like. Though I'm sure Pandora has a few friends she wants you to meet ...' Yeah, I think, forty-something yummy mummies looking for victim number two. Or three. 'Christ,' Trellick says. 'No wonder he's broke . . .'

I follow his gaze out of the window. A bunch of llamas are running alongside the car, inhabitants of Du Pre's petting zoo. We can see the vast ranch coming up and, in the distance behind it, the Ferris wheel topping the full-size amusement park. Parked in front of the house is an array of high-end motors: Hummers, Porsches, a Ferrari. We crunch over gravel and park up. 'Narnia . . .' I say, looking at the word spelled out in flowers in an enormous bed.

Trellick sighs. 'The Paedo, the Rapist and the fucking Wardrobe.'

A huge Samoan bodyguard is walking towards us, reaching for the car door.

Once again – show time.

Now, I have spent much time with the truly famous and I can generally testify to the old adage about their mentalities being frozen at the age at which they became famous. Anyone who gets there much over the age of twenty-five has a shot at some kind of sanity. As you slide further towards youthful success you're on a scale of diminishing returns. Many pop stars and actors get there in their late teens and that's what you're stuck with forever – a screaming fucking teenager. Elvis, who became famous at nineteen, is the paradigm here. Look at his life, forever surrounded by a gang of cronies, watching porn, living on a diet of Coca-Cola, mashed potatoes and burgers, never getting out of bed: basically what happens if you give a teenage redneck free rein. From him right on down to One Direction you're pretty much dealing with people who are by turns truculent, petty, grumpy, exuberant, illogical or whining. So you take someone like

Du Pre: he's been famous since he was fucking *nine*. You're dealing with a nine-year-old billionaire who hasn't much heard the word 'no' in forty years. But with the additional complication that the nine-year-old's cock and balls are fully grown and riddled with spunk and his brain has fused somewhere along the line and he's decided that what he really wants to do, what he *has* to do, is fuck other children. So, you have a slightly overgrown toddler with a God complex. Just listen to him. Listen to what I'm listening to here, sitting in the Kew Gardens-like conservatory.

'And the Lord said "*I will walk with my people*" and I want to walk with my people. It could be so beautiful, Mr Trellick, Mr St . . .'

'Stelfox.'

'Stelfox. I love foxes. I love all animals. Some say the souls of animals do not go to heaven, but I believe the Lord will welcome all of his creatures into his kingdom. Walking, with my people. I want to walk with them. I truly do. All of us in white. You know, Lance, you might want to remind the costume designers about that before I see them in New York. Everyone in white. I had an idea, for the opening bars of "Shakedown", everyone is looking up at this bright light, then I descend out of it . . .' He goes on in his lisping, high-pitched whine.

It's not really a conversation, as such. More of a free-wheeling monologue that could be called 'Things That Are Passing Through My Brain'. Du Pre veers from topic to topic, dispenses with sequiturs, half finishes thoughts, attempts to start sentences three or four times before abandoning them altogether and changing the subject. It is exactly like speaking with a toddler. I should also add that he's wearing sunglasses and some kind of military jumpsuit embroidered with gold, gold lanyards and epaulettes and stuff. He looks like a version of Colonel Gaddafi someone knocked up on RuPaul's Drag Race. While they were pissed. It also strikes me as odd, his penchant for constantly mentioning God and Jesus when he spends half his life out of his mind on gear, pumping his mad dross up the fucking dung funnels of prepubescent boys. Then again, I've never read the Bible. Maybe there's something in there that says all of this shit is fine and dandy. *'And blessed shall be the drug-addled child molesters, for they shall bring succour to their own testes and pleasure to the rectums of the chosen ones.'*

I must also be mindful of Du Pre's upbringing, of the role of his father in all of this. I mean, it's pretty hardcore, isn't it? Your own dad, screaming his head off as he smashes your back door in? Punching you in the back of the head and calling you a dirty bastard, his actual balls banging off your cheeks. That's bound to give you some pretty strange ideas about yourself, isn't it? I mean, pick the change out of that one, cunt.

'. . . and they will touch the hem of my garment as the spotlight —'

'Uh, Lucius? Mr Du Pre? HEY!'

He turns to me, startled. 'You need,' I say, looking directly at whatever passes for eyes behind those black wraparound shades, 'to be quiet now and listen to Lance.'

Du Pre looks surprised, I think, it's hard to tell from the Botox-blasted expressionless mask he has instead of a face, but he shuts up and turns to his manager.

'Lance?' I say again.

'Right. Uh, yeah. OK. So . . .'

Schitzbaul tells him. It takes a little while, his voice is unusually soft and he makes no eye contact, mostly looking at a spot on the marble floor, but he gets it all out. The Murphys, the video, his finances. In almost comical fast-forward we go through the Five Stages of Kübler-Ross. Stage One ...

Denial. 'That ... that's a lie. It ... it's disgraceful. I never ... Connor and I, we have a beautiful relationship. So beautiful. To even think ... these people and their filthy minds, it makes me –' He goes on for a bit.

'Lucius,' Schitzbaul says, looking at him for the first time. I swear there are tears in his eyes. 'Do you want us to play the tape?' Du Pre stops talking. He looks at the tea and coffee things on the low table for a moment. Then he *screams* as he gets up and boots everything – cups, saucers, sugar, milk – across the room and we're into Stage Two ...

Anger. 'MOTHERFUCKER! THAT LITTLE BITCH! AFTER ALL I DID FOR HIM AND HIS FAMILY! IT WASN'T ME WHO STARTED ANYTHING! THAT KID'S THIRTEEN GOING ON THIRTY! SONOFABITCH!' He tries to grab a tall pot plant – some kind of fern – and hurl it across the room too, but it's too big, so he just kind of wrestles with it for a bit, screaming while Trellick and I watch and Schitzbaul says 'Lucius ... Lucius ...' to no avail. 'COCKSUCKER! LOWLIFE PIECE OF SHIT! FUCK!' Finally, his rage abates and he collapses back onto one of the sofas and we're off into Stage Three ...

Bargaining. 'Lance,' he says, dropping from the sofa onto his knees on the floor in front of Schitzbaul, 'you gotta make this go away. We can find the money. Just pay them off. We've done it before. We can remortgage this place. I ... I'll sell

some stuff. We can go to the banks again. We can –' He goes
through a bunch of half-arsed solutions, all of which have
already been exhaustively discussed and dismissed by us. Lance
and Trellick tell him one by one why none of them will work.
Du Pre grows more and more agitated. At one point, when
Trellick is explaining just how much debt he is in, he begins
wailing and tearing enormous lumps of hair out of his scalp,
revealing strange brown/pink patches, the result of the mad
bastard's ongoing project to try and turn himself into a darkie.
After Trellick bats down his final deranged scheme to raise
cash – something about going public and offering people the
chance to buy shares in his future recordings, Trellick having
to wearily point out that no one is going to be lining up to
buy stock in Paedo Inc. – Du Pre slumps to the floor and
begins to sob and we're into Stage Four.

Depression. 'I'm finished. It's all over. I . . . oh my God.
The papers. The trial. I . . . I'll go to prison. I'll never get
justice. A black man?' We all look at each other. 'I . . . can't
go on. I want . . . I want . . . I'm going . . .' the words are
coming between choking sobs now as he sits there, slumped,
destroyed, demented, handfuls of his own hair in his hands,
'. . . to kill myself.'

It's my turn to speak now. To turn the final screw and
edge us into Stage Five.

'Lucius?' I say very softly. 'Lucius?' He looks up at me. His
sunglasses have flown off at some point during his frenzy and
I am looking into the haunted, red, weeping eyes of a broken
fifty-year-old man. 'I can make all this go away. Would you
like that?' He looks at me, a strand of saliva hanging from his
jaw onto one of his gold epaulettes. 'All of it. The tour.
Everything. You don't want to do this stupid tour, do you?'

'No. Oh God no.'

'What do you want, Lucius?'

'I ... I just want everything to be beautiful again.'

'That's right,' I say, moving over, closer, sitting down on the low edge of the coffee table, just a few feet away from him, lowering my voice even further. 'You just want to have some friends, special friends, and your candy, your treats, and be left alone, don't you?'

'That's all I ever wanted,' he whispers.

'Well, I can make that happen. You just have to trust me and do everything I say. You'll never have to worry about anything again.'

'Really?' he says, looking at me like a five-year-old on Santa's knee.

'Really.'

'Oh, Mr Stelfox ...' He collapses forward and starts crying again. Different tears this time, soft tears of gratitude, of sweet relief, the tears due to someone who extends the hand to help you into the final lifeboat off the *Titanic*. He begins kissing my feet, getting drool all over my bespoke Foster & Son shoes.

'There's just one thing, Lucius ...'

He looks up. 'Yes?'

'You won't be able to come back to America for a while. Do you understand?'

He sits back against the sofa and wipes the tears off his face with his sleeve. He looks at each of us in turn, Schitzbaul, Trellick, then, finally, at me again. 'I hate this fucking country.'

And there we have it – Acceptance.

THIRTEEN

Connor Murphy couldn't believe it. His own TV *and* the Sony PlayStation VR! The new TV dominated an entire wall of his tiny bedroom. He was on the floor, with the VR headset pushed up on his forehead as he rooted through the haul of new games scattered around him – *Superhot*, *Rigs*, *Rush of Blood*, *Rez Infinite*. And all for nothing! It wasn't his birthday, or Christmas, or anything. They'd just come in the day before yesterday and told him they loved him and taken him into their bedroom where there were all these boxes waiting. He couldn't remember the last time he'd seen his parents in such a good mood. Now, though, it sounded like things were more back to normal, the shouting coming down the hall, from the kitchen area, where they were meeting with that guy, that creepy lawyer guy. Oh well. Connor hit 'NEW GAME', pulled the headset down over his eyes, put his headphones on, and plunged back into the darkness of gaming, the voices from the kitchen disappearing.

'Jesus Christ, Artie, fucking relax, man. What's the problem?'

'The problems, plural, Glen, are these.' Artie ran a hand through his thinning hair, a sure sign he was trying to keep his temper under control. 'One – conspicuous spending at this stage is bad. Do you understand?'

He looked at Glen and Bridget, this pair of fucking retards, standing there, both of them head to foot in new outfits, looking ridiculous, like they were dressed for the Oscars standing here in this shitbox. He thought of that brand-new black Porsche 911 out front, which had nearly caused him to have a stroke when he pulled up. What? 120,000 dollars? Parked on this street? In front of this place?

'Look,' Bridget said, 'the car's a lease. We traded that Mustang as the deposit!'

'Two,' Artie said, ignoring the dumb bitch, 'you shouldn't have taken that million in the first fucking place. And you what – you agreed to twenty million without even consulting me? Are you crazy?'

'Come on, we knew fifty was high,' Glen said.

'We were in a *negotiation*, Artie,' Bridget whined. 'What were we meant to say to him? "Excuse us while we go call our friend"?'

'Yeah, man. It's not like *Who Wants to Be a Millionaire?* or something.' Glen laughed at his own witless joke. Not for the first time Art Hinkley found himself wondering what the fuck he was doing in bed with these people. And Art was a man whose legal career had seen him happily defending wife-beaters.

'And third,' Artie continued, 'three hundred and thirty-three thousand dollars belongs to me.'

'Shit, we know that,' Glen said.

'What – you think we're going to rip you off?'

Bridget stubbed her cigarette out and opened the cupboard next her knees, below the breakfast bar.

Artie watched in utter disbelief as she took out two brown-paper Ralphs bags, both of them stuffed to the brim with tightly banded packs of crisp hundred-dollar bills. She put them on the counter and started taking stacks out. 'Are you fucking kidding me?' Art said. 'You're keeping a million dollars in cash in FUCKING RALPHS BAGS UNDER THE SINK?'

'Just for now! We were gonna –'

'Right, OK. Enough. Glen, go get me a suitcase. Bridget, stop. Stop that. We're taking this money and putting it in a safety deposit box. And there will be no more spending until –' He looked in the bag closest to him. It wasn't quite full to the brim. 'How much have you spent?' he asked.

'Not much,' Bridget said. 'Maybe ... fifty grand?'

Glen's hand instinctively went to his wrist. 'Maybe, like, seventy?' he said.

'What's that?' Artie asked. Glen sheepishly brought his wrist up to show off his new watch – a chunky Daytona. 'What the fuck?' Artie said. 'You already had a fucking Rolex! The one Du Pre gave you!'

'Yeah, but I never really liked it. I always wanted the Daytona.'

'Fuck me.'

Here was a guy without a pot to piss in last week who suddenly had decided what he really needed to do was upgrade his fucking Rolex. Art sat down on one of the stools at the breakfast bar and put his hands together in prayer fashion.

'Right, guys, please. If you're at all interested in, I don't know, actually becoming *rich* instead of being the best-dressed couple of rubes in jail then, please, listen to me like you've never fucking listened to anyone before.' Glen went to say something, but Bridget shook her head and he shut up. 'We are engaged in a criminal enterprise. We have this appalling video that we chose not to go to the cops with. That's withholding of evidence. We also set up how we obtained that video. Entrapment. Exploitation of a minor. Then blackmail. If your fucking neighbours suddenly think, "That's odd. Glen and Bridget still seem to be unemployed but here they are head to foot in Armani stepping out of their new Porsche. Mmmm ..." that could lead to *bad things happening*. OK? So here's what we're going to do. The cash is going to the bank, the Porsche is going back to the dealership, and we are all going to play it very fucking cool for the time being, do we understand each other?' Silence. God, how Art longed to be out of this dismal fucking house.

Finally, very quietly from Bridget, 'OK.'

'Glen?' Art looked at him. A beat.

'I can keep the watch?'

Artie sucked air in through his teeth. 'Yes. You can keep the fucking watch.

'Yeah. Sure. Fuck it. Whatever you say, Artie.'

'Now go get the suitcase.' Glen headed off down the hallway. Artie took a cigarette from Bridget's pack, lit it, and relaxed slightly, loosening his tie. 'So, this guy you met with. Stelfox? What's he like?'

'He seemed like a nice guy,' Bridget said. 'Cooperative. We can handle him. He knows we got them by the fucking balls.'

'When's the next meeting?'

'Monday.'

'I'm doing it.'

Bridget thought for a moment. 'Might spook him. Change of players.'

'Bridget. I'm doing the fucking meeting, OK? Otherwise I'll take my three hundred grand now and you and the brain trust through there can fly solo from here on in.'

'OK, Artie. Jesus. You take the meeting. You don't need to fucking insult us, man.'

Artie stubbed the cigarette out. What was he thinking? He was trying to quit. This thing was going to kill him. What was he going to do about this pair and their goddamned brat kid? Like they say, four can keep a secret.

If three of them are fucking dead.

FOURTEEN

Saturday morning. 8.23 a.m.

Still cold, out here in the desert. Terry Rawlings huddled down into his parka, sat in his rental car, a nondescript Dodge, looking through field glasses across Joshua Tree National Park. He could see the mountain range in the distance, the Pintos, to the north, reaching an elevation of 4,500 feet above sea level. It was low, but he'd made lower. He was doing calculations on the back of his rental agreement, adding weights together, drop speeds. He'd spent the previous evening reviewing the list the boss had given him that lunchtime (boy had the boss looked tired). It was a list of trips the target regularly made, ones that could be undertaken without arousing suspicion. He'd narrowed it down to three, but this looked the most promising. Several times a year he visited a dermatology clinic in Phoenix, which was directly along this flight path. There was a private airstrip at Palm Springs, only a forty-minute drive away from where he'd leave the car. He'd have to hit that mark in the dark, but he'd hit harder marks. And in the days before GPS. With towelheads taking potshots at him. Yeah, this could work just dandy. He'd need something fast-acting on the sedative front. Couldn't be swinging punches and fighting before he had control.

And there was scale here, he thought, as he looked at the immensity of Joshua Tree, the endless miles of desert. The difficulty of conducting a search in those mountains, in winter. (Well, what passed for winter out here.) The cold. The wolves. Yep, forget those other sites (one north towards Carmel, one south to Mexico), this was it. Now he had to drive up to look at Du Pre's place, posing as a maintenance guy from Bell. Terry checked his notes – Du Pre had the 407. Terry knew the model. It was good news all round at the moment.

FIFTEEN

I wake up a little after lunchtime on Saturday afternoon, having slept for twelve hours straight. I feel re-energised, almost athletic. Over coffee I check my voicemail and return one call — to Terry. He thinks he can be ready to go middle of next week. There is also a reminder from Trellick about his kid's birthday party this afternoon. Christ — what do you take to a kid's party? When I was younger the idea of having children, having a family, made me ... physically fucking ill. Now that I am middle-aged. Well, it's odd. Almost everyone I know has made that jump now. Even the most hardcore bachelors, the Trellicks, the Desotos, they all knuckled down at some point. Got with the programme.

I shower, jump in the Bentley (the GT coupé, black) and run over to Nate 'n Al's for lunch, grabbing the newspapers on the way. But the place is rammed and, unlike almost any other restaurant in LA, trust me, celebrity counts for nothing here. You can't book. Unless you're literally a fucking rabbi who was born in the back you're standing in line. Fuck it. I wander up the road to Le Pain Quotidien, which is quiet. I pick at my omelette and scan the headlines. Theresa May was in Washington, meeting the Donald. There they are – striding across the Whitehouse lawn, her tiny paw in his gigantic wanking paddle. ('*There's no problem there, believe me.*') Yesterday, Donald signed an executive order that bans people from Iran, Iraq, Syria, Yemen, Sudan, Libya and Somalia – all the Muzzers basically – from entering the USA for the next ninety days. The US State Department has just told the *Wall Street Journal* that Britons with dual nationality of one of the seven affected nations would be affected, this includes, say, Mo Farah. This has, pleasingly, caused outrage on the left. I jump on Twitter and spend a couple of minutes firing up the bots with the usual stuff – #gomuslimban #lockherup #draintheswamp #trumptrain. I end up getting into a row with some Jewish feminist. I send her a few Pepe the Frogs and then tell her to get in the oven. She calls me a fucking cunt. I report her. She gets her account suspended. See you later, Sooty.

There are already protests at airports across the country, people going nuts at JFK, where thousands have gathered, waving their placards saying shit like 'NOT MY PRESIDENT' and 'MUSLIMS WELCOME HERE'. (Mate – 1. He fucking is. And 2. You want to go to the town of DogFucker, Indiana, and try your 'Muslims welcome' routine in a boozer. Ironically, it'll likely be a Muslim doctor putting the two hundred fucking stitches in your face.) It looks like what the Donald hoped for – immigration officers basically throwing anyone who looks like a Muslim into the slammer and fisting them for a couple of hours – isn't quite happening because border control officials are uncertain the order is constitutional. I read editorials in the *Washington Post* and the *New York Times* saying he's finally gone too far. He's signing executive orders like it's going out of fashion. Something like half a dozen in his first week on the job.

Not for the first time I reflect on what a fantastic A&R guy Trump would have made. Because he truly understands something all the clowns writing these editorials don't: there is no bottom to where you can go with this stuff. It's like boy bands or reality shows. Find the stupidest, thickest, most mental bastards out there and go directly for them. Shoot someone on Fifth Avenue? Trump could get up there right now and tell his people that Pakis are the sole cause of AIDS and he'd still be laughing. He truly understands something that is a golden rule in the record business: *never destroy your fanbase*. Flipping quickly through the rest of the *Post* I see a small story, buried in the international news section, about a government minister in Bogotá who has been killed in a car crash, bad brakes on a tricky road. I smile.

'Will there be anything else?' The waitress's voice is terse, unfriendly. True, I am not often the dream gig for people in the service industry, but to my knowledge I've done nothing to offend this bitch. 'Thanks ...' I say, not looking up from the paper, just pushing my empty coffee mug towards her. She starts refilling it. I notice bruises in the crook of the arm holding the coffee pot, just visible at the hem of her sleeve – livid yellow and purple. Tiny red pinpricks. Ah ha. Now I look up. Something in her face strikes me. It is like an aged version of a face I used to know. This was undeniably once a good-looking woman, twenty-odd years ago. It dawns on me. I put the paper down and lean back, something very close to joy spreading through me.

'Jesus,' I say. 'How are you?'

'Fine,' she spits.

'You're looking ... well.'

This is a lie. The face is lined and haggard, the cheeks sunken. The tits are bolstered by some titanium bra but I'd go you dollars to doughnuts they're smacking around her belly button when untethered. She'd be, what now? Early to mid-forties? Right on the cusp of true boilerdom.

'Have a good day,' she hisses as she sticks the check on the table and strides off.

'Hey!' I say to her back. 'Hang on! Let's catch up!' What's her fucking name? Mary? Marnie? MARCY! That was it. 'Marcy?' But she doesn't respond, disappears through the employees only door at the back of the restaurant.

A very long time ago, in another lifetime, Marcy was in a band called the Lazies who were signed to our label. They were, very briefly, the hottest band on the planet. I became their A&R guy after I took over the department, after the guy who signed them topped himself. Now, admittedly, and I'll admit this, mistakes were made. Maybe we didn't get the right producer. Maybe we did try and chase a polished radio sound a bit too soon after the rough-edged debut album that everyone loved. Maybe it did cost us their original fanbase before we'd done enough to appeal to a more mainstream audience. Whatever – their second album *tanked*. I mean, talk about shit the bed. I think we went from half a million worldwide on the debut (a good start) to something like 30,000 on album two. Losing about 95 per cent of your customers overnight? That's not bad, is it? (I wonder what

we could have done to lose that last 5 per cent? Made the
CD case out of razor blades? Banged a swastika on the cover?)
Anyway, after that, rest assured, I signed the papers to drop
them faster than Trump signing an executive order. I heard
they made the inevitable indie album for One Hunchbacked
Man Records of Inverness (or wherever) before disappearing
into the vast, dark chasm of Cunts Who Had a Shot.
Occasionally, over the years, you do wonder what happens
to these people whose lives you've destroyed. Whose hopes
and dreams you wiped your arse with like so much toilet
paper. And now we know – they wind up shooting smack
and waiting tables at Le Pain Quotidien on South Santa
Monica Boulevard. I finish my coffee as I look at another
waitress across the room – older than Marcy, around sixtyish,
proper boilerdom – and think about her getting off the bus
here, back in the late seventies probably: the attempt at music
or acting, followed by the stint as a hooker, or in the porn
industry, followed by waitressing. It is hard not to think of
it in this town, as some kindly old dear brings your food, or
tops up your coffee – the frankly incredible amount of cocks
that will have gone off in her fucking face.

The check is a little over eighteen dollars. I lay a twenty
down, stiffing Marcy on the tip, and head off to get a
present for Trellick's kid, greatly buoyed by this chance
encounter, my faith in the fundamental justice of the
universe fully restored.

'Middle of next week,' I say to Trellick. We're standing off
to one side, in the huge, lush garden of his house on
Coldwater Canyon, up above where Sunset snakes through
Beverly Hills. Children run around going crackers, jumping

in the pool, playing on the giant inflatable he's hired in. Waiters move through the adults, offering canapés, cold glasses of Perrier-Jouët. We're drinking Mexican beers from the bottle.

'Is there anyone on the staff needs a heads-up on this?' he asks.

'Absolutely not,' I say. 'Reactions have to be totally natural.'

'Yeah, you're right.'

'Hey,' I say. 'Guess who I saw at breakfast this morning.'

'Who?'

I tell him.

'Nasty,' Trellick says. Then – 'Still doable?'

'Barely.'

'Very fucking nasty.' We both follow our own trains of thought for a moment, both of us slipping back twenty years. 'Poor old Parker-Hall,' Trellick says. We clink beer bottles.

'And what are you boys plotting and scheming about?' Trellick's wife Pandora has appeared. She's mid-thirties, the standard fifteen years younger than Trellick, and is carrying their two-year-old, Henry. Despite the three kids Pan is (obviously) in very good shape: the LA regime of Pilates, yoga, canyon-hiking and eating only a single leaf of arugula every other day clearly paying dividends.

'Oh, the usual,' Trellick says.

'Let me know when I can grab Steven for a minute,' she says. 'There's a couple of ladies I'd like him to meet ...'

'Oh, really?' I say flirtatiously, although most of the women here look to be in their late thirties and forties and are, obviously, undoable.

Suddenly there's an extra-loud splash from the pool followed by shrieking and crying. 'Oh, for fuck's sake,' Trellick says.

'Well, don't just stand there!' Pandora says. Trellick puts his beer down and heads over to sort out whatever rumble is brewing. 'I'd better ... hang on ...' she says. 'Steven, do you mind for a second?' And with that she hands me the fucking toddler and heads after Trellick.

They do this, don't they? Mothers. Hand you a fucking kid as casually as handing you a drink or a dildo. I sit down. The kid is chewing on something, a soft toy of some description, and seems relaxed, calm. I bounce him on my knee and try the usual baby-talk stuff you see other people doing. 'Are you having a good time at the party, Henry? Yes? Is it a good party? What's Mummy and Daddy up to? What are they up to?' The problem with baby talk, like talking dirty, is that you soon run out of stuff to say and fall back on variants of the same thing. Changing tack, lowering my voice, I say, 'Look ... there's that loser from Live Nation. What a loser. Yes he is. Yes he is. Look, see that right old monster over there? In the blue dress? Wouldn't you like to bend her over that gazebo and pummel her arse? Yes, that'd be fun, wouldn't it? Yes.'

'Arsss.' he says.

Fuck. They can talk at this age? 'No no, you shouldn't –'

'Arsss.' He's giggling now.

I look into his eyes as he laughs, his whole face, seemingly in reaction to my horror, suddenly radiant with joy. Something dawns on me, with the force of an epiphany. You can teach them stuff. You tell them things and they retain it and it comes back out. I'll admit, forty-seven is probably fairly late in the day to be having this count as a revelation, but, hey, gimme a break. I've been busy. 'No. Henry, shhh ...' I say. But this only causes the fucker to piss himself laughing. I try reverse psychology. 'Yes. Good. Arse. Continue.'

'ARSSSS!' he says. Oh Jesus.

'Are you having fun with Uncle Steve?' Pandora is back. 'Are you!' She tickles him.

'ARSSSSS!' the kid shrieks in her face. Pandora frowns.

'We were, uh, playing pirates,' I say, turning back to the kid. 'ARRRR!' I growl.

'ARRRSS!' Henry says.

'Oh! Good stuff,' Pan says, picking him up. 'Right, young man, where is your nanny? Time for your nap. Steven, I'll be back in a tick. I want all the latest gossip from London.' She trots off across the grass, Henry looking back at me, over her shoulder, grinning, waving goodbye with his tiny fingers. Something in me turns over. There's a feeling of ... what? What the fuck is this? I look around at the party, straight out of a Ralph Lauren ad. The masters of Beverly Hills and their wives. I look at my watch – 4.30. Nothing really to do until Monday evening, until the Murphys Round Two and final planning with Terry. What the fuck am I going to do with the rest of the weekend? This is the other thing that happens when you reach your late forties childless. Suddenly I remember something. I get my phone out and dial the number.

'Really?' she says. 'Sure. That'd be great. I'd appreciate the help. Danny's going to be there. You can catch up. Want me to book you into the same hotel? No problem. Flight's at eight, you sure you can make it?'

'I'll make it,' I say. 'See you there.'

Fifteen minutes later I'm out of there and motoring down past the Beverly Hilton, heading for the 405 out to LAX. This is the great thing about having no kids and a fuck ton of cash – you can literally do whatever you want, whenever you want.

SIXTEEN

'I mean – just look at that lot. Fuck me. *Fuck me.*'

'Oh man,' she says, laughing.

America's playground.

We're people-watching, through the windows of the Lincoln Town Car as it rolls down the strip, taking us towards the MGM Grand. There's a family of four on the sidewalk, standing there staring up in mute awe at a demented replica of the Eiffel Tower that's all lit up, multi-coloured, red and green and pink and blue. The collective weight of this family of four (mum, dad, teenage girl and boy) must be in excess of a thousand pounds – half a fucking ton of mad toler standing there, cracking the fucking side-walk. Dad and son are dressed identically, billowing tent-like untucked check shirts, three-quarter-length shorts, sandals and baseball caps. (Dad literally wearing a MAGA one.) Mum and daughter match up too – both in some kind of kaftan or muumuu, hiding as best they can the rippling, unimaginable rolls of blubber. They're all clutching those Big Gulp cups, doubtless holding about a quart each of the Diet Coke they all think is going to sort them right out. They're motionless, bathed in neon light, and could well be a sculpture titled *USA*. I *love* Vegas, the ultimate expression of the American dream.

'How did they even reproduce?' Chrissy says of the mum and dad. 'I mean – how do they actually fuck?'

The one-hour flight was actually . . . tolerable. I upgraded us both to first, snicking my credit card down on the check-in counter, and, with eternal good grace and forbearance, even managed to turn flying commercial into some kind of funny adventure. We gossiped and bitched all the way here, me indiscreetly telling her about some of the milder episodes of Trellick's youth, Chrissy in turn telling me about some of his rumoured transgressions in more recent years, at conventions, retreats, when Pandora's been away with the kids. 'What are you really in LA for?' she asked me again, halfway through her second Bloody Mary. 'I told you,' I said, sipping nothing stronger than mineral water, 'I'm just on holiday.'

'Oh, oh, Steven, check this out. Eleven o'clock . . .' she's saying in the car now, pointing out of the window towards two women striding up the steps into the Bellagio. They're wearing tight black cocktail dresses, spiked heels, platinum-blonde hair tumbling down. It's not like the old days here. You can't rock up in leather or PVC with a pair of vibrators for earrings and a couple of hundred condoms and a few litres of KY jelly spilling out of your handbag. This pair are dressed respectably enough to gain entrance, to get through the doors, where they'll lurk in one of the dark bars until Ian from Iowa, Willy from

Wisconsin or Akira from Osaka has got enough Johnnie Walker down him to be talked into a thousand-dollar double-ender.

'Oh yeah. Ostros,' I say.

'What's an ostro?' Chrissy asks. She's wearing a more upscale take on her ususal jeans and T-shirt. Tight black trousers tucked into thigh-high suede boots, a clinging velvet top, her thick red hair worn up. More make-up than usual too. It's good. I'm having it.

'A hooker.'

'Oh yeah. Major hookers.'

Where did the Americans decide to make the epicentre, the ground zero, of EDM? New York? Chicago? Detroit? Nah, fuck that. Let's do it here. In Vegas. The equivalent back home would have been the decision to move London's dance scene lock, stock and barrel up the M6 to fucking Blackpool. You drive down Sunset Strip and you see them, massive posters bearing down, advertising residencies, at the MGM, at Omnia, at Jewel, by toerags you've never heard of – MC Fried Rice, Tetris, the BungeeJumper, DJ Registered Sex Offender – all of these animals pocketing something like half a million shitters a week for banging out the poof doof to a roomful of MDMA-crazed Middle Americans in cargo pants who think that Juan Atkins played for Real Madrid. Again, it is capitalism at its finest.

'Here we are, folks,' the driver is saying over his shoulder, through the partition, as we pull up in front of the enormous golden lion outside the MGM.

It's all business as usual from here: we are given our own personal greeter – Shelley, replete with clipboard and headset – who whisks us past the gigantic line of animals who will be queueing for hours to get in and takes us up into Hakkasan, the relentless thud of the bass drum already kicking our chests as we approach the nightclub. Once inside we are led to a table in the roped-off VIP section by the dance floor, where a huge silver ice bucket holds bottles of Grey Goose and Dom Perignon. All of this is complimentary obviously, a courtesy from the management of tonight's headliners Norwegian Dance Crew. On a night like tonight, Saturday, the vermin at the tables all around us will be paying something like eight thousand dollars just to sit there and then another thousand bucks a bottle, plus an eye-watering gratuity. 'And this is you here,' Shelley says. 'This is Agnes,' she gestures to a smiling, hotter, younger version of herself who has materialised behind her, 'and she'll be taking care of you tonight. Enjoy, Mr Stelfox. Huge fan by the way.'

'Thank you,' I say, having to shout over the blaring cobblers pounding out of the speakers as I slip Shelley a hundred-dollar bill.

'Thank *you*,' she says. You do get treated like a king in America. The only problem is you have to spend like an emperor in order to get this treatment. If you just spend like a king you'll get treated like a prince and so on down the chain until you reach the people who spend normally, who obviously get treated like cunts.

It's a recent development in the entertainment industry, people not wanting to get treated like utter cunts. Turns out, they'll pay well over the odds for that. VIP packages. Small businessmen from Hull, Russian bankers, gook computing magnates, they'll all pay a fortune so they can get a limo to the gig, skip the queue and get to hang out at the soundcheck, where they'll get a thirty-second 'all right, mate?' from Paul McCartney/Sting/An Actual Fucking Rapist while they snap a selfie to put up on Instagram like they've just been on holiday together. That'll be five grand please, Mr VIP. It's too fucking good. (It's so good that Hollywood is starting to catch on. Not for actual A-listers. Don't be stupid. But, if your star is waning a bit and the IRS, or all those ex-wives, are on your case, you could do worse than pocket half a mil for getting interviewed in front of a theatre full of dog-fucking toerags who think your 'that-time-the-DOP-farted-while-I-was-doing-a-take' stories are endlessly fascinating.)

Agnes is pouring us both a glass of champagne when a south London voice booms out of the darkness behind me, cutting through the music.

'OI! OI! STELFOX! YOU FUCKING CUNT!'

I turn to see Danny Rent, coming through the darkness towards me, his arms extended, his mad face beaming. 'Danny fucking Rent ...' I say.

'Fucking hell, mate,' he says as we embrace. 'Been too long! I couldn't believe it when she told me you was coming!' He says this as he releases me and turns towards Chrissy. 'All right, Chrissy?' They embrace too. 'You got everything you need? They taking care of you? Love,' he says to the waitress, 'this pair here. Anything they want is on us, yeah?'

'I've already been told, Mr Rent.' Tolers at the other tables are staring, impressed. We sit down.

'So, what you doing in Vegas, mate?' Rent asks, his broad cockney not at all dented by however much time he's been spending here.

'WHAT?' I say, cupping my ear.

'WHAT YOU DOING OUT HERE?'

'In LA for a bit, doing some consultancy stuff with Trellick, for Unigram, and Chrissy told me she was looking to sign your guys –'

'WHAT?' he says, cupping his ear.

'I'M IN LA FOR A BIT …' I go through it again.

'Sweet. Hey, Chrissy, you better watch this one –' Rent says, hooking a thumb at me.

'WHAT?' Chrissy says, leaning over the table.

'I SAID, YOU –'

'LOOK, DANNY,' I cut in. 'FUCK THIS. CAN WE GET OUT OF THIS TOILET?'

'Yeah, course, mate. Come on backstage. Meet the guys.'

We follow him off, leaving a couple of grand of untouched booze on the table.

'The thing you need to understand about Norwegian Dance Crew is that it was never something we built for profit, man. We always come in and want to make the best show possible, something where we can test and push the boundaries and take bigger risks. We always bring in a big production, even though we might only break even. It's all about being true to the *music* at the end of the day. Not selling ourselves out. It's about energy. Peace …'

This cunt Thorsten goes on in his soft Norwegian accent. Danny and Chrissy are both nodding away like this pile of utter reeking human logs posing as words is coming from the burning fucking bush. Thorsten, very much the leader of the group, sweeps his long blond hair up out of his blue eyes, revealing a tattoo on his neck – some kind of mad

Celtic symbol. His two bandmates, whose names I fail to catch, flank him. Unsmiling. I'm trying to remember the last time I did this: sat in a dressing room and listened to an artist telling me his philosophy. It's been a while. The only thing he's said so far that makes sense is about the necessity of having a big production. Yeah, I want to say. I get why you'd need that – being just three Vikings standing up there playing a fucking CD. In their T-shirts, jeans, beanies and tattoos, Norwegian Dance Crew have the collective charisma of a bunch of Deliveroo drivers taking a break before the evening rush kicks in. It's another brilliant refinement of popular culture. Like they say, for a long time now you could become rich without having any talent, thanks to the scratchcard or the rollover. You could become famous without having any talent, by going on *Big Brother* and wanking a dog off or something. However, you couldn't actually become *talented* without having any talent. That was tricky. So we sorted that one out too. Talent no longer required. It's been headed this way for a while, but these guys, Jesus Christ. They almost make me pine for my youth. Let's face it, in the talent and charisma stakes Norwegian Dance Crew make even a twenty-four-carat chancer like Rage look like the bastard child of Hendrix and Jagger. 'There's a thing with house music,' Thorsten is saying, 'when the level of intensity is so high in a club it almost becomes ... calm. Serene. Like in the eye of a storm.' Another thing – he's not young, this guy Thorsten. Got to be at least thirty-five. Remember when one of the very few prerequisites of being a pop star would have been youth? Well, dance music seems to have taken care of that too. Look over there – the fifty-eight-year-old DJ still cranking it out. They're not even off their nuts any more, half of these cretins. There you are, flying around the world, sober, jacked up on nothing more than Evian and caffeine, standing in front of a mass of pilled-up fools one third of your age and urging them to have it? You're doing interviews where you're banging on about the vibe at X club, about the energy at Y festival. What are you doing, you fucking disgrace? Why aren't you at home with the wife and kids counting your money? Or, more hauntingly, down the pecking order, there's the guys who *never* made any real money, relics from the nineties who never quite banked the big cash, but who still have just enough juice that some Eastern European promoter will book them. A few years back, before I stopped flying commercial, you'd see some of these guys, at Heathrow, at Gatwick, striding across the terminal, shades on, headphones around their necks, larging it on the way to DJ in Zagreb on a Friday night for a thousand quid and a few cans of Red Bull, all the while wishing they were at home with the kettle on, flicking through Sky movies. Nasty. Very fucking nasty.

'What's your favourite track on the album?' one of them is asking Chrissy.

'Track three,' she says. They nod. I do like this girl.

'Guys?' Danny's assistant Jamie is poking her head around the door. 'The girl from *Mixmag* is here to do that interview.' Shit, I think. *Mixmag* is still a thing? Who knew?

'Well, fellas,' I say, standing, shaking hands, 'really great to meet you.'

'Yeah, man,' one of them says. 'That was, uh, pretty amazing on your show, a few years ago. When you had that kid on who thought he was Jesus? I loved him.'

'Yeah,' I say. 'It was something.' People bring this up remarkably often. 'Anyway, really looking forward to seeing your set. Thorsten – nice meeting you. Danny – see you after, mate.'

My phone starts buzzing in my pocket. I check the screen – Terry.

I leave and light a cigarette in the corridor outside the dressing rooms while Chrissy hangs back talking to Danny, about the deal, about the insane amounts of money these clowns are now being offered. 'Terry,' I say.

He says one word – 'Tuesday' – then hangs up. Tuesday for what we've taken to calling Operation Elvis.

Chrissy comes out, closing the door behind her. 'OK,' she says. 'That was great, thank you, Steven. Thanks for coming. I think it really helped.'

'No problem,' I say, pocketing my phone.

'So, shall we grab a drink before the show starts?'

'The show?' I realise she is actually intending to watch these fools. Well, she's young. 'Piss on that. You've met the band. Let's get the fuck out of here and go for dinner. Come on. I made a reservation ...' I take her hand and, kind of scandalised, but laughing, she follows me.

SEVENTEEN

We're deep in the bowels of the MGM Grand, at a corner table in L'Atelier de Joël Robuchon, the only three-star Michelin gaff in Vegas, where we're drinking an exceptionally good white burgundy while I order a lot of food: langoustine fritters with a smudge of basil pesto, prosciutto with toasted tomato bread, poached Kumamoto oysters on the half-shell, sautéed duck liver with minced-citrus gratin. Chrissy is live-streaming the gig on her phone with the sound down and checking a fan site where the records they're playing are being listed in real time. Later, our account of having seen the show will be absolutely seamless. A vast improvement on my days in A&R when you could be in a dressing room telling a band how great the show was only to be asked if you enjoyed the part where a naked tramp invaded the stage and started dry-humping the lead singer, the part you somehow missed, because you were finishing dinner in some fuck-off restaurant. 'Jeez,' she says as the food starts to arrive. 'Hungry much?' It dawns on me that, aside from that omelette served by a junkie whose life I destroyed, I haven't really eaten much in thirty-six hours.

'So, how you feeling about it?' I ask.

'The NDC deal? I think we've got a decent shot. It's, you know, XL are the competition here, they're ... hard to beat.'

She's not wrong. Fucking Richard Russell. '*Who's your label got, mate?*' '*Fucking* Adele. *Suck on this.*' She's sold more records since we started this meal than half the lowlifes you take meetings with will ever sell in their lifetimes. And as if that wasn't enough it's also *oh, and by the way, if that's too mainstream for your tastes, we've got Radiohead and Jack fucking White too.* 'Tough one,' I say. 'What do you do when you're up against that? You could get a videotape of Richard Russell calling the entire band cunts while crouching down and cranking a log out onto a photograph of the lead singer's mother, and the fucking act would *still* sign with XL ...'

She laughs and looks around the expensive restaurant, still capable, at twenty-eight, of being flushed with pleasure at being somewhere like this. Incredible eyes. Really. Her face, not yet hammered senseless by life, loss and cocks. I briefly flash on being her age, wanting to get on, get ahead. Still enjoying things like this, before it all became routine. You fuck someone over, you wreck a life, you order the fifty-six-dollar portion of black cod and you move on to the next thing. Then, more unwelcomely, I flash on something I haven't thought of in a long time: Rebecca, laughing in a place like this a very long time ago. Wanting to get on, get ahead. Now just the remnants of some bones in a suitcase at the bottom of a reservoir in Essex. Maybe not even that. Chrissy catches my look and says in her Texan twang, 'What you thinking about?'

'Money,' I say, which is always, to some degree, true. 'So come on then, Chrissy Price, what's your fucking story?' I ask.

She tells me. It doesn't take very long. What is there to say at her age? She grew up in Austin. Went to a good school on a scholarship. Was the poorest kid in her class, lit a fire within her to show those fuckers. Aced her boards, went to Berkeley, moved to LA right after and got an internship at Capitol, was thinking about law but it looked too boring. Always loved music. Tipped the A&R department off early on a couple of acts who became hot deals, got hired at Unigram as full A&R two years ago, has been close on a couple of big deals but has yet to sign the act that will make her name. Young, smart and hungry in full effect. Something occurs to me. 'What did you major in?' I ask.

'Politics,' she says.

I smile. 'Interesting times.'

She smiles too, but rucfully, shaking her head. 'This fucking guy . . .' She embarks on exactly the kind of Trump speech you'd expect from a hip twenty-eight-year-old resident of California. I let it all go, let it wash over me, occasionally nodding in agreement, or sombrely quoting idiotic bits of fake news I've read in the *Guardian*, on the *Daily Beast*, in the *Washington Post*, as I savour the rich white wine and tiny, expensive plates of fish and meat, surrounded by the fine lunatics of America, all of whom, like me, think she's talking utter cobblers.

Later, in bed, alone, I reflect on how difficult it is to do boilers when you're not off your nugget. We went back just as the set was ending. We hung out briefly with Danny and the band ('Amazing set. I couldn't believe it when you dropped X into Y. The energy in that place. Let's meet again in LA next week.' And so on and so on), then limo'd back to our hotel where we had a debrief in the bar over a whiskey, a chaste peck on the cheek, and then took different elevators to our rooms – me to a suite on the exec floor, her to a regular shoebox. Back in the old days this was all very different of course. Much more straight-forward. You'd drink yourselves senseless, bang a mountain of racket, and get your cock out. Simpler times. I lie awake and find myself thinking about the fact that I'm forty-seven and she's twenty-eight. Isn't there a formula that the ideal age for a girlfriend is half your age plus seven years? That would be someone, what, thirty-one for me? Our age difference is nineteen years. So when I'm fifty-five she'll be thirty-six. When I'm sixty she'll be forty-one. When – oh God.

I sit up and turn the light on.

I know what all of this means.

Christ, I don't need this level of complication right now.

EIGHTEEN

Art Hinckley, ordering another Diet Coke, lighting a cigarette, sitting outside a coffee shop in Los Feliz. He checked
his watch, just after eleven. The guy was late. Had he got
the right place? The fucking balls on him. No, LA traffic,
he'd be there. Calm down. Cool. In control. He was holding
all the cards here. Be strong. He stilled his internal monologue as a black Bentley pulled into the parking lot. He
watched the guy get out. He'd be about Art's age, but there
the similarities ended. Where Art was pasty from endless
days spent under the fluorescent tubes of his office, this
guy was tanned. Where Art had an extra twenty pounds
hanging around his midriff this guy was lean and toned.
Where Artie was sweating through his suit this guy looked
cool and relaxed in some sort of thin cashmere sweater.
Head to toe in black. He sat down opposite and extended
his hand, saying, 'Hi.'

'I'm Art.'

'So, what happened to your ... colleagues?'

The guy was almost smirking. Take control. 'I thought it was time you met the first team,' Art said, immediately regretting it, hearing it as it left his mouth sounding like bad movie dialogue.

'I see.'

'So let's get off on the right foot. No more negotiating on time or money. You have the deal. You pay us the twenty million today or have fun tuning into the six o'clock news tomorrow night.'

'Friday.' Saying it matter-of-fact, in his British accent. No hint of apology.

'What?' Artie says.

'Friday. You'll have the money on Friday.'

'That's not what I asked for, you fuck –'

'Listen, Mr Hinckley. Art. Artie. The money is being put together. It'll be in the account you've specified by close of business on Friday. There's nothing else to say.' He reached over and took a cigarette out of Artie's pack. Lit it.

'Help your fucking self,' Artie said.

'Cheers,' this Stelfox said, exhaling smoke. 'You must be worried about them.'

'Huh? Who?'

'Your colleagues. The Murphys. I mean the collective brain power of that pair . . .' He whistled.

'One, they're not my fucking "colleagues", and two, they've done their part.'

'Well,' he said, tapping ash into Art's empty Diet Coke can. 'There's also the question of trust, isn't there?'

'Trust? Trusting who?' Art was beginning to see what Bridget meant. It was like there was nothing riding on this for him. Like he didn't give a fuck.

'Art, come on. You're really going to trust a pair who'd get their own son to videotape a half-Fergal ploughing his fucking farter, are you?'

Ploughing his farter? And what the fuck was a half-Fergal? What the fuck was this guy talking about? Artie took off his sunglasses and leaned forward. 'Look, maybe I'm not being clear. Forget about the Murphys. Worry about me from here on in, OK, buddy?'

Now he took off his sunglasses too. And, for the first time, Artie recognised that he was feeling something more here, something more than just a sense of not being in the driving seat. His eyes were dark, black, bottomless. Yes, fear. Artie felt fear. 'I'm not worried, mate,' he said. 'Neither should you be. By Friday you'll be a rich man. Thanks for the cigarette.'

'Hey,' Artie said, casting around uselessly for something to say, feeling he should be the one to end the meeting, trying to regain some kind of authority. 'Just don't try any fucking funny stuff. OK?'

'Sure, Artie. You're the boss. See ya.' He walked off towards his car, whistling, leaving Artie feeling like anything but the boss. He looked at his watch again.

Steven Stelfox had been there less than two minutes

NINETEEN

'YOU KNOW I HATE FLYING! I WANT MY MILK! GET DR ALI! SHIT!' A tray full of expensive toiletries went sailing through the air and smashed into the shower stall.

The monthly early-morning chopper ride, over to Phoenix, to the Blezzard Clinic. Things had gone wrong with Lucius's skin. He had to admit it. On a good day he could pass for a very light-skinned black man. On a bad day, or when he mismanaged the frankly incredible amount of medication he was taking, he had patches that were pink, white, black and brown all within a few inches of each other. Today was not a good day, on many levels. Sadly, tiredly, Schitzbaul watched his client methodically smashing up the bathroom. In normal circumstances he'd have caved of course. Dr Ali would have been on his way over right now, preloaded hypodermic in hand. But Stelfox's guy had given clear instructions – no propofol twenty-four hours prior. It might interfere fatally with what he had to do. Lucius had no idea what was coming. Famously capricious, it had been decided that it would be best all round if everything came as a total surprise to him. It was also necessary that it happened this way for reasons of witnesses, flight logs, etc. There would be some breakage of course. But the families would be compensated.

'Lucius, come on. Not now. You can have some right after. Take a Xanax.'

'NO! I WANT MY MILK!'

'Or a Percocet.'

Crash, bang, smash. More stuff going over, a mirror breaking. 'Jesus Christ, man, come on, the chopper's ready. The boys are ready.' Schitzbaul, in the doorway, nodded towards Marcus and Jay, coats on, sitting in the hallway.

'I hate you,' Lucius sobbed. 'You don't care about me ...'

Lance controlled his temper and fished in his pocket, for the small brown tub he kept for emergency use only. They were already nearly an hour late and dawn was starting to break. 'Here,' he said. 'Just one ...' Lucius looked down into his manager's fat fist to see one tiny, pale orange pill nestled in the middle of his palm. Dilaudid, 4mg. His red, damp eyes brightened a fraction as he scooped up and dry-swallowed the opioid.

'OK, let's go' Lucius said, suddenly decisive. Schitzbaul gave the signal to Jay and a chain of walkie-talkies crackled into life – 'Number One is moving.'

They hurried out of there, Jay and Marcus following, falling into step behind them, Schitzbaul barking orders, telling one of the maids about the wrecked bathroom on the way through the great hall, the inner circle moving with purpose, as they used to move through the concrete depths of football stadiums and basketball arenas, back in the days when the name Lucius Du Pre meant one of the most visceral entertainers in music, instead of ... whatever he was now.

Out the back door and down the steps towards the lawn, the helipad just a hundred yards away, the rotors starting to turn as she fired up, the pilot having been the last stop on that walkie-talkie chain. Several of the staff (witnesses) were lined up on the steps, wishing Lucius a safe flight. (Again, all of this was routine. Everything about this had to be routine.) 'Bye, Mr Lucius. Safe flight.' 'See you later, boss.' 'Have a nice trip.' And so on.

When they were on the grass, just fifty or so yards short of the helicopter, Schitzbaul stopped and put a hand on Lucius's shoulder. This was as far as he was going. (Again, routine – he never came to Phoenix.) 'HAVE A GREAT FLIGHT,' he roared over the rotor blare, wind whipping him in the face. Lucius just nodded and turned to hurry on. Schitzbaul felt the need to say something more, something to mark the moment. 'LUCIUS?' he shouted, holding him back. 'TAKE CARE, OK?'

'Yeah,' Lucius said. He turned and doubled over as he walked the last stretch under the whirring blades, Jay guiding him, holding his arm. Oh well, Schitzbaul thought. Not the most profound way to end a thirty-year relationship, but there it was.

Jay helped Lucius up into the front seat, next to the pilot, where he always sat, and then got in the back with Marcus, putting his headphones on.

'Good morning, gentlemen,' the pilot said in a clipped, aristocratic English accent. 'Seat belts all on please? Good.'

'Hey,' Marcus said, buckling up, 'where's Nate?'

'Off sick, I'm afraid,' Terry Rawlings said, flipping switches, throttling back, the whine of the engine sharpening in pitch. Lucius didn't notice the change of pilot. He rarely spoke on these trips and felt no need to do so now, with the golden thrill of the Dilaudid just starting to kick in, accentuating the whooshing rush he felt as the grass rocketed away beneath them. It always reminded him of being on the Ferris wheel, which he could see below him now, going up, imagining the shrieks and whoops of children in his ears. Terry hovered high above the property for a moment, the ocean out there, sparkling in the dawn to his left, before he dipped the nose, putting the machine into a turn, and headed off, flying due east, into the rising sun.

Forty-four minutes into the flight – his three passengers dozing gently (as expected, this really was the middle of the night for them) – Terry saw the Pinto Mountains coming up in the distance. He checked his watch – 7.11 a.m. – and took a few deep breaths (not for drama, just on instinct, following training, slowing his heart rate down) as he checked the altimeter, four and a half thousand feet, put her into a gentle ten-degree dive, and engaged the autopilot. He unbuckled his seat belt and took the small hypodermic out. Terry leaned over and, in one motion, clamped his right hand over Lucius's mouth and jabbed the syringe into his thigh with his left hand. Lucius stiffened in his seat, yelping soundlessly into Terry's palm. A few seconds of struggle, his sunglasses falling off, Terry seeing panic in those haunted brown eyes, and then he slumped forward, unconscious. Terry undid Lucius's belt, pulled him out of his seat and sat him in his lap. He weighed next to nothing, about 110 pounds, Terry guessed. The bodyguards in the back hadn't even woken up. Terry worked fast with the webbing belt, fastening the sleeping Lucius tightly to his chest. Those mountains up ahead, getting closer now. 'Okey-dokey,' Terry said softly, to himself. He blew the door – explosive bolts cracking, the door flying off into the slipstream of the chopper – and leapt out.

Jay and Marcus, waking up as one on the bang, freezing air rushing in, filling the cabin, both of them looking around, wild with terror – at the now empty front seats.

Terry in free fall, counting in his head, a fine balancing act, having to wait until he was clear of the rotors, falling fast, weighing nearly three hundred pounds with the addition of the Emperor of Pop.

Jay screaming, Marcus trying to climb over the seats and into the front, desperation making him claw for the stick, even though he had no idea how to fly a helicopter. Suddenly an alarm sounded and a metallic voice started barking at them – 'TERRAIN! TERRAIN! PULL UP! PULL UP!' Jay looked ahead through the cockpit and saw the mountains – huge and getting closer by the second.

Terry, popping his chute at just under two thousand feet, feeling the hard tug on his shoulders as they rocketed back up into the early-morning sky.

Marcus's fingertips almost reaching the cyclic control as he heard Jay screaming 'FUCK!' somewhere behind him. He looked up in time to see the mountainside – his eyes fixing ridiculously on a small bush. Now it was a bigger bush. Now it was huge. He just had time to say 'Momma', before –

Terry saw the fireball erupt on the mountainside in the distance just as he hit the ground.

A clean, professional roll-out, even with the encumbrance on his chest, and he was quickly gathering up his chute. Terry unstrapped Lucius and laid him sleeping on the desert floor while he stuffed the chute back into the pack and strapped it on his back. He shielded his eyes against the morning sun and looked west. He calculated he'd only missed the drop site by about half a mile, not bad in the circumstances, bailing out of a helicopter at low altitude, but it could be fatal if someone happened to be out this far for a dawn drive or hike. This was the most dangerous, the most exposed, part of the whole operation. He picked up Lucius, threw him over his shoulder, and started running. Terry – a man whose training had involved running fifteen miles uphill in a hailstorm in the Brecon Beacons, carrying close to a hundred pounds of weapons and equipment – covered the half-mile in just over four minutes. He unlocked the Dodge, threw Lucius and his parachute into the boot and slammed it shut. He checked his watch once more – 7.19 a.m., eight minutes from start to finish – and tore off in a shower of dust and gravel, heading south-west, towards the private airstrip outside Palm Springs, around forty minutes away.

Stelfox got the first call from Terry a few minutes after 8 a.m. Just five words. 'Elvis has left the building.'

Stelfox rang Lance Schitzbaul and told him the same thing. Lance sat down and waited for the phone to start ringing.

James Trellick had made sure he was in the office even earlier than usual that morning, at 7.30 a.m., just the cleaners and that idiotically gung-ho new kid in marketing in the building. He'd thought about his speech over and

over. It would be brief. He went over the backstory
they'd agreed on: he'd gotten the first call, from
Schitzbaul. He'd had a little while to process his shock,
so he could afford to look somewhat composed. All of
their thoughts were with Du Pre's family and friends
and of course with his legions of devastated fans. He
was a truly unique, inspirational artist whose legacy
would be measured in generations. All that kind of balls.
A little after eight he turned the TV on in the corner
of his office, to CNN. But, as was often the way, he saw
it first on his Twitter feed: 'Lucius Du Pre feared dead
in helicopter crash.'

Art Hinckley was in the car, driving over to Silver Lake
for a 9 a.m. meeting with a prospective, housebound client,
an elderly lady who was looking to sue a pharmaceutical
company. Man, he would be glad to soon be free of this
shit. He flipped between stations, getting Boston doing
'More Than a Feeling', and turned it way up. He was about
to scream along with the first chorus when an urgent voice
cut into the track, a news bulletin. 'We're bringing you
some breaking news now,' the guy said. 'There are reports
that a helicopter carrying Lucius Du Pre has crashed near
Joshua Tree National Park east of Los Angeles, with the
loss of all life on board. We're now going live to –' Art
pulled over into the parking lot of a 7-Eleven, his heart
pounding, his hands trembling. He dialled the Murphys'
and got 'please leave a message'.

Breakfast time in the Murphy household. Mum and
Dad, still in bed, hung-over, Connor Murphy channel-
hopping on the sofa while eating a bowlful of dry Cap'n
Crunch. (No milk in the fridge. Again.) It was almost

nine and he was late for school. Fuck it, they were all about to be rich, weren't they? He wouldn't need school soon. As he pumped through the channels – '*now available with zero per cent financing ... are your teeth sensitive to hot and cold? ... we were on a break! ... if you've been injured at work through no fault of your own ...*' – something caught his eye, on CNN. It was a shot, taken from a distance, of a desert hillside, with white smoke pluming up from a patch on the face of the mountain. But that wasn't what caught his eye, it was the caption below it – '*LUCIUS DU PRE AND THREE OTHERS FEARED DEAD IN HELICOPTER CRASH*'. He turned the volume up as some man, in overalls, was being interviewed. 'I just heard this buzzing sound and by the time I turned around, it ... it just went right into the mountain.'

Connor ran down the hallway and straight into his parents' bedroom. 'MOM! DAD!'

'Jesus Christ,' Glen said automatically, 'what time –'

'Turn the TV on! Now!'

'What the fuck, Connor?' Bridget snapped.

'*Now! The news!*' They saw he was nearly crying, standing there with balled fists. Bridget fumbled for the remote and clicked it on. An aerial shot, of the crash site, someone saying, '... just after dawn this morning.' And then his face came up on the screen – Du Pre, smiling on a red carpet somewhere. Before he knew what was happening Glen was in the bathroom, on his hands and knees, hearing his vomit spattering into the bowl. Bridget just kept staring at the screen – now showing the model of helicopter believed to have crashed – and repeating the word 'no' over and over again: 'No no no no ...' She turned her phone on and saw she'd already had four missed calls from Art. Dialling his number she became aware that her son was crying. 'Connor? What is it?'

'I loved him!' the boy wailed.

March

TWENTY

Hollywood, California. Monday 13 March 2017

It's been a while since I've been involved with one and, to be honest with you, I'd forgotten just how much I'd missed it – being at a record label that is in the process of having a great, big, fat, stinking, enormous hit. You see everyone walking the hallways with an extra spring in their step. Genuine laughter around the water coolers. Macho bonhomie in the boardrooms and in the executive offices, like the stuff Trellick and I are indulging ourselves in right now as we stand up by the windows of the Unigram conference room high over Hollywood Boulevard, moving around the long table, looking at artwork.

'Are you kidding me?' I say, throwing a glossy mock-up into the rejection pile.

'He looks like he's got fucking AIDS in this ...' Trellick says, holding up another one. The head of marketing and the creative director cower before us as we continue to eviscerate the stack of proposed album covers for the next Du Pre album, a collection of unreleased (indeed until now unreleasable) out-takes and odds and sods. The only problem being – we don't have a single as yet. This may take some doing . . .

The current Du Pre album, a straight-up greatest hits collection titled *Remembrance: The Lucius Du Pre Story* (the title took me a while. Inevitably the joke title whiteboard I set up in Trellick's office ended up being fuller than the serious title board. Joke titles included *Get Black*, *Half-Darkie*, *The Buggerer* and *I Fuck Kids*), is number one all over the world.

What a difference six weeks makes.

I have to say, the outpouring of national grief for the cunt has been *staggering*, far in excess of anything we had anticipated. Even now, weeks after the event, there on the TV screen playing silently in the corner of the room, are the fans: housewives, children, the clearly mentally ill, some of them dressed up like him, all of them bent and twisted with grief, their faces soaked with tears as they gather in impromptu vigils all across the country to sing his songs and celebrate his memory. I mean, Trellick and I haven't laughed like this since Diana died. And that time, unlike now, we weren't Mercury. We didn't even have the record. We fucking do now. The Top Twenties on both Spotify and Apple Music are entirely composed of Du Pre tracks. He is the most searched artist on the Internet. We're even ruling with the CD. The *fucking* CD. Sales for that poor, forgotten coffee-table relic of Generation X have topped a million copies in the US alone. No CD has done this in years.

The other thing that has astounded me has been the absolute lack of blowback. We fully anticipated a bit of this — some smarmy liberal fucks on chat shows trying to get a discussion going about the 'darker' aspects of Du Pre's personal life. Probing articles in the newspapers about rumours and improprieties.

We were, of course, fully ready to combat this stuff with our own 'fake news' blitz. But not a bit of it appeared. No one gave a fuck. I even watched an arts and culture programme where a woman journalist, talking about how well Du Pre did everything at his peak — sang, danced, wrote songs — said that she liked the idea of a 'cookie-cutter' Du Pre: you could pick out the bits you liked and leave the rest. Excellent! I'll take the singing and dancing and just leave the troublesome inserting-your-penis-in-a-child stuff. This approach, the national mood of total love and forgiveness, suits us down to the ground of course and has been a major contributing factor in how well I have been able to deal with the Murphys and their good lawyer ...

The four of us met, at Hinckley's office in Pasadena, the week after the accident, several days after they had been scheduled to have been paid, days in which, needless to say, I had not returned any of their increasingly frantic phone calls. To say you have never seen three people so broken by grief is an understatement. They stared at me dumbfounded as I laid it out for them. 'Look, guys, he's dead. No one was expecting this. I ... we just can't pay you right now. It's chaos, the estate, the whole thing. Let us get things in order, put the greatest hits out, make some cash, and then we'll come to an arrangement.'

'No, we're going to the media,' the lawyer said.

'Fucking A,' Glen said.

'That's your prerogative,' I said. 'But just think . . .' I got up, walked across his small, fetid office and turned on the TV, to CNN. 'Look at this . . .' They were covering a Du Pre vigil in New York, in Central Park, thousands of them screaming and wailing like Muslims at a fucking funeral. 'Look at the papers. The guy's getting treated like a cross between the Pope and Martin Luther King. No one wants to be hearing he was a fucking paedo right now. If you go out with your stuff obviously we'll deny it. We'll "fake news" it. Say it was a lookalike in the video. Whatever.'

'Stop it,' Hinckley said. 'It's clearly, undeniably, him in the video.'

'Is it?' I said. 'Look at the inauguration. The biggest crowd in history at that, right?' Those photographs – Obama's crowd stretching into infinity. The acres of white, empty space at Trump's. Spicer up there with his blow-ups, telling everyone a banana was an apple. A jackboot was a glass slipper. Fucking genius. 'Millions of fucking Americans believe that.' Bridget and Glen looked confused. Hinckley saw where I was headed. 'You know,' I said, gesturing to the TV again, to the weeping multitudes in Central Park, 'it's incredible what you can get away with when you have a hardcore fanbase . . .' I could see their minds working, the doubts slowly taking hold.

'You wouldn't da—' Bridget began.

'Now don't get me wrong,' I went on, cutting her off. 'I don't want to go down this route. Because you're right, you might win, but remember – Art, you're a lawyer – you'll be dealing with his *estate* at that point, you'll be dealing with debtors, creditors, family members, probate, the whole nine yards. It'll take forever. I *want* to pay you your twenty million. It's cleaner. Easier. Everyone wins. We just need some time.'

You could see them, the gears turning, weighing up their options, until, finally . . .

'How long?' Bridget said.

'Well, we've got to get the record into production, put an ad campaign together, all that crap . . . a few months. Say until the end of May. Memorial Day. Let us maximise sales. Let this press cycle end and wait until everyone's bored and looking for a new angle. We all win.'

They looked at each other. 'You've got till the end of May,' Hinckley said, relishing what the utter fucking clown thought was the chance to turn the screw. 'I strongly advise you not to test our patience any further than that.'

'Yeah. And . . . and we want another fucking mil in the meantime,' Glen added. 'A good-faith payment.'

'Done,' I said.

I tune back into the artwork meeting, where Trellick is holding up another mock-up and saying, 'Now, this one I don't mind . . .'

I take it from him. The proposed cover shows Du Pre's face in profile, in black and white, heavily airbrushed, making him look like a light-skinned black man, rather than a child molester from a nightmare who's just had acid thrown over them. His hands are clasped in prayer and his eyes are closed in penitent meditation or some fucking thing.

'Very nice,' I say. 'Simple. Elegant.'

'Oh, that's totally my favourite,' the creative director purrs. 'It'll look great on billboards.'

'Yep, gets my vote,' I say.

'Seconded,' Trellick says.

There is one particular aspect of the artwork that pleases me greatly. It's very small, tucked away on the back cover, down in the bottom right, below the various songwriting and producing credits:

Executive Producer: Steven Stelfox

Four simple words. One for each percentage point I have negotiated myself on all of Du Pre's posthumous releases. I mean, Trellick's a mate and all that and I like doing mates a favour. But, a *favour*? Do me a fucking favour.

'Dinner?' Trellick asks.

'No can do,' I say. 'Got plans.'

He smiles. 'And how's all that going?'

'All good,' I reply, slipping my jacket on. 'Laters.'

I walk out of his office, say goodbye to Sam, and stroll down the long hallway. I make a left along the corridor of A&R hutches, stop at one and lean in the doorway. She looks up from tapping away at her computer. 'Hey, you,' she says.

'Ready to rock?' I ask.

'Where are we going?'

'We have a reservation at Animal, on Fairfax.'

'You know what I'd really like?' she says, turning her computer off, stretching as she gets up and comes round the desk towards me. 'How about we just order in and go back to your place?' Chrissy puts her arms around my neck, looking straight into my eyes.

'Sure,' I say.

We kiss.

What a difference six weeks makes.

TWENTY-ONE

It was so *hot* in paradise.

Even with the fierce air conditioning, even with the chilling cocktail of opiates that coursed through his veins, Lucius found he broke into a fierce sweat whenever he had to do something more strenuous than lifting a glass or crossing a room, as he was now, to stand at the windows of his palatial bedroom and gaze out at the glittering Olympic-sized pool, at the palm trees casting shadows on the aquamarine water, at the lush gardens, gardens so vast you almost forgot that beyond them lay endless miles of desert. (Photographed from the upper atmosphere the Sultan's estate looked like a postage stamp of bright green set in the middle of an enormous beige page.) He pressed a glass of ice water to his forehead, yawning, and watched two men loading baskets of dirty laundry into a van. It amazed him that anyone was capable of doing such work in this heat.

But he couldn't complain. He loved it here.

He couldn't exactly recall how he'd got here. He'd woken up stretched out on a sofa in a jet – a Gulfstream like his, but not as opulent – and the last thing he could remember was a sharp stabbing pain in his thigh, while he slept on the helicopter. Some terrible dream about falling.

Dr Ali and a couple of people he didn't know were on the jet with him and he was told it was done. It was all happening. Mr Stelfox's plan. Ali gave him a nice drop of milk and he went back to sleep and when he woke up they were here, welcomed into their new home like Roman emperors returning from a long, hard-fought war.

Dr Ali had his own set of rooms somewhere on the other side of the courtyard, the two of them occupying what was essentially a small mansion (25,000 square feet) set within the grounds of a larger mansion. Their days over the last six weeks had, as promised, passed very pleasantly. Indeed, the differences from his previous life in California were very hard to detect. Lucius would rise at his usual time of three or four in the afternoon. He'd slowly come round, sipping water and coffee, slowly recovering from the major-surgery-grade anaesthetic he'd taken in order to sleep the night before. Around six o'clock he'd have breakfast brought to him in his room, the only meal of the day he really ate, and even then not really. (The habits of a lifetime spent watching his weight were hard to shake.) He'd usually eat alone, although sometimes Dr Ali or Abdullah, the Sultan's son, would join him. After breakfast there would be a shot of candy and a couple of drinks to get him into the party mood for the evening's entertainment: whatever collection of beauties had been arranged for him that night. They were all young, twelve to fifteen, all very handsome and dark-skinned and (and this was a definite difference from back home) they were all *fully compliant right away*. No cajoling or threatening, no promised treats or sly administering of the Jesus Juice was needed here, in paradise. There were no Lexuses to be bought for guardians. No enormous 'goodwill' cheques to be cut to suspicious parents. The boys turned up, they all had a good time, the boys went away, a new consignment arrived a couple of days later. It seemed to Lucius an unimprovable deal. And running below all of this, underscoring his happiness like a bassline, the first thing he thought about every day, was this: *he didn't have to do those stupid goddamn shows any more*. (Admittedly now and then he would be requested to put on a display for the Sultan's son, show him a few old dance moves, lip-sync along to one of his hits. Nothing too taxing.) Even though he sometimes missed his special friends – even Connor, that little traitor – when Lucius thought about how, right now, he might well have been in final rehearsals, preparing for the mammoth runs of concerts in New York and London, it was all he could do not to weep with joy, to go outside and kiss the hot Arabian dust with gratitude.

A gentle knocking at the door, Lucius's 'come', and two of the staff were wheeling his breakfast trolley in. They set it up at the end of the bed, facing the TV that was permanently tuned to the Disney Channel, just the way he liked it. There was French toast with strawberries and blueberries and a thick dusting of icing sugar. There was a champagne glass full of the morning's pills – a cocktail of seventeen different caplets and tablets that Dr Ali prescribed to keep him 'balanced' until that evening shot of real candy. Lucius washed them down with a swig from a frosted beaker of freshly squeezed orange juice, and smacked his lips with satisfaction. There was another gentle knocking at his door and a moment later, Abdullah popped his head round. 'Hi, Lucius,' he said. 'Is it OK if I watch TV with you for a little while?'

'Sure, Abby,' Lucius said, using the nickname he'd bestowed upon the guy, something Abdullah had mistaken for a sign of affection when it was in fact simply less bothersome for Lucius to remember than the tricksy trisyllable.

Abdullah hopped up on the bed next to Lucius. 'What you watching?' he asked, adjusting one of his epaulettes. (He was almost always dressed like Lucius from a certain period of his fame. This morning it was the military pimp look of his *Ceasefire* period of the late nineties.)

'*Beauty and the Beast* . . .' Lucius replied, nibbling a tiny corner of French toast.

'Oh, I like the part where they have the dance,' Abby simpered.

'Me too,' Lucius said.

'Beast's so good-looking . . .'

'Ewww. Oh, you mean when he changes?'

'No! Even when he's Beast!'

'Ewww!'

Anyone reading a transcript of this conversation would certainly have identified the interlocutors as being girls of around seven or eight, not a twenty-two-year-old and a fifty-year-old man. Abby lay on the bed beside Lucius while he ate and they went on talking about Disney films and how much they liked maple syrup and what they were going to wear for that night's party when Lucius became aware of a certain … pressure on his thigh. He looked at Abby – who was biting his bottom lip as he pressed what was clearly a monumental boner against Lucius's leg.

'Excuse me, Abby,' Lucius said primly.

He went into his bathroom, where he clutched the sink and took a few deep breaths. *Oh my God. Abby was, like, ancient! He had to weigh two hundred pounds! I mean – AS IF!*

And here it was, just like the Bible said.

In paradise – a serpent.

TWENTY-TWO

A girlfriend. That's right. Fuck you. Yeah, I know what I've said in the past but, but ...

It just kind of happened. We went out a couple more times, to talk about the NDC deal. Well, we soon gave up on the pretence that either of us really gave a fuck about that and, one night, after dinner and drinks, we fell hungrily into each other in the basement parking garage of the Chateau Marmont while we were waiting for my car to be brought out. We woke up in bed together the next morning and I had the strangest urge. Or rather, I *didn't* have the usual urges. I didn't want to slip from the bed and creep out without waking her. Or call the doorman, or the maid, and get them to show her out. I wanted her to stay. How fucking perverted is *that*? It is weird though. Waking several mornings in a row with the same girl. One you have not violated in multiple, barely credible ways. One for whom you do not have to invent a meeting – or give a stack of bills – to make go away. (A common misconception when it comes to hookers: you don't pay them to come. You pay them to *leave*.) Don't get me wrong, the habits of a lifetime are hard to shake. Sometimes in the last few weeks I've caught sight of us, in the mirrored wall of a restaurant, or an elevator, in the smoked glass of a limo, and thought what any sane person would think – *why are that pair of cunts so happy?*

And we do the things couples do. We have breakfast. We go into the office together, the twenty-minute drive east along Fountain filled with chatter, industry gossip, celebrity nonsense and so forth. We go to the market. We go to parties together, making our debut at the bash Unigram threw at the Roosevelt to celebrate the number-one position for *Remembrance*. Chrissy's friends all coo over her new-found happiness while undoubtedly hating her for having a boyfriend who is worth hundreds of millions of dollars and secretly bitching about the fact that he is nearly twenty years older than her.

Some things about Chrissy: she is a Texan who is almost a vegetarian. She's an indie rock kid (her playlists, fuck me, Modest Mouse, Saint Etienne, Mogwai – the kind of music that makes you want to own a slaughterhouse, or join the NRA) who works at a major label. She's a Democrat who voted for Hillary but really wanted Bernie. She likes to read, is a cunning, fiercely competitive tennis opponent and she can cook. But why? Why am I doing this? Why her? Why now?

Well, maybe, it was just time. I'm certainly conscious of one thing. There's no two ways about it, if you're still single at my age – no matter how many models you do, how many stonking-hot boilers you're photographed falling in and out of parties and nightclubs with, no matter how many romances you're linked to in the tabloids – people do begin to wonder if you're either a ginger beer or the full fucking Du Pre.

I can hear you asking – so how does this work? How does it go with this quasi-vegetarian, indie-rock-loving, Hillary-voting girl? I find many of the obstacles in these areas can be overcome by a very simple strategy: not listening to a fucking word she says. I mean, most relationships end up there anyway, I just accelerated it a little. You would not believe the amount of mileage I get from the phrase 'that's interesting'.

Like now, for instance, on this warm, March Sunday morning as we drive out to Malibu for an afternoon at Soho Beach House. We have the top down, which Chrissy thinks is *so* ostentatious. And it's true, driving this kind of motor – 200,000-dollar price tag, six-litre engine, about a mile and a half to the gallon – does get you some dirty looks from the bearded, hipster cycling communities if you venture much out of Beverly Hills or Hollywood, but, to be honest with you (and there's not much point in being anything other than honest at this point, is there? We've come so far together. Shared so much), if I could get away with it, I'd have murals of starving children painted along the sides of the car, the tyres made out of moulded hundred-dollar bills that are visibly burning off as you drive by. *Fuck them.* 'That's interesting,' I say again to Chrissy, who is scanning the weekend newspapers, laid out in her lap in the passenger seat as we come through Palisades.

'It's not "interesting"! It's outrageous!' she says. 'You're not even listening!' She laughs – scandalised.

That's the other thing: she seems to know how truly appalling I am (well, she *thinks* she does. Obviously if she was party to three or four minutes of a frank conversation between me and Trellick she'd be spending a couple of months in therapy) and doesn't care. Chrissy is banging on about the big news story of the week, the one that dominates the fake news this weekend. Trump has accused Obama of bugging his offices at Trump Tower during the campaign. 'Terrible!' the Donald said on Twitter. 'Just found out that Obama had my "wires tapped" in Trump Tower just before the victory. Nothing found. This is McCarthyism!'

'I mean,' Chrissy fumes, 'what *proof* does he have for this?'

'A lot of people are talking about it,' I say, loving it.

'Oh, for Christ's sake ...'

Chrissy and her friends are obviously going bananas every day at the moment. They are going mad all the time. This is because they are still living in the Old America. I myself, even before the election, always lived – happily, sanely – in the New America. The America of realpolitik. What's the deal in the New America? Well, it's got nothing to do with proof or evidence or due process or any of that bollocks. You know what it's got to do with?

Massa told everyone Chicken George was a devious liar. And they're listening.

They've been *dying* to listen for eight years. Eight years staring slack-jawed at the TV – in their trailers, in bars where they drink domestic draft, in Southern police stations – and watching a *black man* in the White House, a black man who talked like his dad ate a Harvard lawyer. *Did the Trump campaign go too far? Did it damage the discourse?* These are the questions Chrissy and her friends keep themselves up with at night. I thought the campaign was fairly restrained myself. Let's face it, he could have gone with a poster of Obama dressed as an actual cannibal (loincloth, human bones around his neck), grinning as he stirred a huge cooking pot swirling with white babies, aborted foetuses, bloodstained dollar bills and topped off with the tag line 'DO YOU WANT SOME FUCKING MORE OF THIS, WHITEY?', and 30 per cent of America would have stood up and fucking cheered.

Chrissy's phone rings and I half listen as she takes it. She says 'Oh shit'. And 'When?' and 'Are you sure?' and stuff like that. She hangs up and sighs.

'What's up?' I say when she hangs up.

'Yep – they're signing to XL.'

'Have signed or are going to sign?'

'Going to.'

'OK. You're not dead yet.'

'Fuck! That weasel Danny Rent! He said –'

'Calm down. Where are they?'

'With the deal?'

'No, physically. Where are the band?'

'I, uh, I think they're in Miami this week. For the Winter Music Conference.'

'Jesus Christ,' I say. 'That's still a thing?' I went to the WMC a few times, way, way back in the day.

'Yup.'

'OK then – let's doorstep the cunts. Make a last-minute offer-you-can't-refuse.' Actually, thinking about it, I quite fancy a trip over to Miami. I could look up Dick. He might be able to get me in there, up at Palm Beach. Just for lunch or something. Now that would be a laugh.

'Steven,' she says, 'I think it's over. We lost.'

I try to picture my name in the same sentence as this odd, alien word – '*Yeah, stelfox lost the deal.*' '*Stelfox lost.*' '*Stelfox is a loser.*' I find it can't be done. Also, and this is further proof of what an appalling soft wreck I'm turning into, I want to help my *girlfriend* out here. 'Don't worry, baby,' I sing, mock Beach Boys as we turn into the drive of Soho House, me enjoying the look of awe and respect on the black valet's face as he approaches us, taking in the car, Chrissy, everything. You get none of the crap you get back in England out here. No one keys cars. Everyone reckons they'll soon be sitting where you are. Why would they fuck with that? 'We'll get hold of Danny.'

'Yeah?' she says. 'And do what? Kill him?'

I just smile as I hand the keys and a fifty to the grinning kid. I'm looking forward to eating beside the ocean, to some grilled squid out there on the deck, some hamachi, maybe a little white wine, and then the drive back to Hollywood in the gathering dusk, sex later, then falling asleep in my emperor-sized bed high over Hollywood, looking forward to the royalties starting to pour in from the Du Pre record, to continuing to be rich and white in the land of the free.

TWENTY-THREE

'... hardwood floors throughout, this would obviously make a great den, opening up onto the gardens through here ...' The realtor, Barbara something, slid the doors open to show a green expanse of lawn sweeping away from the house. 'Now they're asking three-point-two, but I know they're keen to sell ...'

Bridget Murphy stood in the open doors and pictured this three-bed, four-bath in Brentwood being her new home. Pictured herself coming out of these doors in summer, heading towards the long dining table over there, set up beneath a canvas awning, carrying a plate of something nice. (Because obviously she'd have learned to cook in this new life of hers.) Their friends (new friends, the kind you get when you're rich) cooing, oohing and ahhing in awe over the house, the pool, the gazebo thingy.

'Where are you at the moment?' Barbara asked.

'We're, over, ah, we're in the valley. Temporarily.'

Barbara showed no disgust. 'And are you selling?'

'No, we're ...' Bridget couldn't bring herself to say 'renting'. 'It's a cash buy.'

'Oh.' This signalled a change in attitude. 'You know I've got a couple of very nice places east of here, fringes of Beverly Hills. You're nearer five million then, but –'

'You seen the size of the fucken kitchen?' Glen, lumbering in down the hallway. He saw Barbara. 'Sorry. Excuse me. Just, it's a big kitchen.'

'The house is great for entertaining,' Barbara said, trying to place this tacky pair. Entertainment? Retail? 'What line of work are you in, Glen?'

'Oh, this and that.'

Jesus, Bridget thought. *Try and sound more like a drug dealer.* 'We're in PR,' Bridget said, inspired.

'Oh, super. Anyone I'd know?'

'Well, until recently.' Glen lowered his voice. 'Lucius Du Pre?'

'Oh. I'm so sorry.' Barbara looked at the floor, shook her head. 'So tragic.'

'Actually,' Bridget said, shooting Glen a look, 'we'd rather not talk about it.'

'Guys, I'm so sorry. I didn't mean to –'

'That's OK. If you could just give us a few minutes, Barbara.'

'Of course. I'll be out front making some calls.'

The front door closed, leaving the two of them alone in the big, empty house. 'What the fuck, idiot?' Bridget said.

'What?'

'Why even mention him?'

'You started the bullshit! I was just ... improvising!'

'Why don't you leave all that to me?'

'You're getting worse than Artie ...' Glen huffed, stomping off, the rubber soles of his biker boots clumping and squeaking on the dark hardwood.

Ten per cent deposit, Bridget was thinking. *Lowball them at two-point-nine, put around three hundred thou down now*. They had a little over one-point-two million dollars in the secret account, their two-thirds of the two mil they'd received so far, minus around a hundred grand that had gone on 'treats' in the past couple of months: the new car (a Lexus SUV – they'd returned the Porsche and simply not told Artie about the Lexus, parked it around the corner the one time he came over for a meeting), clothes and vacations. Disneyland with Connor, a suite in the hotel there. There'd been a long weekend at the Four Seasons out at Santa Barbara, just the two of them. The ease with which they'd signed cheques, picked up new cashmere sweaters in the gift shop, charging them to the room. Eaten lobster and drunk champagne. Done good blow after dinner and stared at the ocean. It all felt right to her. It felt like – *so this is where we were meant to be*. All that other stuff, the life they'd led for the four decades leading up to this, it had all been training for what every American felt was their birthright. They weren't quite there yet of course. Maybe twenty years ago you would have been. But a million didn't mean shit any more. So you were a millionaire. So what? But they were close. Tantalisingly close. Memorial Day. Less than a couple of months away.

Connor had been sad at Disneyland. The place had reminded him of Narnia. It had been a difficult time gener- ally with Connor, with Du Pre's face in the papers and on the TV and all over the Internet all the time. His music constantly on the radio. It had been difficult with Glen too, who had been less than sympathetic to his son's complex emotional response to the death of the man they'd been blackmailing. ('*Why the fuck is he fucking crying about that asshole who fucking raped him again? Fuck him, Du Pre, the sick twisted mother fucker, I'd kill him myself if he was still alive, the fucken jagoff.*') Bridget's response to Du Pre's death, like her son's, had been more complicated. She pictured herself, in years to come, trying to answer questions about what had happened to Connor, on talk shows, in interviews. How, as a mother, could she live with what had happened? She'd done a lot of reading on the subject. '*Well, Oprah …*' she'd say. '*I'd long known my son was gay. Yes, thirteen / fourteen is young, but look at the men we look up to when we see them with girls of that age: Jimmy Page, Bill Wyman, these guys. And did you know that the ancient Greeks venerated the practice of younger boys sleeping with older men? To them it was a sacred thing. So —*'

Yeah, that shit might not fly on Jimmy Kimmel. Sometimes she wondered if she could come right out and say what most people were thinking — '*Yeah it was a fucken disgraceful situation and I'm glad he's dead but you know what? We got paid, bitch.*'

Memorial Day.

One way or another, they were getting paid.

TWENTY-FOUR

His plan came to him gradually, as it had for Moses – '*And he was there with the LORD forty days and forty nights; he did neither eat bread, nor drink water. And he wrote upon the tablets the words of the covenant, the ten commandments.*' Lucius wasn't sure if had been forty days and forty nights, one way or another – the handfuls of pills, the injections, the endless parade of dark flesh – he'd kind of lost track of time. But there had been several epiphanies that had led up to the confrontation. The first was sexual, some weeks ago. Lucius had been panting, staring at the back of the boy splayed on the bed beneath him. Lucius was kneeling, having just brought forth his seed with all the mighty vengeance of the Lord. He was staring, panting, at the nameless brown back, and the thought had occurred to him – '*I don't really like fucking Arab boys.*' And it wasn't racism – Lucius loved *all* God's children – it was something harder to articulate but that might have been boiled down to this: there was no fight. No seduction. Lucius realised that part of what appealed to him was the gradual winning – and the subsequent betraying – of trust.

The second epiphany was directly ego-related. He'd been stretched out on bed, channel-hopping, when something had caught his eye: a fat youth, white, American, crying and talking to an interviewer. The youth was dressed exactly like Lucius had dressed around the period of *Outlaw*, in the mid-eighties. Black leather with rubber accessories. (Although a good deal more leather and rubber were involved in this kid's outfit.) The chryo running across the bottom of the screen had read: '*LUCIUS DU PRE FAN CRAIG SAYS HE'S LIVING IN HELL.*' Lucius never watched the news, the incredible lies they told about him. He'd spent the last few years studiously avoiding all media. But he'd thumbed the volume up in time to hear this Craig saying, 'I still can't believe he's gone. I ... I can't sleep at night. I wake up crying ...' The interviewer's voice took over as Lucius drew nearer the set, '... And it's not just Craig who's feeling that way. As the huge outpourings of grief at Du Pre rallies all across the country have shown ...' The image had cut to a sports hall, filled with thousands of kids dressed like him. They were crying, hugging one another, while his music played 'Although for some fans,' the voice had said, 'like Tracy Mueller, there is still hope ...' It had cut to another fan, a woman, in her early thirties, Lucius guessed, being interviewed in the sports hall. 'I keep telling people. He's not gone.' Someone off camera tried to say something, to argue with her. 'He's NOT, he's not gone. He's out there. He just had to get away from all this ...' she gestured to the camera, the mike, 'this whole circus. And he's going to come back to us and it ... it's going to be *so beautiful.*' Lucius had fought back tears as he'd nodded in sombre agreement. Yes, Tracy from Indiana, it could be so beautiful.

On top of the epiphanies, there were practical problems. Like the increasingly tiresome Abdullah. As the weeks went by he kept finding more reasons to knock on Lucius's door. To invite Lucius to join him in pastimes Lucius had no interest in – tennis, chess, ice skating, racquetball, all of which were available at private facilities within the estate.

The final factor had become apparent as winter, such as it was here, became spring. It had occurred to Lucius when he decided to take a walk the other afternoon. Not a *walk* of course. Just a stroll, through the gardens and down to one of the many swimming pools. He'd gone just a few steps before he'd had to take shelter in the shade of the house. There was a thermometer on the wall beside him. It read 35 degrees. I mean, really. Seriously? In *March*? He'd gone to see Dr Ali.

'You want *what*?' Ali had said. He'd been standing in his vast bedroom, dripping from the shower, a towel around him, either just back from, or on his way to, the golf course.

'I want to go home,' Lucius had repeated.

'I . . . Lucius . . .' Ali had begun. Where to begin?

Ali had been surprised by this hot Arabian province. Even though you could only play in the early morning and early evening, the golf course was sensational – a 6,800-yard gem, modelled on Pinehurst, with beautiful Bermuda grass, fast greens and some luxury improvements as yet unheard of on American golf courses: little refrigerators built into every tee-box, filled with water, Cokes, beers and champagne. You were given not one, not two, but *three* caddies – one to constantly attend you with a sun umbrella, one to go ahead and look for your ball, and one to drive the cart and give you yardages. Ali was only mildly surprised they hadn't gone as far as to revert to having 'jam boys', black kids slathered in jam or honey, who walked a little way ahead, to attract the flies and stinging insects away from you, like they had on Southern American courses in the old days. Yes, Ali had played on all the Trump courses back home, but this ... this was some serious luxury. He had a good regular four-ball too – the Sultan, his cousin and one of the Sultan's doctors. The cousin was a seriously good player, a two-handicapper. Under his tutelage and with playing twice a day nearly every day, Ali reckoned he had shaved a little over three strokes off his 15 handicap in the time they'd been here. By the time they went home at the end of May (not that Lucius knew this was the plan yet. He was on a strict need-to-know basis, as per Stelfox's instructions) he might just have achieved his lifelong goal of getting into single figures.

Then there was the food and drink – an endless, sumptuous banquet every night – and the women: incredible, compliant creatures delivered to (and removed from) his rooms whenever he desired. Yes, fair to say the doctor was enjoying his vacation. He had looked at Lucius, sitting on the edge of his bed, fidgeting with the TV remote, not making eye contact, speaking very quietly. Yes, he looked like a guilty child, but that could change in an instant with the provocation of the dread word 'no'. Ali would have to tread carefully. He had gone over and sat on the chaise near the bed.

'Lucius, we talked about this. I thought it was clear. We ... it's difficult.'

'I'm bored,' Lucius had said.

'Well, is there something you want to do? The Sultan can arrange pretty much anything we –'

'I want to see my fans.'

'Your fans?'

'They miss me.'

'Of course they do. But part of the reason we're here is because, you know, those comeback shows. Remember? You really didn't want to go through with all that, did you?'

'Sometimes I think, maybe I should have ...' Lucius had whispered.

Christ, Ali had thought. Should he let the powers that be back in LA know about this?

'Lucius,' he'd said, patting his patient's leg, 'you're thinking too much. Let's just enjoy ourselves. Now ...' Ali had glanced at his watch surreptitiously. He was off the tee in twenty minutes. He switched to physician mode. 'Would you say you were feeling very anxious or just a little depressed?'

'Well, this morning I was anxious. Now – maybe just sad?'

'Hmmm. Hang on a minute ...'

Ali had crossed the room and gone into the walk-in wardrobe that also served as his pharmacy. He'd got his black medicine bag out from under the shoe rack and rooted through. He'd knocked four orange Dilaudid into his palm. Then half a dozen shiny white Demerol. He'd walked back into the bedroom and handed them to his patient. 'Here, take a white one if you're feeling a bit sad, the orange if you're really anxious, OK? We'll review in a couple of days.'

'OK.'

'And let's have dinner tonight, yeah?'

'Sure,' Lucius had shrugged.

'Cheer up,' Ali had said. 'Remember – you could have lost everything. We're here saving it. We're saving Narnia.'

'Narnia,' Lucius had repeated. He had been so happy there.

Lucius had returned to his room and gone into the bathroom, an expanse of sandy marble and soft lighting. He'd stood before the mirror, a glass of water in one hand and an orange tablet in the other, staring at his face for a long time. Even with the scant amount of time he'd spent outside he was already pleasingly darker. Dr Ali hadn't actually said the word. The hellish monosyllable 'no' had not escaped his lips. But, even so, Lucius had clearly expressed a desire. He wanted to go home. In the old world, when Lucius expressed a desire, whether it was for a movie, a car or a flock of emus, the desired object was placed in front of him. Another epiphany had come to him – '*Then he blinded the eyes of Zedekiah; and the king of Babylon bound him with bronze fetters and brought him to Babylon and put him in prison until the day of his death* ' Jeremiah, 52.11. He had been tricked. That clever British guy.

Lucius was a prisoner.

Him. Lucius Du Pre. What could he do about it? He knew the first step he would have to take if he were to escape the clutches of his oppressors. It would be difficult. A hard road. But, like his brave forefathers – like Martin Luther King, like Malcolm X – he would screw his courage to the mast. The hardest step was always the first. Lucius had looked at his own trembling hand, already halfway towards his mouth, the orange tab of Dilaudid already seeming to glow with impossible promise, the promise of taking away all his doubts and fears.

Lucius had dropped it into the sink.

He had turned on the faucet and, with the rush of water, watched the opiate vanish.

TWENTY-FIVE

'He got hit on the head, got amnesia, can't remember anything.'

'Oh, oh – he wandered for miles and wound up living with some family in the desert. They nursed him back to health.'

'Too complicated. You'd have to hire someone to play the family. Then you're into all that.'

'When he realised he'd survived the crash he ... he knew it was an opportunity to ... to escape his life. Oh – maybe this is stupid ...'

'Hey!' Ruth says. 'Remember, kids – *there are no stupid ideas when we're spitballing!*'

We're brainstorming. Spitballing.

Present around the huge Carrara marble dining table in my apartment (the current meeting is way too hot to be conducting it within ten blocks of the label) are Ruth Blane and her two protégés Les and Jenny. Ruth is a legend in this business. New York Jewish, fifty(ish), sharp as the edge of a box-cutter and utterly devoid of scruple, sentiment or shame. Remember that basketball player who got caught with those fifteen-year-old twins at a motel in Reno? The former member of that boy band who killed two pedestrians after his car mounted the kerb outside Moonshadows? The married-with-five-kids chat-show host who got caught blowing the seven-foot Colombian transvestite? Basically if you're in the NFL and you find yourself DUI and performing CPR on a MAW who's about to be DOA and you know you'll soon be looking for PR – Ruth is the ultimate expression of the art form in the twenty-first century. We have worked together several times over the last fifteen or so years, ever since Ruth helped with damage limitation after the Jesus kid fiasco on *American Pop Star*. Les and Jenny are both in their early thirties and are mini-Ruths, having been sucking at her intellectual teat since they left college. These three are being paid an incredible retainer for their skills and discretion in helping with phase two.

'He, the shock, in his shock, he found God,' Les says.

'He's already found God, ya schmuck.' Jenny doesn't look up from her screen, monitoring the bot accounts. 'Or how about,' Jenny goes on, 'he survived in the mountains for months, living wild. Then –'

'Sorry,' I interrupt. 'I know we're spitballing here, but that *is* a fucking stupid idea. Have you seen the cunt? He couldn't survive in the mountains for three minutes. I mean, the guy hasn't bought a carton of milk in thirty years.'

'COME ON, YOU HICKS!' Ruth yells at her guys. 'THINK!'

'Jesus,' Trellick says. He's been pacing in the background while all this is going on. (Only the people in this room know where this thing is heading next. The new way — a small, utterly committed team controlling the national narrative.) 'I don't know. I just don't know about all this.' The PR team look up from their laptops.

'What don't you know, James?' Ruth asks.

'Just, I mean, what? We're going to unveil him at some press conference and say "Surprise! He's not dead! He's been living in New Mexico with amnesia"?'

'That's not bad . . .' Ruth says.

'How fucking dumb do we think people are?'

For all Trellick's cynicism, part of him, like Chrissy and her friends, is still living in the old world, where certain laws applied. Truth. Reality. He has not yet fully made the leap into the new world, where uttering these words has become like saying 'penny-farthing' or 'blunderbuss'. What's that you've got there, you fucking libtard clown? Oh, a picture of some gas chambers? Didn't happen. Here's a screenshot of Pepe the Frog giving you the thumbs up and telling you you've been schilled. A million people appear to have retweeted it. *This Is My Truth Tell Me Yours*, those Welsh socialist miner fucks sang, way back in the day, before all of this happened. Nowadays? This Is My Lie Prove Me Wrong. 'Trellick,' I say. 'Prove it. *Prove* to me that something like this isn't what happened.'

'Something like what?'

I lean back in my chair, clasp my hands behind my head, and precis the most convincing take we have yet. 'Lucius was thrown clear of the crash and knocked unconscious. He can't really remember much about what happened then. The next thing he knew he woke up in this guy's home. Some sick, crazy redneck hillbilly fuck, some John Wayne

Gacy motherfucker who tortured Lucius in ways he will never fully be able to recount –'

'Until the autobio and the book tour,' Ruth chips in.

'– who kept him prisoner for months until he was finally able to escape. And here we are.'

Trellick sighs. 'Everyone will know that's utter bollocks.'

'Who?' I ask. 'Who'll know?'

'Every sentient person with an IQ over eighty-five,' he says.

Ruth just laughs at this.

'Jenny,' I say without turning, 'what's the Internet saying?' She turns her screen around to show Trellick. The hashtag '#LUCIUSLIVES'. The Facebook pages devoted to conspiracy theories: he was murdered ... he didn't actually die in the plane crash ... the CIA did it. Blah blah blah. Some of these are just genuine nutters, madmen out there, braying at the world, howling at the silver moon. But many, of course, are our own bot accounts, guys in a basement in Eastern Europe, helping the nutters along, telling them what they need to hear, giving them memes and hashtags and, most importantly of all, telling them what every lunatic needs to hear – *You're right. You're not alone. You are not mad, my friend.* All of it is nonsense of course, all of it muddying the water, softening the ground, paving the way, lubing the anus, for the outrageous cobblers, the monster cock to follow.

'When we drop this,' I say, 'it'll be almost July. We're going to have the biggest-selling album of the summer, the biggest in history.'

'We don't have a single ...' Trellick says flatly.

'Oh, on that subject, get onto A&R again. There must be more in the vaults. Have them dig out *everything*. Every last out-take we have. Seriously – song sketches, abandoned demos, jam sessions, soundcheck recordings ...'

'I'm telling you,' he says, 'there's nothing there.'

'I've even got the title.'

'Go on,' Trellick says.

I smile. '"The Resurrection".'

TWENTY-SIX

'Fucking hell.' Danny Rent drained his beer and set it down on the counter of the poolside bar at the Delano Hotel, his market-trader accent standing out like a cat at Crufts. He looked around at the girls of the Miami Winter Music Conference – brown bodies, sheathed in diaphanous white silk wraps and shirts, in bikinis and tube tops and shorts – and said, 'There's some fucking birds in here ...' before adding, hastily, 'no offence, Chrissy love.'

'None taken,' Chrissy said, following his gaze around the pool. She knew these girls. They traipsed the world, representing brands, organising events, looking after models and DJs and whatever, following the sun and the fabulous people from Glastonbury to Ibiza to Miami to wherever, their lives a blizzard of the three Cs: clubs, cocaine and cock. They earned a pittance but then they didn't need to earn anything: they didn't eat, the flights and the room were paid for, and one of the guys who followed in their wake would pick up the drinks tab. It was a life of sorts, Chrissy thought, until they hit forty: their skin like sandpaper, their wombs dried up like used condoms left on the beach over there, under the Florida sun.

'Where's Steven by the way?' Rent said, changing tack.

'Oh, he's around. Said he'll catch up with us later.'

'This your first time working together?'

'Well, we're not really working together, Danny. He's a consultant for Unigram. Takes an interest in the odd project.'

'Yeah, I bet he fucking does ...' Rent said, grinning. Danny liked Stellfox. He did. They'd had some laughs together. But Danny remembered all too well the end of the Songbirds' short career. He remembered how, after the success of the first album, when the second record started stiffing, the girls had gone from being 'Steven's band' to being 'our band' to suddenly being 'Danny's fucking band'. Steven didn't take prisoners and he didn't do failure.

'So, Danny,' Chrissy said, putting her glass down, tiring of the fun and games. 'What do we need to do to get this deal signed?' Christ, she needed this. These guys had built their own fanbase and cultivated their own image. They had developed it to the point where they could headline Brixton Academy or Hammerstein on their own. They had done it all by themselves. You wouldn't need to do a fucking thing except spend more cash. They were the perfect major-label signing. 'We can't go any further on the money. Christ, we're at seven hundred and fifty grand now. We've matched the competition step-for-step. Have you any idea how big an advance that is in the current climate?'

'It ain't about the money, Chrissy. I'd sign it tomorrow, love,' Rent said. 'But for the guys, for an artist, you know,

XL are hard to say no to ...' Danny liked this girl. He did. He'd have loved to make it work with them, he really would. But sometimes, well, the manager was just the messenger, wasn't he? He had been building up to how to tell her. Fuck it, just rip the Band Aid off, it was never pleasant. 'Look, Chrissy, I like you, I like Unigram, but –'

Here it came. The hammer blow. The phrase she'd already heard several blood-chilling times in her short career: 'but we're signing to Island/Capitol/Matador/Whoever ...' Right then Rent's phone pinged loudly on the bar, the cheerful digital tone cutting through the party din, cutting off whatever he was about to say. He looked at the screen and frowned.

'But...?' Chrissy said.

'Just a sec ...' he said, holding up a finger as he opened and read the message, his frown deepening then fading as he poker-faced it. 'But ...' Rent resumed, trying not to stutter, trying not to let his face colour in reaction to what he was reading, 'I ... think it's just going to take the band a little while longer to come round to my way of thinking ...'

'So ...' Chrissy said, stretching out the vowel cautiously, experimentally. 'We're still in this?'

'Yeah. Course you are. Ain't over till it's over. Look, love, I gotta shoot right now. See you at the party tonight, yeah?' He went to lay his room key on the bar, for the drinks.

'I got these, Danny.'

'Yeah? Sweet. Laters.' He pecked her on the cheek and headed for the lobby.

In the elevator, on the way up to his room, Danny Rent read the text message again, to make sure he wasn't dreaming.

No, there it was, in the bright green box: *'We'll double the XL advance. 1.5 million. Offer open for 24 hours. SS.'* Fucking hell. It wasn't about the money and all that. But, at the same time, it was *always* about the money.

In his suite, a couple of floors above where Rent was now getting off the elevator and hurrying to his room to call the band and their lawyer, Steven Stelfox was pouring two glasses of Cristal. As he finished Chrissy stepped into the room, her phone ringing. 'Sorry,' she said to him, answering it. 'Hello?' He watched her, enjoying the moment, sipping his champagne. *'What?'* she said. 'I didn't auth … wait, James, that's … that's crazy money! Is this any way to get the fucking deal? I … he's here right now.' She looked at Steven, sitting calmly in a club chair by the window onto the balcony. 'OK.' She hung up and looked at him, folding her arms. 'What the fuck is going on? That was Trellick. We've just offered one and a half fucking million on the NDC deal? That's just nuts! It says we've got nothing to offer but money. What if XL match it? What if –'

'Chrissy,' Stelfox said, 'calm down, sit down, listen and learn. One – we're not going to pay one and a half million. Two – we *don't* have anything to offer except money. And three – there's no way XL are going to match it.'

'But –'

'You want this deal, right? You want to get on? Sign a big, hit act? Then trust me and come over here. We've got an hour till dinner. Come on. Take that off. Here …'

TWENTY-SEVEN

Gold and marble. Marble and gold.

'I mean, he must have cornered the market in these two substances, right?' Dick says, laughing through a mouthful of Caesar salad. I lean back in my (heavily gilded) chair, taking the dining room in.

It's restrained decor-wise compared to the lobby, but still. It's busy too, on this warm Sunday lunchtime, a lot of the guys still wearing chinos and polo shirts – Lacoste, Ralph Lauren – red-faced from the golf course, frowning into the heavy menus, cutting their thick steaks. The women are all painted, freeze-dried hair, silicone-racked, airbrushed in the way of ageing dick-and-dollar worshippers the world over. Dick's a golfer. A member here. When I knew I was coming to Miami I rang and made him bring me for lunch. I've left Chrissy back at the Delano, an hour south, working the conference. I just told her I had a meeting. Safe to say she wouldn't have approved of this side trip. Me? I just wanted to breathe the same air, so to speak. Get inspired ...

Everywhere in the building you hear the whispers (*'he's on the fourteenth ... he just made a birdie!'*) and you see the guys: dark suits, sunglasses, bulging armpits. The security to get in was incredible. (Although not, Terry would probably tell you, impregnable.)

Dick and I go back to the show, to *American Pop Star*. A TV veteran, he knew the networks and I knew music (or at least knew the drama that surrounds the making of music) and together it all worked. Dick made a fortune too when we sold up and now he winters in Palm Beach. At sixty, this place is definitely more his speed these days than the Delano or Soho House. I look at my plate. I have ordered the meatloaf and mashed potatoes, out of respect, because they say it's one of his favourites.

'So,' Dick says, 'I noticed you got a producer credit on the Du Pre record. What's with that?' He cocks an eyebrow.

'Nothing. Seriously. Trellick asked me to help out. I just advised on sequencing, oversaw a couple of remixes ...'

'You got points?'

'I just did a mate a favour.' I can see from the way Dick sips his ice tea that he knows this is about as likely as one of these women around us sucking a cock without having first been bought a Rolex, but he lets it go. Granted, I didn't do much on the Du Pre greatest hits to earn a producer credit. No. That was a reward for my 'conceptual' input. The input that resulted in Du Pre currently being out of sight on the other side of the world. (Schitzbaul is checking in regularly with Dr Ali and the Sultan. Everything seems to be fine and dandy out there.) However, rest assured I will most definitely be earning my producer credit on the next Du Pre record, the comeback album, *The Resurrection*.

I have spent the last few days in LA combing through the years of Du Pre out-takes, trying desperately to find something unreleased that could be moulded into a hit single, to drive the sales of whatever drivel we put on the album. It has been a fascinating exercise in its own hellish way. There were hours of cover versions of old Motown tunes. Half-realised arrangements of some of his greatest hits. Endless 'jam' sessions, the band churning a riff over and over while Du Pre tried to come up with a top line. There must have been several hours alone of Du Pre singing acappella versions of the 'Star-Spangled Banner', the national anthem being the tune he always used to warm up his vocal cords for a gig or a recording session. Hours of him intoning *'Oh say can you see, by the dawn's early light ...'* in his fragile, delicate voice. Interesting enough stuff for the rabid fan or completist, the kind of satanists who read *Record Collector*, but in terms of finding the raw materials to manufacture a hit record, it has so far been about as useful as tits on a bull, as Chrissy would say.

'He was fucking weird that time we had him on the show, right?' Dick says. We had Du Pre on as a guest artist, on season two or three, way back when. I wasn't much involved, Dick handled all that stuff, but I heard about the endless rider requests, the usual demands that no one make eye contact with him. The separate dressing rooms for his personal chef, personal trainer, personal banker, personal llama and so forth. Standard stuff. 'You think the rumours are true?'

'Which rumours?' I say.

'Come on,' Dick says. 'You can't libel the dead.' No, I think, but you can dent their record sales. All publicity is good publicity? Not when it involves your demented self-blackened balls banging off some kid's arse cheeks. 'The whole fucking little boys stuff. You reckon there was anything to it?' I think of the grainy footage, badly lit, Du Pre's face, distorted and mad at the point of orgasm.

'Nah, mate,' I say, pushing my plate away. Signalling the waiter for coffee. 'It's all bollocks.'

Just then, a charge shoots through the room, a hushed murmur, a collective intake of breath, the air seeming to tighten around us, as if the available oxygen is being sucked out to feed something whose needs are far greater. It is something I have experienced before, when you walk into a place with someone who is very, very famous.

Dick and I turn our heads at the same time, just as a collective cheer goes up, and we see him – on the other side of the room, surrounded by those guys in the dark suits, with the bulging shoulders, making his way to his table, shaking the outstretched hands, smiling, patting shoulders.

The man. The. Fucking. Man.

He's wearing chinos, polo and red MAGA hat, the candy-floss straw of the hair flying out beneath it. Now, don't get me wrong. I've met everyone. I've been around enough famous people to know how to handle shit like this. But I find that even my heart is pounding like a fourteen-year-old boy who was half asleep in front of *Fantasia* when he realised Lucius's hand was inside his pants and clutching his boner like a fucking gearstick. People are beginning to clap. '*Holy shit …*' I whisper to Dick.

'*He does this*,' Dick whispers back. '*He loves it.*'

And, as in a dream, before I quite know what's happening, he's passing right by our table. We're standing at his point, clapping along with everyone else. Grinning. He's maybe five feet away from me, a Secret Service guy in the way. 'President Trump,' I shout, thrusting my hand out, raising my voice above the din. He turns to look at me – the eyes pale blue, piercing, a real, proper hit of *Führer Kontakt* – and, just for a second (or am I imagining this?) the president's fixed grin seems to falter, to flicker like a bad connection as he takes in our table: Dick and me, two men, dining alone together. No families. No boilers hanging off us, making us, at best, losers, and, at worst, queers. 'We love you in Great Britain!' I say. He claps me on the shoulder and says, 'Brexit, right? Brexit. Good job . . .' and then, in slow motion, it's happening: he takes my hand, skin-on-skin, four digits sliding across my palm, the thumb coming around the back, up over the knuckles, the bone-crushing pressure as he pumps it. And all at once I am filled with rage and hatred at the liberal media. Because it is clear, perfectly clear, as my regular hand is engulfed in this thing, this huge, thick-fingered paw.

Lies. All lies.

And then he's being urged on by the Secret Service, getting swallowed up by the crowd as he moves off across the members' dining room of Mar-a-Lago. I stare at my hand – the schoolgirl who just met the pop star. 'Fuck me,' I say to Dick as we slump back into our seats. 'Did that just happen?'

TWENTY-EIGHT

The following morning I do not join Chrissy on her commercial flight back to LAX as I have some pressing business to take care of in New York. I kiss her goodbye in the lobby and take a car to Miami International and then a NetJet – a poxy, ancient G550 which I am forced to share with one other passenger, some pro golfer, but the only private flight available – to New York, where I spend a tedious but very necessary afternoon on Wall Street, in a conference room at Stern, Hammler & Gersh, surrounded by lawyers and investment bankers, all armed with P&L reports, earnings projections and cash flow statements.

The Sultan came through. It took some doing though. A shell company had to be set up first. The shell company then transferred funds to the International Bank of Cyprus. The IBC then invested the funds in several new corporations registered in the United States. These new corporations are about to lend money to me.

Do you know much about corporate financing? About reverse buyouts? Leverage? Junk bonds? Money is cheap right now. It's not quite the crazy, golden days of the mid- to late eighties but, with the right credit line, you can buy pretty much anything. It's all a question of when to get in and when to get out. Of identifying undervalued assets.

You need to understand this stuff to a certain extent, but don't get me wrong, it's not like I *like* this shit, unlike everyone else in this room. I yawn and fold my hands behind my head as the talk of pure money flows around me – '*soft money … hard money … long bond curve … LIBOR … COMEX … beta rate …*'

Like most of my contemporaries I made my first real cash flipping property, back in the day. You'd buy an under-valued toilet in Hammersmith, or Kensal Rise, get a squadron of Poles in, lick of paint, bit of seagrass matting, turn it and burn it at great profit and on to the next one. You did this three or four times and – bosh – a million quid in the bank, which seemed like so much money back in 1999. I got out of this racket ages ago, when Trellick's then PA Lucy left her job to become a property developer. When the fucking *secretaries* are reckoning they can be players, what you have there is market saturation, my friend. See you later, Sooty.

But everything is looking good here in the conference room of SH&G. Everything is looking doable. There's a couple of i's needing to get dotted, a couple of t's for crossing. And I can't pretend that having to invest close to two hundred million of my own cash (close to all my liquid assets) isn't making me more than a little nervous, but, assuming a couple of things go my way – and they fucking will – it'll be a very merry Christmas indeed, Mortimer.

We take a break and I stand up at the window, drinking lukewarm coffee, looking west across Lower Manhattan, towards the Hudson, towards the sun, sinking behind where the World Trade Center used to be. I am thinking about the guys on the first plane, the only ones who knew what was coming, screaming their fucking heads off as the fat belly of the jet hunkered down over the rooftops of Queens, the glittering towers unspooling towards them as they gave it maximum '*ALLAHU AKBAR*' in the instant that everything around them carbonised at a billion degrees. I am thinking about how anything is possible if you are prepared to go all the way.

I check my watch. I have an early, off-the-record dinner with a journalist I know at the *Wall Street Journal* before I fly back to LA. A couple of the tips I gave this guy before Du Pre's accident – about how Du Pre's upcoming tour would be cancelled, about how the company was desperately overpaying on deals like Norwegian Dance Crew – helped to drive Unigram's stock down even further while I quietly bought large blocks of shares. I need to keep feeding him. But discreetly. This is, after all, proper insider trading now.

May

TWENTY-NINE

Quatain, Persian Gulf. Friday 19 May 2017

Late spring, gradually moving towards summer.

The temperatures in Quatain climbing into the forties.

Could he do it? Lucius wondered. If you had told him a little over twenty minutes ago when they brought the plate in that he'd soon be wondering whether or not he could finish the lot all by himself, he'd have said you were insane. But apparently you wouldn't have been. He'd eaten nine pieces of fried chicken – just one plump, juicy leg left on the salver. He picked it up and let his teeth sink into the crisp, fat-drenched skin, a spurt of grease soaking into the thin cotton of his shirt. Well, let's be honest, 'shirt' wasn't covering it any longer. What he was wearing here was closer to a bell tent. Granted, his mind was clearer than it had been for years. But it had undeniably come at a cost. It was incredible what giving up opiates after years of addiction would do to your appetite.

It had begun right after he'd started flushing his morning pills down the sink and passing on his evening injections. A strange, almost forgotten feeling, a keening, nagging tug down in the pit of his stomach that, at first, he naturally mistook for fear, anxiety, before he realised the malady had a simpler cause: hunger. Lucius was *starving*.

How he'd begun to gorge on all the things he hadn't eaten since childhood (for many years because he wasn't allowed them, always dieting to fit into one skintight stage outfit after another, and then, later, because his digestive system had been pummelled into shutdown by the side effects of things like, well, having a general anaesthetic every bedtime), torturing the Sultan's team of chefs (after all, Lucius was effectively the only resident of a six-star hotel) with half a dozen or more requests every day for things like spaghetti marinara covered in cheese, mountains of mashed potatoes silky with butter, French fries by the bucketload, six-egg omelettes stuffed with onions, bell peppers and ham, and, his current favourite, endless platters of fried chicken. Then there were the desserts, consumed at night, the calming, soporific effect of these starch-and-sugar marathons helping him towards sleep in the same way the propofol had before. Key lime pies just visible under thick whipped cream, cherry and vanilla cheesecakes washed down with quarts of milk, chocolate brownies, marble cake and pavlovas. And, in between all of this, the boxes and bars of candy: Hershey bars, Snickers, Junior Mints, anything that tasted of home. So, certainly, he'd gained some weight in the last two months. A few pounds.

Actually, about eighty of them.

Five feet six inches tall and now weighing in at just under two hundred pounds, Lucius Du Pre tossed the remains of the leg onto the plate and waddled into the bathroom, where he regarded himself in the mirror.

His face, it ... it had just vanished. His eyes were there all right, just two bright, black pebbles marooned in a puddle of flesh, his mouth a tiny 'o' somewhere below them. He washed his hands and wiped his lips, rinsing grease off them with cool water. Yes, all of this had taken its toll on his frame in the past couple of months. But the mind, the mind was *sharp*. Sharper than it had been for years. 'Hah!' Lucius barked out loud, alone in the bathroom, before adding 'OOMF!' and 'GROO!' and then a quick bark and growl session. Yes, there had been some side effects to coming off his meds as swiftly as he had (simply dumping his champagne glass full of anti-anxieties and antidepressants down the toilet every morning now), but Lucius would argue that, despite troubling lapses like the other afternoon when he had a fifteen-minute conversation about Moses with his nightstand, his mind was definitely clearer now.

And the things his mind was planning

Three weeks ago, knowing Dr Ali would be long gone at the golf course, Lucius had waddled over to his set of rooms and had a good look around, for one thing he knew his plan would require. And, boy, had he found it. Thick rolls of dirhams stuffed into the pockets of trousers and shirts, sitting out in plain view on the dresser, on top of the TV. And then, in the bedside drawer – jackpot. Stacks of American dollars in banded wads of hundreds. It had been so long since Lucius had had any need for the stuff he was surprised to see Benjamin Franklin still on there. He'd furnished himself with several thousand dollars in cash before his wanderings took him further into Ali's chambers, into his dressing room off the main bedroom. The black medicine bag hadn't really been hidden, just tucked away behind a pile of shoes. In times only very recently gone by the discovery of the goodies in this bag would have constituted a very different kind of treat for Lucius, but now, already panting hard from the effort of kneeling down among the smell of leather brogues and laundered suits, it hadn't been drugs he was looking for. He had been wondering about something else entirely. Sure enough, right down in the bottom, hidden beneath the brown tubs of barbiturates and glittering spansules of amphetamines, there it was: a passport. It had his face on it (well, the face he used to have) but the name of a Mr Fergal McCann. Fergal. What an odd name. More was to come. Tucked inside the passport, in the photo page, was a single, thin slice of plastic: a Platinum American Express. A card that also bore the name of Fergal McCann. He had returned the passport and Amex to exactly the spot he'd found them and then did the same with the medicine bag. Lucius had some work to do before he could take advantage of these finds, work he was returning to now as he set himself up in his usual spot by the windows with pen, pad and watch, his yellow-and-gold Rolex, the one with the second hand. Lucius was keen to see what kind of time his boys made today. It was usually very standard, within a minute or two every week. But there had been variations. He needed to know how often and how much. He had to be precise. He would only get one shot at this. Lucius glanced towards the mini-freezer beside his bed. He knew there was a pint of Ben & Jerry's in there. Phish Food. Those chunky little dark chocolate minnows studded though the ice cream. Mmmm. Could he really be hungry again already?

But no time for that now. For here they came, the van rumbling up the drive. 'BRRRR!' he spat, clamping his hand over his mouth to silence himself. He wrote down the time and started watching the second hand. This time next week, he'd be ready ...

THIRTY

My Bentley – still chirruping and gulping as the engine cools – looks incongruous in the parking lot in front of the Pasadena offices of Art Hinckley, attorney-at-law. It's one of those mini-malls you see off the freeway: a 7-Eleven, a nail salon, a cellphone accessories store, a laundromat, a Subway. One of those places that screams 'America'. The only other car here, parked at the far end, is a nondescript Dodge.

Also screaming 'America' are the expressions on the faces of Glen and Bridget Murphy as they stare at me: stunned, floored, flummoxed, looking for meaning in a situation suddenly beyond their comprehension. Hinckley himself, sitting behind his ridiculous faux-antique dark-wood-and-green-leather-inlay desk, is faring a little better at pulling off a game face. He's wearing tinted glasses, which help to hide the anger and confusion in his eyes, but they can't conceal the trembling rage with which he's gripping his pen. I mean, I don't blame them. Memorial Day is next week.

They rocked up here for the 7 a.m. meeting I called (me fresh from a 5.30 a.m. stint in the gym, Hinckley bleary-eyed and badly shaved, the Murphys looking as if they might well have been up all night) expecting to pretty much be asked 'where would you like us to send the cheque?' and now they're hearing all this. The three of them look like Ned Beatty, wandering around glazed and numb after he's been gang-beasted by those hillbillies in *Deliverance*.

'I'm sorry,' Hinckley says, trying to keep his cool, 'can you say that again?'

I cross my legs, shoot my cuffs, and repeat the statement I opened the meeting with, with great deliberation. 'Du Pre is alive. We faked the crash. Next week, we're bringing him back from the dead. There's going to be a new record to follow.'

'I ... you ... where is he?'

'I'm sorry, Bridget, that's on a need-to-know.'

'Need to know?' Art says.

Being the stupidest of the group, it is Glen who is roused to anger first. 'YOU LYING FUCKING PIECE OF SHIT!' he screams. 'WHERE'S OUR TWENTY MIL?'

'Be quiet, Glen,' I say softly, not taking my eyes off Artie, flicking an invisible piece of lint from my trousers. For a second I think Glen is going to go for me and part of me wants this to happen, but Bridget places a calming hand on his forearm, restraining him. I give them a moment, watching the collective wheels turn. Artie puts his pen down and sits forward. 'You're going to bring him back and say ... what?'

'He was thrown clear of the crash. He wandered in the mountains with amnesia for a few days before he was found by a fan. A crazed fan. A fan who kept him hostage in a cabin for months. You know – a Fritzl-meets-*Misery*-type deal – before Du Pre gradually regained his memory and was able to escape his basement prison and get to a phone.'

As I speak I'm aware of the bewilderment on their faces, of how utterly mental this pitch must sound, hearing it for the first time, when you haven't spent weeks working on it, honing it. Yeah, well, go tell George Lucas that 'a kid living on a dead-end planet turns out to be the son of the dark ruler of the galaxy and he uses mystical powers to defeat evil' sounds mental. I continue, staring Artie down. 'The only number Lucius could remember was his manager's – Lance Schitzbaul. He rang Lance, who, understandably certain his client was dead and fearing an impersonator and a scam, also not wanting to alert the media, decided to send private security to investigate. The fan-slash-captor was killed in the ensuing shootout and Du Pre was rescued. He's heavily traumatised. Sedated. Not speaking to the media. Blah-de-blah, bish bash bosh, my old man said be an Arsenal fan.'

Silence for a moment. And then Bridget starts laughing. 'That's ... you're fucking insane.'

'Why ... why have you done this?' Art asks finally.

'Because I figured it was doable,' I say. 'You know what I asked myself, kids? What if Elvis really wasn't dead? And imagine you were Tom Parker. Imagine you were RCA?' I warm my tone up, making them feel like equals, like co-conspirators, as I get up and pace around the small office, helping myself to some tar-like black coffee from the dripping pot, the liquid making those tiny hisses as it hits the hotplate. 'How much fucking money would you make?'

'If you got away with it …' Bridget says.

'Got away with what?' I say.

'If no one finds out, like, *the truth*?' Glen says.

That stupid fucking word again.

'So what you're here to ask,' Art says, getting to it, 'the reason you're finally telling us all this, is "will we play ball?"'

'Yep.' I'd rather they did play ball, for now. I am mindful of the fact that they have that footage stashed away somewhere. That could definitely interfere with Du Pre's glorious comeback. If they don't play ball, trust me, they really don't want to meet the consolation prize waiting for them in the parking lot.

'What's in it for us if we don't get straight on the phone to every newspaper and TV station in the country the moment you walk out that door?' Artie says.

I reach into my jacket and throw a CD onto the desk. Artie picks up the copy of *Remembrance* by Lucius Du Pre. 'Look at the back,' I say. 'Down at the bottom.' His eyes track down and find the words 'Executive Producer: Steven Stelfox'.

'That'll be the three of you. I'm offering you a credit and points on everything Du Pre does after the comeback. There'll be the new album, then another greatest hits, then who knows what? There'll be touring and merchandise and product tie-ins.' I perch on the edge of Art's desk and sip coffee. 'I'm offering you guys a piece of the pie across a 360-degree deal that will make *hundreds of millions of dollars* in the next few years.' I'm kind of free-forming at this point, but so what? 'You want, what, twenty million dollars? You know what? Given the fact that the only thing the American public has so far proved resistant to forgiving is getting caught with your actual cock up a child's arse, given the leverage you have, I'm stunned you're aiming so low. Because let me tell you something about being rich – it costs a lot of fucking money. Here ...' I throw my chequebook onto the desk. 'I'll write you a cheque right now for twenty mil. I can write you that on my fucking *current account*. So you'll get what? Six and a half mil each plus change? I'm assuming you don't want to go and live in Costa Rica? Wanna stay here in LA, right? So, Artie, I'm guessing you've already got a scheme in place to set up a little company, Black Mail Inc. or whatever, make the three of you directors –' Artie says nothing – 'declare the money "fees for professional services", pay the IRS the minimum you can get away with and keep on rocking? Right? Great –' Glen goes to say something – 'Don't interrupt me, Glen. So with some decent accounting you pay twenty-five to thirty per cent in taxes, leaving you with about four million each. You buy a nice house, move out of that shitbox of yours, right?' I slap Glen on the shoulder. He glares at me. 'There's a couple of million gone, minimum. You've got two million each. Then you start with all the flying first class, staying in nice hotel suites, shopping at Barneys, putting little Connor into a good school, all that crap. You know what? You're broke in three years. And what are you going to do then? I'm guessing you don't have another kid who a rich celebrity has chosen to use as a human spunk bucket. Trust me – a few million dollars is not rich any more, guys ...'

I sit back down and light a cigarette.

A moment while Artie looks at his clients. I smoke and watch the three of them. Trellick thought this meeting, my whole 'full and frank' strategy, was an incredibly bad idea, but I have no doubt as to the outcome.

Well, I say 'full and frank' but, of course, there's full disclosure and there's *full disclosure*. There are still certain things that, for these guys, will remain on a need-to-know basis. They do not need to know, for instance, that yesterday I bought another half a million shares of Unigram stock. They do not need to know that the shell companies SH&G set up with the Sultan's money have also been quietly buying up Unigram shares, shares they will sell to me when the timing is just right, shares that will add up to a stockholding position that, when combined with Trellick's block, will present a very compelling picture. And the reason I do not doubt the outcome of this meeting? Because I think I've divined the characters of the participants correctly. Art – the failed music lawyer. Glen – the failed agent. Bridget – the failed actress. Forget about the money, these people want what every fool out there wants. They want to be part of the most beautiful thing America ever created. the entertainment industry. They want to be on the inside, they want to see their names among the credits and in the trades. They want to get good tables in restaurants and have people whispering behind their menus, saying shit like – 'Oh, those guys over there work with Lucius Du Pre.' They want to be *players.*

'Look, we, we're going to need a moment . . .' Artie says.

I wander outside and yawn and stretch in the morning light while I check emails on my phone. It's just after

7.30 and this dismal stretch of southern California is beginning to come to life. Lights are going on up and down the main drag, in offices, in coffee shops, in a Jiffy Lube. Soon these buildings will be full of people who will work there all day long for pocket change before returning to their toilets in Pasadena, Glendale, Orange County and other places – poorer, even more terrible places – that I will never know about. It feels good to stand here watching the rush hour begin and to know you will never be part of it. That you will never eat a three-dollar burrito for lunch, gulping it down in your allotted half-hour in some dismal canteen, standing on the oil-stained cement floor of a garage, sitting at your desk trapped within the grey, open-plan honeycombs of a maze you did not design. Here they come now in their green Hyundais, their brown Camrys, their yellow Mazdas, the traffic sweeping by on the road, sending wind gusting into the lot, catching the fast-food wrappers, soda cups, bits of newspaper and cigarette ends, the garbage chasing itself around in churning circles, much like what is happening behind me where, through the glass window that says '*A. Hinckley, Attorney-at-Law, Pro Bono work considered*', I can just hear the raised voices as the three partners attempt to reach an agreement. How very out of their depth they are, how thin the ice they are standing on is, and, below the ice, waiting to tear them to pieces, the sharks. Terrible sharks with rusted hypodermics for teeth, the chambers of the syringes filled with plague, anthrax and AIDS. This thought feels familiar to me, like I had it before, a very long time ago. Across the lot, that consolation prize sits at the wheel of the Dodge, drinking a styrofoam cup of coffee and reading a newspaper, looking for all the world like a regular guy waiting for the laundromat to open up. Terry glances my way as he turns his page. Experience has taught me that it's better to have an ex-SAS mercenary on hand and not need him than it is to need him and not have him. Will he be needed this fine morning in Pasadena? While I would certainly draw no small amount of pleasure from watching Hinckley, Bridget and Glen beg for their lives before Terry pulled the trigger on his silenced Ruger and blew them all away, tarping up their bodies and later dissolving them in acid, I'm still hoping that won't be necessary. But Terry's always worth having around, I reflect as I read an email from one Tommy Groont, a private investigator based in Oslo I hired on Terry's recommendation. And a fine recommendation it has proven to be: these photos Groont has attached, taken on some Norwegian high street, have remarkable clarity given they are nearly twenty years old, taken well before everyone travelled with a digital camera in their pocket. Yes, just look at the hatred and rage on those faces. I forward the photographs on to Ruth, along with some instructions. She's handling this as a favour, given the eye-watering retainer she's getting on the Du Pre account. I click 'send' just as I hear the door opening behind me and turn to see Bridget holding it open.

I walk back in and stand in the middle of the room, very much not sitting down.

'We want paper,' Artie says.

'Iron-clad fucking contracts,' Glen adds uselessly.

I smile. 'Not a problem,' I say.

As I walk back to my car I pass that Dodge. The window is down. 'All good, boss?' Terry says, not looking at me.

'Yup,' I say. 'Time to bring Fergal home ...'

THIRTY-ONE

Late spring in Vegas. Utterly indistinguishable from pretty much any other time of the year. Danny Rent sipped his tea – poxy American tea – as he scrolled through the message boards full of chatter about his act. Chatter that had intensified since they made their decision. It had been a surprisingly short conversation with the band. As soon as he'd told them that Unigram were willing to go to 1.5 million dollars they'd looked at each other for a few astonished seconds before Thorsten – man of integrity and credibility – had smiled and said, 'Hells yes!'

It had not been a call Rent had been looking forward to making. As a manager you hated pissing off a label you knew you would want to do business with again, but it had to be done. He'd rung the band's lawyer, who'd rung XL's lawyer, who'd rung XL and told them how flattered the band were by their offer, how much they loved the roster and all that but, sorry, they were signing to Unigram. Surely, Danny knew, it would only be a matter of time before XL were on the phone to him, demanding to know what the hell had gone wrong, increasing their offer and so forth. But this call had not come.

However, someone had been talking to someone. The industry websites and message boards were already full of vitriolic gossip, like the posting Danny was now reading in his suite at the MGM Grand from a user called Musichead1975.

> *Unigram paying 1.5 million for the NDC deal? Just goes to show how over that company is. Nothing to offer but cash. When did they last break a new artist? If it hadn't been for Lucius Du Pre's death they'd have posted their worst year in history. XL would have been the smart choice for the band. Guess they got greedy ...*

It was a sentiment echoed in the other tab open on his laptop, an article on the *Music Week* website, in the business section, where, just that morning, a further drop in Unigram's share price had been announced.

> *... while Unigram's cash flow has been helped by the phenomenal sales of Lucius Du Pre's back catalogue, analysts seem to be taking the view that this is a temporary blip. The* Wall Street Journal *continues to report talks of a takeover bid brewing. The only bright light for the company in terms of new talent has been the news that they are rumoured to have won the hotly contested battle to sign EDM act Norwegian Dance Crew ...*

Fuck sake. Were they making a mistake here? Should he just get Richard Russell on the blower and deny everything?

Danny looked down at the fuming streets of Vegas, criss-crossing away from him into the shimmering heat haze of the desert. Nah, calm down. It'd be all right. Stelfox was dark, fucking dark. But they'd had the offer. They'd bank the cash. They'd be all right. Unigram wasn't going anywhere, was it? It was a fucking institution. Focus on the important stuff. 1.5 million. Like Bo Diddley used to say – take that dollar and fuck the rest.

An email arrived. From Ruth Blane. The PR woman. Danny knew her a bit, from conventions, gigs. The header read 'Have you seen this?' Danny hesitated, fearing spam, before curiosity overcame him and he clicked on it. There was a link and, above it, the words 'Holy shit – someone forwarded this to me. Thought you should know ...' He clicked on the link and went from puzzled, to astonished, to enraged as his gaze tripped down the few lines of text. His anger mushroomed into genuine fury tinged with terror when he looked at the photograph. What the fuck? No ... no, this couldn't be true. But it did look like him. Oh Jesus. Jesus Christ. Who'd seen this? *Oh fuck ...*

THIRTY-TWO

Trellick and I are in his office, discussing which triggers we pull and in which order. Timing is crucial. Everything impacts on everything else. 'How low can the share price go?' I say, repeating his question aloud.

'I think there's a dollar, dollar-fifty still to go,' Trellick says.

'Bollocks. Needs to go lower than that for this to work.' I'm watching CNN with the sound down over Trellick's shoulder.

'More like a two-dollar fall?'

'Three,' I say decisively.

'Three? Fucking hell, Steven. What's going to cause that?'

I look at him. He raises a hand. 'Actually, I don't want to know. It'll take a fucking miracle though. How on earth you think ...'

Trellick drones on, but I've drifted off, my eyes wandering to the TV set in the corner, CNN flickering soundlessly, still constantly showing images from yesterday's bombing in Manchester, the cordoned-off arena, the cops, rerun footage of people fleeing. Trump's Twitter avatar comes up on the screen and I thumb the volume up. It seems the Donald has weighed in on Twitter, calling the terrorist 'losers'.

'How presidential,' Trellick sighs.

There was more of this, earlier today. Trump visited the Holocaust memorial at Yad Vashem and wrote in the guest book: 'So amazing! Will never forget!' There has been much chatter today, in the press, on social media, about how poorly this compares with Obama's long, eloquent note in the same book a few years earlier. About how stunned people are that the seventy-year-old president of the USA often sounds like a teenage mean girl. So fucking what? Like the Trellick of a few weeks ago, these people are all still mired in the old world. They're walking around in flares. They're strolling around St Petersburg in November 1919 saying, 'Hey, we can keep *some* of our stuff, can't we?' 'No, mate. That's over. Not only will you not be keeping anything, you see that wall over there? Well, in a minute, we're going to take you, and your wife, and your kids, and we're going to line you up against it and fucking shoot you.' And while everyone's going bananas about all this crap, about fucking tweets, the real shit is quietly happening behind the scenes. This morning the White House released Trump's first budget proposal – billions for the wall, for the military and, most importantly, for massive tax cuts. I am fucking *drooling* at the possibility of this. Obviously, to pay for all of it, there are going to be billions of dollars of cuts to shit like Medicaid, food stamps, meals on wheels, whatever. What a total fucking result. This is the new reality: we do what we fucking want and there will be no accountability. I mean, eloquence, articulation, being 'presidential' … the Donald doesn't give a gypsy fuck about that shit. What does he care about?

Loyalty. Trust. The rarest, most precious of resources.

I look sideways at Trellick, watching the TV. We are now deep into some very dark shit. Do I have his loyalty? Can I trust him? I *think* so.

My phone starts ringing – 'RENT'.

I hold the screen up to show Trellick. 'That'll be the miracle you ordered,' I say. I hold a finger to my lips as I slide the bar over to take the call, sticking it on speaker and putting on my most sombre, serious voice. 'Danny,' I say.

'Steve, I got a bit of a problem here …'

'I know. I'm looking at it now.' My tone is glacial as I bring the photo up on my laptop and turn it around for Trellick to see.

'Eh? Fucking … how?'

'Ruth, she's a mate. She knew we were in on the NDC deal and thought I ought to know.'

'Fuck. It's … I …' I can hear him, literally scraping the stubbly skin off his head in lieu of hair.

'It's a fucking nightmare is what it is, Danny.'

'I get that, mate.' *Mate*, no less. I pump an imaginary cock in Trellick's direction. 'But, look,' Rent goes on, 'we've got a deal, right?'

'Danny, if this gets out, have you any idea what's going to happen?'

'It ain't getting out. I'm on it. I'm gonna find out who's sent it to Ruth, what they're fucking after, pay them off, whatever. It ain't a fucking problem …'

I look at the photograph on the screen, the photo that the investigator in Oslo sent to me, that I sent to Ruth and that Ruth then sent to Danny.

It shows Thorsten Lunt of Norwegian Dance Crew, back in the nineties, when he was in his late teens. In the photograph he is not the smiling, beatific, pot-smoking champion of universal love and house music we met backstage in Las Vegas. Oh no. In this photograph the young Thorsten's blond hair is much shorter and severely cut, his blue eyes are blazing, his features are composed into a vicious snarl and his right arm is thrust ramrod straight into the air, the palm flattened, the fingertips straining for the sky. He is wearing a leather jacket and a white T-shirt, the T-shirt emblazoned with the cool, levelling gaze of Adolf Hitler, the whole ensemble topped off with a swastika armband. There's no way around it . . .

The cunt was a fucking Nazi.

Obviously this turn of events has awakened in me a deep and new-found respect for Thorsten Lunt, but that's neither here nor there. '*It ain't a problem*?' I repeat to Danny. 'Danny, Unigram is a publicly traded company. When Trellick finds out about this,' Trellick is now nodding, holding a thumb up to me, 'he'll have to tell the chairman, the board. There's no way –'

'Steven, *I'm going to fucking kill this thing*!' Danny says.

'Well, good luck with that, mate. Get back to me, yeah?'

I hang up.

'Fuck me,' Trellick says.

'By the time this photo does the rounds,' I say, 'the share price will be in the crapper. We're the label who signs Nazis. By next week Rent's going to be in here begging us to sign those Scandinavian pederasts for a dole cheque and a crate of fucking Red Bull.'

'My hat,' Trellick says, 'is off. Just out of interest though, how does the lovely Chrissy feel about the, um, strategy you're currently employing in pursuit of her deal?'

'Ah, I didn't think she needed to be troubled by the finer points. I'm just trying to help.'

'So considerate ...'

'Right, so day after tomorrow we send the jet for Ali and Lucius.'

'What are you going to do about finding your Fritzl-meets-Annie Wilkes?'

'Terry's on it,' I say. This being all that needs to be said. 'Come on.' I pick my jacket up off the back of the chair. 'Let's go get lunch. I'm fucking starving.'

'Jesus,' Trellick says. 'I don't think I could eat a thing. Fucking knot in my stomach. None of this bothers you?'

'None of what bothers me?' I say, looking for my car keys, distracted.

'Oh, I dunno, manipulating share prices? A little insider trading? Blackmail? Perpetuating the biggest hoax in the history of popular music? Take your pick.'

'Yeah, hell of a day at sea, huh?' I say.

THIRTY-THREE

'Look, guys,' Chrissy said, her voice low in a corner of the Chateau garden, near the tiny smoking area (the one that frequently contained the only four smokers in LA), 'I still love the music, and, Thorsten, I know it was a long time ago. We all do stupid stuff when we're young. But that's the way the company feels right now. Politically, it's just too difficult ...'

'Fucking hell, love,' Rent said, 'tomorrow's fish and chip wrappers and all that.' He laughed, reached for his drink, trying for levity.

'It was twenty fucking years ago!' Thorsten offered, again. 'I was just a fucking kid.' Unusually he was drinking, throwing another Patron back. The other two members of Norwegian Dance Crew grunted at him in Norwegian.

Yeah, Chrissy thought. A fucking *Nazi* kid. 'I think you're both right,' she said. 'And if this was a hundred grand we'd be signing the contracts tonight. But, a mil and a half? It's a big news story, the board and all that. The shareholders

... I'm sorry.' She kept her tone cool as she got up and signalled for the check, having drunk precisely half her glass of sparkling water. (All of this per the Stelfox handbook for this meeting: be firm, neutral, don't drink, leave early.)

'Hey,' Rent said, 'leave it. We'll get the check. We got plenty of other deals on the table, Chrissy.'

'We go with fucking XL then. *Like we wanted to*,' one of them — Sven the Viking — sneered at her.

Chrissy just smiled, snapping her bag shut. (Celine, red leather. A gift from Steven.) 'They're a great label,' she said. 'Good luck. Bye, guys.' She headed off, her heels ticking on the flagstones.

A few seconds later Rent caught up with her in the lobby, literally grabbing her by the elbow. 'Chris, Chrissy, wait up.' She turned.

'Danny.'

'This is final then?'

'I'm afraid so.'

'Where's Steven in all this?'

'Nowhere. It's my deal, Danny.'

He held her gaze. 'Right. Give him my best, eh?'

'Sure.' Chrissy turned and headed down the stairs. She'd catch up with Steven later, after her doctor's appointment.

Rent walked slowly back towards the band's table, where he could already hear some debate breaking out between the three members. Voices being raised in their native language. *Just go back to XL?* You stupid Scandi cunts. Like that wasn't the first fucking thing he'd thought of. If he heard the words *'Richard knows you called. He'll get back to you'* one more time ...

Now Danny would have to begin the tedious process of ringing around all the long-rejected labels, the second-tier contenders, cap in hand. Forelock tugged. Bollocks. He was trying to remember exactly who he hadn't been cool with to the point of no return when he was snapped out of his reverie by shouting in Norwegian as he approached their table. A few heads turning to look. Thorsten and Erik, jabbing fingers at each other now as the band's argument climaxed, Thorsten shouting something at Erik, throwing a huge shot of tequila back, and then he was getting unsteadily to his feet, smashing his heels together, extending his arm, pointing those rigid fingers skywards and shouting 'HEIL HITLER!'

Oh fucking hell.

THIRTY-FOUR

At the exact moment Steven Stelfox had been parking his Bentley GT in a Pasadena mini-mall, a little over eight thousand miles to the east, it was 6 p.m. and movement of another kind was afoot: Lucius Du Pre was hiding in some bushes, sweating like, well, like Lucius Du Pre hiding in some bushes, as he heard the trundle of tyres on gravel and took a deep breath. He'd timed it well. Ali, his doctor turned chemical jailer, was finishing up on the back nine of the Sultan's golf course. The Sultan and his loathsome son were away for the night, at a horse race somewhere. Around 5 p.m. Lucius had ordered a vast amount of food to be brought to his suite (well, it would once have been vast. Nowadays the marathon of fried chicken, potato salad, slaw, fries, beans, corn, gravy and biscuits followed by a tub of ice cream or a box of Dove bars simply constituted his nightly dinner) and left word that he was not to be disturbed. He put a DVD of *Fantasia* – his favourite – on repeat and checked the essential kit he'd packed.

1,100 dirhams in cash.

3,642 US dollars in cash.

1 × false passport in the name of Fergal McCann.

1 × Platinum Amex in the name of Fergal McCann.

1 × lip balm.

1 × blister pack Valium.

He'd caught his reflection in the mirror as he slipped out of his room and had briefly had time to reflect that, yes, he did look totally crazy: a 200lb half-black man wearing wraparound Gucci shades and a billowing kaftan with a fanny pack lashed around his waist.

He crouched down further now among the sweet-smelling eucalyptus leaves and watched as the laundry guys got out of the van and made their first run, down to Ali's suite. (And Ali's laundry needs were voluminous, going through two golf outfits a day most days.) Here they came now (two minutes twenty-two seconds later, slightly faster than usual), jabbering to each other in Arabic as they swung the heavy hamper into the truck, climbed up and pushed it along. They jumped down and strolled back into the palace. This trip, to Lucius's quarters, would take them a minimum of three minutes and fifty seconds.

Lucius sprang into action.

Yes, 'sprang' was a stretch here. 'Sprang' was pushing it. Lucius, a man once described as 'the most athletic performer since Michael Jackson', scuttled out of the bushes looking like a giant constipated crab. He threw himself up onto the tailgate of the laundry van and, groaning, lashing more sweat with the effort, his forearms straining and aching, finally managed to pull himself up onto the wooden floor of the van.

He lay on his back for a second, panting, before getting onto his knees and crawling towards the huge wicker hamper, lifting the lid, smelling something troublingly fragrant, and was about to congratulate himself on the whole thing having taken less than a minute when he patted his waist and stomach and dropped to his knees. The fanny pack! Gone. He ran back to the tailgate – there it was. Lying on the gravel, torn off by the effort of pulling himself into the van. *Oh Lord, help me.* He jumped back down and grabbed it, the mad crab glancing around frantically, no one to be seen in the gathering Arabian dusk, but voices audible from somewhere down the service hallway behind him, the laundry guys, coming back. Lucius felt a rush of adrenaline – like he used to feel when he ran onto the stage of a stadium, like he used to feel when Ali pushed the plunger on a sweet shot of candy – as he *leapt* back up into the van a second time, ran the length of it, lifted the lid again and threw himself inside, pulling damp, soiled clothes over him. He tried to still his pumping heart, slow his breathing as he heard the men at the tailgate, climbing up and coming towards him. He heard their guttural chatter, heard the second laundry hamper (the one he'd been sure to overfill, to make as heavy as possible) thumping down beside his, their footsteps banging on the wooden boards, their feet crunching on the gravel as they hopped back down and then their voices receding once more as they made their final run into the house, for the kitchen whites.

Another couple of minutes passed, Lucius chewing on a calming Valium there in the dark, his nostrils full of the sweet, fungal smell of damp polo shirts, chinos, socks and underpants. Then the sound of doors being slammed, the vibration as an engine kicked into life beneath him, and the crunch of tyres as they moved off down the gravel. Once the van was moving at speed Lucius climbed carefully out of the hamper. He had to do it right away because he had no idea how long they would be driving. Crouching unsteadily in the darkness of the swaying vehicle, he began to transfer much of the contents of his heavy hamper, the boots and leather jackets and the rest of his wardrobe he'd packed in there, to Ali's far lighter one. Then he got into his own, just covering himself with a few towels and sheets, equalising the weight between the two, and closing the lid.

You see, he'd thought of everything.

They had been driving for about forty-five minutes, he reckoned from the glowing green hands of his Rolex in the darkness. Lucius entertained himself by giving free play to the voices in his head. With many a 'GRR!' and an 'OOMF!' and an 'ANNG!' he conversed with Jesus. Jesus was trying to tell him something, something he had to do. Lucius had even made up a little song to help him. '*I love Jesu, he loves me. Me and Jesu are so happy!*' He sang the comforting refrain over and over as Jesus told him things.

And then they were turning, slowing down, the tug of brakes as they came to a stop and then the clank and clang of doors opening, voices.

They lifted his basket, one of them at each end, and he felt himself rise into the air a few inches, and then a thump as he was dropped back down. He heard a few puzzled words being exchanged in Arabic and, for a second, he feared the worst – the lid opening, the towels and sheets being thrown back, the astonished faces. But no. Grunting as he was lifted back up and half carried, half dragged to the tailgate. A heavier thump as he was dropped onto concrete, sending a smashing jolt through his back, almost causing him to cry out in pain. Then lifting again, being carried further and then dropped again. There was light now, seeping through the thick wicker, and the sound of activity, shouting, machinery, men. He could smell chemicals, disinfectant. He heard the men exchanging a few words with a woman and then the footsteps were fading away and it was quiet. He waited. And waited. The noise of machinery was constant, but far in the distance. This would be the most difficult part, but he had to do it. Taking a deep breath, Lucius pushed the lid of the hamper up just an inch and peered out. He was in a long concrete corridor, lit by fluorescent tubes overhead, surrounded by dozens of other laundry baskets. At the end of the corridor, in a brightly lit area, he could see people in overalls and facemasks working, upending wicker baskets and sorting through the contents in front of huge industrial washers.

Behind him, much closer, was a loading dock and, beyond it, a yard. Beyond that, open streets. Freedom. Lucius climbed out of his basket, checked his fanny pack was secure, and turned towards the loading dock. From nowhere a young boy came around a corner and almost walked straight into him.

The boy and Lucius regarded each other. He was about sixteen, Lucius guessed, carrying two tubs of some kind of detergent. They both stood there for a moment, frozen. The boy took a step back, clearly on the verge of raising the alarm. 'No! No!' Lucius said, pressing a finger to his lips as the boy's mouth started to open. Lucius fumbled, hurriedly scrabbling at the zipper of his fanny pack, and took out a strange banknote. He held it towards the boy.

The boy looked at it – ten dirhams.

Lucius smiled – hopefully, encouragingly – as he proffered the three-dollar bribe.

It was fair to say Lucius and cash transactions had not been on intimate terms since the late 1970s. He remembered a recording session a few years back, one of his last. The engineer, the producer and the musicians had wanted things, small things, cigarettes, beer, some sandwiches, and a tape op was being dispatched to fetch them. Unusually Lucius had had some cash on him that day and in a show of *noblesse oblige* he'd offered to pay for everything, graciously handing the tape-op a ten-dollar bill, telling him to keep the change. Later, after Lucius had expressed puzzlement as to why his largesse had received such a lukewarm reception, Lance had explained to him that in 2012 ten dollars wasn't really leaving much change after beer and snacks for eight people. Somehow this memory came back to Lucius now, in the breeze-block corridor of a Middle Eastern industrial laundry, as the boy stared nonplussed at the banknote. Lucius took a huge wad of dirhams out – pinks and browns and blues – and thrust them towards the kid. The boy paused for a second, then inclined his head in a bowing motion as he took the notes and said, '*Allah yusallmak.*'

'Praise Jesus,' Lucius whispered, bowing back, adding for good measure, 'PURRR! GRRALL!'

Ninety seconds later Lucius Du Pre stood at the intersection of a busy city street, experiencing something he hadn't experienced in almost forty years.

Being alone, out in the world.

He was near some kind of market, or bazaar. The air was thick with the smell of spices and grilling meats, and Lucius realised he was ravenous, having sacrificed dinner as part of his grand plan. He briefly considered grabbing an armful of kebabs to sustain him on the next leg of the journey but remembered that he was technically on the run. No time for a picnic. He was also trying to come to terms with another strange sensation – no flashbulbs popping. No shouting, screaming mobs. He was getting the odd strange look from people but he soon realised they were probably the kind of looks given to a 200lb man in a kaftan with a fanny pack strapped around his waist, rather than an inter-national megastar who'd sold hundreds of millions of records. While all of this was certainly hurtful to the ego it – and the encroaching darkness – definitely helped him waddle unmolested for the few hundred yards taking him to his next goal: the long line of taxi lights he could see at the far end of the square.

'The airport. NGGG!' Lucius said, squeezing his bulk into the back seat of the tiny, foul-smelling car. The driver barked something in Arabic. Lucius repeated the word, doing the mime – arms extended, making the whooshing sound of jet engines, saliva bubbling on his lips, holding up another fistful of local currency.

The guy nodded and turned the key in the ignition.

THIRTY-FIVE

This is the one, Terry thought. He'd been all over the area for the last week, driving along single-lane tracks, taking turnings off to ranch houses and cabins, knocking on doors. He always used the same story – his GPS wasn't working up here, could they give him directions? He'd met a fair few cranks, eccentrics. The kind of people who tended to live off the grid way up in the Pinto Mountains. But this one, Mr William Tandy, he was ideal. For the last three days, Terry had observed his habits, from a distance, through powerful German binoculars. He was in his sixties and lived alone. His place was three miles from the crash site, set on around five acres, his nearest neighbour over a mile away. In the early evening, before it got too cold, Tandy would sit out drinking on the porch of his cabin. Terry had done a records search and discovered that the man had no living relatives, another huge bonus when it came to dealing with blowback. (No tearful relatives bothering the police endlessly.) He'd done other homework too – it sat in stacks of files on the back seat. He poured himself some more coffee from his flask and watched the cabin and waited for night to start falling. He was good at waiting and planning. You had to be. They were 80 per cent of the job. Finally, the moon started to rise and Tandy, Terry saw before he lowered the binoculars, finished his beer and went inside.

Terry turned the key and drove the mile or so down the track before pulling into Tandy's drive. He parked in a copse of pine trees, not visible from the road, got his kitbag out and strolled up the path. Three sharp raps on the wooden door. A muffled voice from within, footsteps, and then pale yellow light spilling over Terry as the door opened. 'Can I help you?' Tandy said.

'I'm so sorry to disturb you –' Terry's clipped English accent an instant point of entry – 'but I just hit a deer and it's rather messed up my car. Do you think I could use your phone?'

'Damn,' Tandy said. 'You gotta watch out for 'em. Big buck through the windshield and that'll be all she wrote, young fella.'

'Was a bit of a shock actually.'

'Well, come in. Come on in.' Tandy led him inside and Terry brought his fist up with the syringe in it and plunged it into the back of Tandy's neck. The old man turned, an expression of outrage and surprise on his face, his hand already going to his neck. Before he could utter whatever expletive was forming on his lips the powerful tranquilliser kicked in. Terry caught Tandy before he hit the floor. Didn't want the old boy hurting himself just yet. Terry carried him across the room and laid him on the sofa. He took the place in – dusty and crammed with bric-a-brac. Lots of books and photographs, the accumulation of a lifetime. A big stone fireplace, not yet lit.

Along the hall, open the door, and down into the basement. Terry knew from the schematics he'd examined as part of his research that there was a basement, that had been another essential requirement. It was chilly down here, but there was a little pot-bellied stove in the corner. Ideal. Terry dragged a mattress down from the spare bedroom and then went back upstairs for its owner, carrying the unconscious Tandy down over his shoulder and laying him gently on the mattress. Using webbing, Terry tightly bound him to the mattress and gagged him with a piece of towelling and some duct tape. It took three trips to the car to get all his files. Then Terry really got to work.

William Tandy woke up a few hours later – the middle of the night – and struggled to orientate himself, his vision swimming. He seemed to be in the basement. It was cold. He couldn't move. Was he dreaming? He seemed to remember opening the door to a man. A British man. Cultured-sounding. His vision cleared and he looked up to see the man. He was in the process of sticking something onto the wall. Tandy looked around – Jesus Christ. Nearly every available inch of his basement walls had been covered in stuff: posters, newspaper cuttings and the like. They were almost all of a singer, someone he recognised. That fella who had died some months back, in a helicopter crash, not far from here. They'd closed some of the roads. But not all the pictures were of him. That was, what was … ? Tandy looked at another picture on the wall: two men, engaged in an act of sodomy. Another poster of a nude man. And another. Now there, on top of that old dresser: five or six big dildos. What the hell? Tandy made a grunt of outrage. The man turned around from his work.

'Oh. Look who's up!' He came over and dropped onto his haunches, quite close. 'Listen, I'm very sorry for the inconvenience. Should all be over in a few days, OK?'

Tandy grunted against the gag, enraged now, trying to speak. 'MMMF! UNNGGHH!'

'That's a good fellow. Excuse me. Must get back to it ...'

THIRTY-SIX

An hour or so of darkness on the highway – the radio blaring mad raga fizz, the driver making no attempt at conversation – and then, up ahead, a pyramid of light was materialising out of the desert night. They pulled up at the kerb and Lucius simply started handing the man banknotes until he held his hands up saying 'Enough!'

He stood underneath the glowing sign for 'INTER-NATIONAL DEPARTURES'. There had been no air conditioning in the car and sweat was pouring in rivulets down his arms, coursing across his face, his great belly. Wandering a market square filled with locals in the dark had been one thing, stepping in here was going to be quite another. When had Lucius Du Pre (and it is worth noting that the third person was the default setting of even Lucius's inner monologue) last set foot alone in such a place? Through the thick, lightly smoked glass he could see great crowds of people going back and forth, saying hellos and goodbyes, grappling with baggage, staring at the boards.

He looked at his watch: 8.45 p.m. He had been gone less than three hours. They wouldn't even have noticed yet. He could get in a cab and ... how? How to get back into the grounds? No. To go back was ... something about being more difficult than to go on. And go back to what? Then he remembered the TV reports – his fans, crying. They needed him. He checked his sunglasses were in place and took a deep breath ...

Lucius stepped gingerly into the terminal, like a gazelle or an ocelot escaped from the city zoo might pad into a busy branch of McDonald's, almost certain of the astonished looks that would greet him. It was overwhelming – the noise, the lights, the bustle and mayhem. He began tiptoeing across the marble floor, terrified, his eyes darting back and forth behind the thick, polarised lenses.

'Sir? Sir?'

Lucius stopped and turned around – a man in uniform was looking at him. This was it. 'Sir?' the man repeated. Lucius now saw he was gesturing to the empty trolley he was holding. 'Bags?' the man said. Not police – porter.

Lucius shook his head, muttered 'Help me, Jesu, POWEE!' and hurried off, deeper into the throng, his head craning this way and that, something gradually dawning on him – he had no idea what to do. Lucius had never bought a plane ticket in his life. His interactions with reality had been mediated since he was a nine-year-old.

All the signage was unfamiliar, much of it in Arabic. The noise around him was increasing, reaching a crescendo in his head. He clutched his fanny pack tighter, wondering if he could just crunch a couple of Valium, wondering if ... and then he saw it. Two letters, one red and one blue, the twinned mountain peaks (poor Jay, poor Marcus) of the two 'A's: AMERICAN AIRLINES. Lucius felt an instant connection to the motherland. He had even done a commercial for American, many years ago, in the late seventies, with OJ Simpson and one of the Burts, Lancaster, or Reynolds. He waddled towards the desk, where there was no line. An employee girl in uniform and full hijab sat, her fingers whirring on her terminal keyboard. '*Ahlan*,' she said, turning to face him, her eyes faltering just a fraction as she took in Lucius's sweating bulk.

What did one say? Lucius wondered, automatically looking around for PA, for tour manager, for bodyguard. 'I ... I need ...' he began.

'Can I help you?' the girl said, her face Arabic but her accent American.

'A-A ...' Lucius stammered. 'America.'

'America?'

'I go to America.'

'Do you have a ticket? A booking reference?'

He shook his head fiercely, droplets of sweat flying. The urge to start singing 'I LOVE JESU!' in this woman's face was very strong, but he sensed conventional behaviour was required here. He took a deep breath and just grinned insanely at her.

'So you want to buy a ticket?'

Nodding now, his bulldog jowls flapping.

'But to where?'

'America.'

'But –' she pointed to the huge board hanging from the ceiling behind him – 'Washington, Philadelphia, Detroit, New York ...'

'New York!' Lucius exclaimed. The city of his comeback!

'New York City . . .' the girl said, her fingers already flying across the keyboard. 'Okaaayyy, there's room on the 22.30. Gets into Kennedy 17.15 tomorrow evening. Coach OK?' Lucius looked at her. 'Is coach OK?' she repeated.

'Airplane, fnargh,' Lucius said firmly. What the fuck was this with a coach? No, wait, he'd heard of this, many years ago. The early days, the first tours with his brothers, it was a thing. Where all the people sat. What was the other thing called? The girl was starting to look at him like he was truly crazy now. It came back to him. 'First,' Lucius said, pleased with himself, like he'd been picked out by teacher and asked a difficult question. 'First *class*,' he embellished proudly.

'First?' the girl said doubtfully, taking him in, her fingers dancing on the keyboard once again. 'You're in luck. There's one seat left in first on that flight. And coming back?' Again he just looked at her. 'Sir . . . are . . . are you . . . ?' She leaned forward, lowering her voice. Here it came. The autograph book. The phone for the selfie. The declaration of undying love. 'Are you OK?'

What to say? What was normal? 'Tired.'

She nodded. 'When are you returning?'

Lucius shook his head.

She sighed. This was already a long night. 'One way?'

'Way?' Lucius said.

'You're not coming back?'

'No. Never back.'

'OK . . . one way. First class. With taxes that comes to . . . fourteen thousand and fifty-seven dollars.'

She looked at him, part of her expecting this to be the end of the conversation, for the madman to just shuffle off back to the streets. But no, he surprised her by reaching into his fanny pack and, with a snick, laying a credit card down on the counter. She picked it up and looked at it, surprised to see a Platinum American Express and not a supermarket loyalty card, a library card. 'Praise Jesu!' Lucius said.

'And your passport, Mr ... McCann?' Lucius handed it over. She looked at the photo. Then at Mr Fergal McCann. Then back and forth again. And again. 'Are you, do you know ... you *really* look like Lucius Du Pre? Here, I mean, in this photograph.' She left the 'not now' unsaid.

'I ...' Lucius said. 'When I was younger.'

Yes, you could really just see it – the face of the man in the photograph, just visible in the fleshy puddle staring numbly at her now. It was an old passport, issued seven years ago. Jesus, this guy must have been hitting the buffet hard. Fuck it, she started issuing the ticket. 'Luggage?' she asked.

Would this horror ever end? Lucius was thinking, having no idea of the true horror that he was about to endure as he experienced another first – going through general security.

Later, reclining on his flatbed throne, a frosted tumbler of vodka in his paw and two Valium dissolving under his tongue, soothing Motown coming through his headphones while the stewardess went through the safety routine (the humorous indulgence reserved for first-class passengers, an air that says '*of course all this doesn't really apply to you guys, it's for the fools in the back, but let's go through the panto-mime*'), Lucius began to calm down.

He shifted in his seat, still stinging, still uncomfortable, still the wet, greasy tang down there ...

First there had been a long grilling with a man in a glass booth, who seemed to find it difficult to believe that he was taking a fourteen-hour one-way trip to America with nothing more than the clothes on his back, a credit card and a few thousand dollars. But the American passport, it seemed, was still a powerful tool, something that could cow and intimidate. Finally, grudgingly, granted permission to continue, Lucius had imperiously snatched back his documents and strode through some kind of passageway, ignoring the clearly insane maniac who was shouting stuff at him about liquids and laptops and shoes and belts. Whereupon all hell had broken loose – alarms going off and hands upon him.

The episode had concluded in a brightly it windowless room with the snap of a rubber glove somewhere behind him as he looked up into the unsmiling face of the security man he'd shoved back ...

Now, Lucius had inserted his finger into many anuses. With KY, with saliva and even dry, he'd forced many a recalcitrant flower to blossom for him, had engineered his way into countless puckering anemones. He'd had it done to him too, by his father of course – the reek of whiskey in the Comfort Inn, the trucks smashing by on the interstate on the other side of the drywall – or by brisk proctologists over the years. But this had been something of a different order. The brief icy dab of jelly and then – boof – the sensation of filling up, of needing urgently to defecate.

Oh well, he thought, it was over now. He was returning home. To his people. How they needed him. He looked at the small TV screen on the robotic metal arm in front of him, which was showing some kind US news programme. A man Lucius did not recognise – he had an orange face and a crazy wedge of candyfloss hair, presumably an actor playing a bad guy – was talking soundlessly on the screen. At the bottom of the screen the text said, '*President Trump says he decided to dismiss James Comey prior to recommendation from the Attorney General's office ...*' Oh, wait, was this *Donald Trump*? The real estate guy? Lucius had met him, back in the nineties, maybe backstage at Madison Square Garden? With his kids. The boys had been nice, but already too old for Lucius. What was he president of? Did they have real estate guys on the news now? Ah, real estate. His beloved Narnia. He would see it again soon.

But first he had business to take care of, in New York. He was going to get this show back on the road. He drained his glass as he felt himself being pushed back in his seat, his legs rising into the air. Ahead of him the great nose cone came up and the black ribbon of the runway unspooled fast below them as the jet reared into the night, banking, the lights of the airport quickly reducing to pinpricks in the desert as they climbed and turned, seeking America.

'*I love Jesu, he loves me. Me and Jesu are so happy ...*' Softly, over and over. In this fashion Lucius sang himself to sleep.

THIRTY-SEVEN

'And he sounds panicked, like real scared, so I don't know what to do. I know if I call the police it'll be all over the media, and who knows if it's even real? Right? What if it's all a hoax? Just some schmuck?' Lance stops for a drink of water (he's at least making a show of sobriety) and runs a trembling hand through his thinning silver hair before continuing. 'I mean, a lot of people can do a pretty accurate impression of Lucius. Just watch the talk shows, right? So I decided to send one of our people up there to –'

'Very good, Lance,' Ruth says. 'Though you might want a little more hesitation. Show confusion.'

'It was good when you ran your hand through your hair like that,' I offer.

'Yep, nice touch,' Ruth agrees. 'OK, now you, Fred. Go ...'

'Right, so, I drive up there and I get out the car and start walking toward the house. Before I know it Lucius bursts out of the porch and starts running toward me. He's screaming, terrified. Then Tandy, he comes out waving a –'

'How do you know he's called Tandy?' Ruth says.

'Right. Shit. This guy I later learn is Tandy comes out waving a rifle. So I pull my gun and tell him – "Drop it, mister." Next thing that happens is he ... I mean I ... ah fuck. Sorry.'

Media training. Ruth and I are in her office, taking Schitzbaul and his bodyguard Fred through their paces. They are both going to be interviewed hundreds of times in the coming days and they need to be on point. I'm not too worried about Schitzbaul – he's been managing major artistes for forty years, lying comes as easily to him as breathing. He's the kind of guy who, as they say, will lie to you even when it's in his best interests to tell the truth. But Fred, Fred needs some coaching. He's extremely loyal to Schitzbaul, having worked for him for fifteen years, and loyalty, that golden virtue, is the reason he's been chosen. But he's not a natural actor. 'Fred,' Ruth says gently, but with an edge, clearly feeling the pressure, 'keep it simple. You just need to learn the essentials of the script. Let's try again. From the top ...'

We'll be bringing Du Pre back soon. Right now Terry is preparing the final details, up there in the Pinto Mountains. The next few days will not be pleasant for Mr William Tandy as he is kept captive in his own home while Terry transforms his basement into what the tabloids will call a 'shrine' to Lucius Du Pre, with a goodly smattering of hardcore gay and child pornography thrown into the mix. Nor will things improve much for old Bill when Terry takes him out onto the porch and shoots him in the chest with the SIG Sauer P320 belonging to Fred before placing Tandy's own hunting rifle in his cold, dead hands.

So far so good. But we then need Fred – playing Du Pre Personal Security Guard Sent to Check Out Surely Bogus Claim that Du Pre is Alive – and Schitzbaul – playing Near Hysterical Manager – to do their bit. And it is clear Fred is struggling with the enormity of the bullshit that is being asked of him. This rankles a bit as he's being paid one million American dollars for his part in this.

'I ... I saw he was armed, he meant harm, and I ... I ...'

'Fred,' I say, getting up, 'what do you know about lying? In its purest form.'

'Well, I –'

'Get this – you are not lying. If you *think* you are lying then we are fucked. You need to imagine this scene all the time. Imagine yourself getting out the car, seeing Lucius running towards you, terrified, then this maniac wielding a fucking great blunderbuss is coming at you. You're pulling your gun. You're in the mountains. Your hands are cold and you can see your breath steaming. After you shoot him his blood will steam in the air too. This happened to you as surely as you had breakfast this morning. But most important of all ...' I sit down on the conference table, very close to him now, 'the whole time you must be thinking this: *the person I am talking to has no way of proving me wrong.*' Fred nods, seeming to get this. 'Here,' I say, picking up the remote, 'watch this ...' I hit play on the compilation of clips I've put together. The four of us watch some of the greats: Stalin talking about how well collectivisation is working while millions of his own people starve, Goebbels talking about how the Jews are having a right old laugh in the Third Reich, Clinton saying '*I did not have sexual relations with that woman*', Alan Clark telling Parliament with a straight face that we sold Iraq 'machine tools', Lance Armstrong, looking Larry King right in the eye and giving it '*I've said it for longer than seven years. I have never doped*', literally off his nugget as he says it, his one mad ball dangling somewhere beneath the desk, Berlusconi smiling, saying 'I've never threatened anyone', Jonathan Aitken, incensed at the accusations he met with arms dealers, hitting back with righteous fire as he delivers '*If it falls to me to cut out the cancer of bent and twisted journalism in our country with the simple sword of truth and the trusty shield of British fair play, so be it. I am ready for the fight*', all the while knowing he's been meeting with arms dealers like it's going out of fucking fashion. And, interspersed between every other clip, the Man. The King. He's saying stuff like '*I didn't want to go into Iraq*', saying '*between three and five million illegal votes caused me to lose the popular vote*', saying '*professional anarchists, thugs and paid protesters are proving the point of the millions of people who voted to MAKE AMERICA GREAT AGAIN*', and saying, over and over again, uncountable times, '*there was no collusion …*'

I'm watching Fred, bathed in the light of the screen, strapped into all this, like Alex in *A Clockwork Orange*, his eyes pinned back, the lies and the bullshit and the evasion flooding him, rushing into him, when my phone starts ringing – Dr Ali. Finally calling me back after the message I left hours ago. Fucking clown. Probably on the golf course. I slide the bar. 'Ali. Fucking finally. Good news, pal. Get ready to co—'

'Steven. I ... we've got a problem.'

'What?'

'He ... he's gone.'

Oh shit. The cunt's done him on meds is my first thought. Too much of that fucking propofol, the juddering paedo heart in that tiny, wrecked body, just going 'pop'. Game over. See you later, Sooty.

'He's fucking dead?'

'No. He's *gone*. Vanished. Escaped.'

I drop the phone.

THIRTY-EIGHT

Lucius marvelled again at the queue – snaking away in front of him, endless, full of his fellow Americans in all their shapes and sizes. (And now he was one of those shapes, one of those sizes, that might, from the evidence on display here, be called 'American Standard'.) He'd been through John F. Kennedy before of course, many times. But this was different. No security-manned golf buggy straight from the gate to the champagne pod of the VIP centre. No. Just an unsmiling Homeland Security official pointing him towards the queue marked 'US Passport Holders'. And praise Jesus that it was this queue. While it was certainly long and slow, the other queue, the one marked 'Non US Passport Holders', seemed to end somewhere out on the tarmac. It was filled with Chinese, Hispanics, Africans, Poles, Russians, Turks, Greeks. All of them jabbering away in their own language, all seeming cheerful enough, unfazed by the fourteen-hour wait they were enduring. Up above Lucius a baffling portrait hung – Donald Trump again. They really did worship real estate here in New York. Finally, after much shuffling along, for the second time, Lucius confronted a man in a glass box. This man was American Standard himself – he filled the box, looking like a reptile that has grown far too large for its aquarium. He was staring at Lucius as if something was expected of him. Lucius smiled back innocently. 'Hello,' he said.

'Uh, passport?' the man said.

Much fumbling in the fanny pack. Lucius handed it over and the man frowned at it. 'You're kidding, right?'

'Hello,' Lucius said, again.

'This is you? Man, you look like Lucius Du Pre in this ...' The official tried to correlate the postage-stamp-sized face in his hand with the sweating mound of blubber in front of him. Now he noticed the entry stamp on the passport – Quatain. 'And you've been out of the US for ... almost four months? Mr ... McCann?'

'Yes. Jesu. Months,' Lucius nodded, having no idea what was going on.

'And what was the purpose of your visit to Quatain? Put your hand on the scanner please. Yeah, no, just there. OK.'

'Purpose?'

'Why were you there? OK. You can take your hand off now.'

'I ...' Lucius found himself unable to speak. Why had he been there? Because there had been a problem. Connor. Connor who betrayed his love. Because people could not understand how a man and a boy, how they could ... only Jesus could ... Deranged though he might be, Lucius sensed that honesty might not be the best policy here. However, he figured that if good old-fashioned celebrity still carried some clout anywhere, then it did so here, in America. The guy was running his passport through some sort of scanner now too. Lucius stepped closer to the glass and lowered his voice ...

'Sir, I must be honest with you. I'm – urrr, gnnn – I'm travelling under an assumed name, for security purposes. I ... I am Lucius Du Pre!'

Great, another fucking wack job. The Homeland Security officer looked at the 200lb sweat-soaked atrocity in front of him. Then at the huge queue of weary travellers still to be dealt with. His computer chirruped a healthy green, showing that the passport was good and that the bearer was on no watch lists and had committed no crimes.

'Yeah, yeah, and I'm George Clooney. I just work here 'cause I like to meet people, you know? OK, Lucius, here you go. Welcome home.'

'Thank you, sir, God bless you.'

'OK. Right. Next!'

And like that Lucius Du Pre was back on American soil.

Fortune continued to beam down on him with a smile more powerful than a television evangelist's. Having stumbled out of international arrivals – having got over the shock that there were no crush barriers holding back rows of screaming fans, no NYC cops watching the fans, chewing gum, hands on hips, just over the cowboy jut of the holstered pistol, no microphones being thrust in his face, no scrum of photographers running backwards, snapping away – Lucius was grappling with the very real question of 'what do you do now?' when he saw a counter with a sign above it. The sign proclaimed: 'AAA Car Service. Limos, SUVs and Town Cars. New York's Finest.'

What a fuss people made of how difficult it was to manage life! Lucius snuggled down further into the grey leather, feeling proud of his own resourcefulness, his ingenuity and can-do spirit. When he got back to Narnia he might let some of the staff go, start doing more for himself, economising like Lance had been urging him to. Less than ten minutes after seeing the sign and following the exchange of only three hundred of his crumpled American dollars Lucius was sitting in the back of an eight-seat stretch job with full bar and TV. Having established that he had no baggage the cheerful black chauffeur had held the door open for him and asked, 'Where to, sir?' For the first time in the duration of this awful trip Lucius had felt the surge of his old life returning. But where to? What was the name of that place? The place where he normally stayed when he came to New York? That was it!

'Yessir! The Plaza Hotel! All right!' The chauffeur had grinned, lit up by the promise of a hefty tip to come.

At dusk on a beautiful late-May evening, Lucius slid through a borough he did not know the name of (track housing, stone cladding, pizza joints and liquor stores, America always showing you its coal before you get to its gold), across a bridge he did not know the name of, over a river he did not know the name of, and suddenly there it was, glinting in the gathering darkness – the burnished towers of Manhattan. Somewhere in there lay Madison Square Garden, the place where he had been due to make his great comeback, before things got ... derailed.

They rolled through the deep valleys of Midtown and then, suddenly, the explosion of greenery as Central Park appeared and then they were pulling into the circular drive of the hotel just as night fell. Lucius handed the driver an additional hundred-dollar bill (*thankyousirppreciateit*') and fought off the advances of the three bellboys who tried to take his non-existent bags as he made his way up the steps and into the lobby. Emboldened by his recent triumphs with airlines, immigration officers and car services, he strode straight up to the desk.

'Welcome to the Plaza. How may I help you?'

'One hotel room please. I love Jesu!' Oops. That had slipped out.

'Do you have a reservation, sir?'

'Ah. One hotel room please.'

'Yes, I ... how long will you be staying for?'

'Uh ... a month? PTOO!' The man looked at him. 'I mean,' Lucius added, 'a week?'

'One week ...' He did his thing with the computer. 'I'm sorry, sir. We're very busy. I'm afraid the only room we have available is a one-bedroom penthouse suite.'

'Yes. A suite.'

'A suite? Not a room?'

'Yes.'

'OK ...' He ran an eye over the filthy kaftan, the fanny pack strapped over it. And, Jeez, this guy could use a shower. 'That's forty-two hundred dollars a night, including taxes, comes to ... twenty-nine thousand, four hundred dollars for the week. How will you be pay—'

The snick of the Amex going down.

'Just one moment, Mr ... McCann.' He ran the card. It lit up green all the way across the board. As ever in America, the entrance of true money into the arena changed the timbre of things. 'Excellent. Thank you, Mr McCann. You know ...' He leaned over, lowering his voice. 'We also have one of our Metropolitan suites available. Two and a half thousand square feet with views over the Park. The rack rate is eight thousand a night but I could give you twenty per cent off that ...'

Lucius beamed. 'Jesu loves me!'

THIRTY-NINE

I haven't smashed up an office in a *long* time. Ruth's conference room looks like fucking Godzilla came through here, with a few of his mates, on a stag night, mankinis on, ten pints deep, into the shots now, Jägerbombs clamped in tiny claws, shouting 'WHO WANTS SOME?', nothing mattering.

After I hung up on Ali I went for the whiteboard first, ripping it off the easel and throwing it across the room. But you can't really do much damage with a whiteboard. So I picked up a chair and put it through the TV – freeze-framed on Trump's face, his bottom teeth bared in that underbite snarl, his thumb and forefinger forming that 'O' in mid-air – savouring the dull electric bang, the splintering screen. Now that felt better. At this point Ruth ushered everyone out of the room and closed the door behind them while I *really* got to work. I swung the black pyramid of the speakerphone unit around by its cord, smashing it off the wall until the plastic shattered and circuitry flew everywhere.

Using one of the broken chair legs as a baseball bat I turned Ruth's drinks trolley into a nest of broken glass, vodka, gin, whiskey and tiny flecks of glass showering my face. I threw decanters at the walls, tore the DVD player out from beneath the smoking TV and hurled it the length of the room where it obligingly met with a framed, original Led Zeppelin tour poster, the glass exploding all over the carpet. Then I picked up another chair – a heavier job, steel and leather – and cracked it off the corner of the conference table again and again and again until the table splintered and my hands were vibrating. And all the time I was doing this I was screaming 'BASTARD!' over and over again at the top of my lungs. Finally spent, I slid down the wall and considered the full horror of the situation I had managed to get out of Ali – who I will almost certainly be having killed very soon.

The staff went to take Du Pre's breakfast tray in around lunchtime as usual. Some movie was playing on his TV but he wasn't in the bed. They searched his mansion. Then the Sultan's palace. Then the grounds. Nothing. He's gone. He cannot drive and has no access to a car. He was last seen around 6 p.m. the night before, wandering in the palace gardens. The palace itself is surrounded by what Terry calls, what soldiers call, 'MMFD'. Miles and Miles of Fucking Desert. They are now searching the desert. The enormity of my situation dawns on me. Sitting here on the carpet, numb, stunned, I realise that my phone has not stopped ringing for the last fifteen minutes. I look at it. Chrissy. *Will you still love me when I'm poor?*

'Hey,' I say, my voice thick, raw from all the screaming.

'Are you OK?' she says.

'Yeah. Just, not a good time right now.'

'Shit. OK. Well, I'm afraid what I have to say probably isn't going to improve your mood.'

'Look, Chrissy, right now I don't give a flying fuck about the Norwegian Arse Bandits fucking deal or whatever the fuck the cunts are called.'

'It's not about that.'

'What, for fuck's sake?'

'I ... I'm pregnant, Steven.'

Of course. Obviously. *Natürlich*. Totes. Good one.

'I ...' I say. Silence. 'I'll talk to you later.'

I hang up and sit there for a bit, on the floor, amid the wreckage. Two pieces of good news swim into my vision. One is a full bottle of J&B that somehow survived the carnage. The other is the intercom box. I unscrew the cap on the pale whisky and drink a good draught down. Then I hit the intercom.

'Ruth, can you send one of the kids in? Les or Jenny?'

'Sure. Are you OK?'

'Yeah.'

'How bad is it?'

'Bad. I'll pay for everything. Sorry.'

'No, fuck the room. I mean Du Pre. What's happened?'

'It's ... bad. I just need to think. Put everything on hold just now.' I hang up and take another pull of whisky as the door opens a few inches and Les puts his head in, taking in the American Carnage.

'Jesus,' he says. 'You OK?'

'Les, get me an ounce of very good cocaine.'

'Do you think that's a good –' He looks at me – insane, covered in broken glass and liquor, surrounded by match-wood – and thinks better of it. 'Gimme an hour,' he says.

Pouring neat Scotch into a tumbler, I call Terry. It takes about five minutes to give him the rundown. 'Right,' he says, cool, professional. 'I'll get on it. But I'll need to get out of here. What do you want me to do with Bill?'

'Who?'

'Mr Tandy.'

'Who the fuck is Bill Tandy?'

'The chap I'm holding hostage in his own basement right now. Do we still need him?'

'Fuck. No. I shouldn't think so. Just ... use your best judgement.'

I hang up and really start drinking.

FORTY

Terry Rawlings hung up the phone and walked back down the creaking wooden stairs into the basement, where Mr William Tandy – the gag, the rope binding him to the chair – watched him approach with wide eyes, this terrifying stranger who had not spoken a word in forty-eight hours. Tandy's judgement was not what it once had been. He had not eaten and had soiled himself many times. Terry was whistling, having found the only silver lining in this situation – he would not have to clean Tandy up now prior to the staging of his death. Tandy watched him open his bag and take out some sort of medical kit. Terry eased a syringe into a small, clear glass ampoule and drew the plunger back, loading it up with a massive 400mg of morphine sulphate. While unflinching in performing his duties, Terry Rawlings was never needlessly cruel. There was no reason to hurt this man unnecessarily, this poor unfortunate man whose only crime was to be in the right place at the right time. Tandy started to struggle uselessly against his bonds as Terry approached and began rolling up his sleeve. 'It'll sting a little,' Terry said as the needle went in. Tandy was shouting at him through the gag, angry, confused, begging. And then, very suddenly, he wasn't doing any of that stuff. He was on the crest of a rainbow-coloured wave, rushing up and up, crystal water tickling his back as he exploded into the sky, kissing the face of God for an instant before, almost smiling, he died.

Terry got to work, opening the door of the pot-bellied stove in the corner, building the rudiments of the fire that would consume the basement, the house and Tandy himself. A fire that would fool any insurance investigator.

FORTY-ONE

Lucius stood at the window of his suite at dawn, savouring the view of Central Park, the strings of lights going off, already the crowds of milling tourists. To the east he could just see the dun block of Trump Tower, the sun rising somewhere behind it. He understood all about that now. He'd been watching bits of the rolling news channels, finding, now that his mind was fresher than it had been for many years, that he could catch up on world events. Trump was the president. Weird. The new president, Lucius saw, also loved the word 'beautiful'. Maybe they could meet. Trump might like to come to the shows at the Garden once they got them rescheduled. Lucius needed to speak to Lance about that. He was definitely going to call Lance soon, right after he'd dropped a few pounds ...

It was hard, dieting. It called for discipline, willpower, self-control, all areas where, it had to be acknowledged, Lucius had historically struggled a tiny bit. He picked up a slice of twenty-eight-dollar room-service pizza and chewed on it thoughtfully. He'd try to cut his number of daily meals down to three from six or seven. And he'd definitely cut out eating after midnight. That was gone. His bedtime snack last night for instance, a simple club sandwich or two washed down with a quart of Diet Coke, and all over by 11.30. The problem was, for the time being at any rate, the candy and the milk and the boys were all gone. What did that leave him? Food. He folded the slice of double cheese and sausage over onto itself and crammed it into his mouth thinking something like — *Lucius Du Pre brings so much pleasure to so many millions of people, why shouldn't he have the odd treat too?* As he ate, Lucius was engaged in another act he found comforting — watching his old videos. The cable music channels seemed to have one on every fifteen minutes or so, sometimes playing two or three of them in a row. He was watching the video for 'Sexx Man', from the early nineties: his dance routine, the blur of feet, the juddering hips, like a man plugged into the electrical grid. He looked down at himself, at the gut churning as he chewed, trembling under the Plaza robe. (He really had to get around to getting some new clothes — another thing to talk to Lance about.) The video for 'Sexx Man' faded out and into the video for 'December', his tremulous torch song that had been number one for six weeks over the Christmas holidays of 1988, Lucius sitting at a white grand piano, stroking the keyboard dreamily, singing about how cold it was now that she was no longer here. A thought . . .

Maybe there could be a new Lucius?

A new kind of show. Leave the dancing to the dancers and focus on just *singing*. Pavarotti didn't do anything except sing, did he? He could even use a stool. Wear a tuxedo. Concentrate on the ballad end of his repertoire – 'She's Gone', 'The Rain Don't Miss Me Anymore'. That kind of thing. Yes, he'd run this by Lance. Tomorrow. He'd definitely call Lance tomorrow. He was probably worried about him. Dr Ali too. He'd be wondering where Lucius had got to.

He tossed the last pizza crust onto the plate and reached for the room-service menu. Dessert. The sundae here was superb – three scoops of ice cream, chocolate brownie bits, whipped cream, chocolate sauce, a ton of M&M's and a maraschino cherry on top. All for just eighteen dollars! Then again, the coconut lady cake and the vanilla cheesecake both had strong merits of their own. Decisions. This was why you had people like Lance. They answered on the first ring.

'Yeah, uh, hi. Yeah, it's me.' A guilty giggle. 'Could, could I get the sundae please? Oh – and the coconut cake? Great. Oh oh – *and* the vanilla cheesecake? Thank you.' Hotels were so beautiful.

The presentation of the show. How to do something remarkable, something that had never been done before? But here Jesus had been helping him with that too. It had come to him earlier that day, when he was singing his little song, in the hall closet, naked, with toilet paper stuffed in his ears (to help him only hear Jesu) and bits of hotel stationery with 'JESU' written on them fastened all over his body with his own saliva.

White. There would be so many of them.

And they would all wear white.

June

FORTY-TWO

I really want to fire a gun, something big — a .357 Magnum, a Desert Eagle — just to feel the release of capping off some massive fat rounds, but they won't let me on the shooting range in Burbank because I'm reeking of booze and I guess I have cocaine flecked around my nostrils and some blood on my face and, whatever, they're not fucking having it. I tell the pair of Chinks working there to go fuck themselves and storm out, staggering back to the limo, the bright afternoon sunlight scorching my retinas even through my sunglasses.

'Where to now?' Mike asks as I fall into the back seat.

'Just fucking drive,' I say. I'm back with Mike at the wheel again, Mike who started this whole adventure with me, what, three, four days ago? I've kind of lost count. I know I've been through a bunch of limo drivers though. I made the second guy drive me for pretty much twenty-four hours straight, during which time he had no food, water, bathroom breaks. I was pushing him hard, I'll admit it, as we hit the bars of East Hollywood. Then Silver Lake, then Echo Park, then Washington Heights, all the time getting further and further away from anywhere I might encounter anyone I know as my condition, well, I don't want to say deteriorated, but ... *I'm off my fucking nugget.*

Les came through with the bugle, an ounce – twenty-eight grams – of very good blue flake Peruvian cocaine. I've been doing it pretty much constantly for at least seventy-two hours now and there still seems to be a fair bit of it left, here in the limo, in the baggie stuffed in the little icebox in the back.

I haven't done all of it by myself of course. I've had some help at various points. There was the bunch of escorts I hired for a while on day one, three or four of them. We drove around, hitting bars and nightclubs from Hollywood all the way to Santa Monica. Pumping and sucking and grinding and snorting and doing all the usual stuff behind the tinted glass while the big grey stretch glided down Melrose, through the Canyons, along Ventura. Then one of the brasses started talking about how much of a fan of Lucius Du Pre she was and I kicked the fucking lot of them out onto the sidewalk somewhere in Beverly Hills, throwing a fistful of hundred-dollar bills at them as the car peeled away. Then there was a bunch of Mexicans I met in a bar on day two. I partied with the beaners for a while until we wound up back at one of their places – some toilet in Encino – and I went into the bathroom and stared in the mirror for a long time until my face turned into an anus and the anus began talking to me, I freaked out and climbed out the bog window and took off in the limo, crunching Xanax and doing bumps all the way back into the city.

We drove around downtown for a while, all over Skid Row. Now and then I'd get out and methodically burn a high-denomination banknote in front of some bums. A mob nearly came at me but whoever was driving at the time (Greg? Tab? Burt?) got out and let them see the swelling beneath his armpit and they all backed the fuck off.

'CUNTS! FUCK YOU! SUCK ME OFF!' I shout through the open window at no one in particular, at the traffic, as we join the 101 at Burbank and head back to Hollywood. On the back seat, on the other side of the little armrest, is a pile of the trades I picked up at a news-stand. Oh, it's out. The front-cover story on *MusicWeek* screams: 'STELFOX BUYS UNIGRAM'. The headline is, of course, oversensationalised as the detail in the story inside makes clear ...

... on Tuesday the troubled industry giant, which has long been the subject of takeover rumors, announced its sale to a group of private investors headed by former American Pop Star *producer Steven Stelfox. Stelfox began his career as an A&R scout at Unigram in London in 1994 ...*

Oh fuck oh fuck oh Jesus fuck. Buyer's regret. Have you experienced it? You've gone out and spunked a couple of grand on a coat you can ill afford. Some nice shoes. A car. Imagine you've spent the best part of a *billion quid* on a shitbox company you were going to turn around overnight by bringing the biggest pop star in history back from the dead only to have the cunt *just fuck off.* My mobile starts ringing again – Trellick. For the umpteenth time. He must be losing his mind. There's a few million shitters of his personal cash in all of this as well as his block of Unigram shares. I let it go to voicemail (I now have nearly two hundred missed calls) as I recall the last conversation I had with Roddy Myerson, the head of investment banking at Stern, Hammler & Gersh, just the other day, as we were finalising the deal. He said: 'Steven, you better really have something up your sleeve, because the only way we can see of paying off the investors within the agreed time frame is the immediate liquidation of Unigram.'

'Yeah, yeah,' I told him. 'Relax, Roddy.'

Now and then, even through the monstrous amount of nose-up, tranquillisers and booze, the enormity of the situation I am in will dawn on me. *I am on the line for over two hundred million dollars of my own fucking cash.* I have invested this money – almost all of my liquid assets – in tumbling Unigram stock. Using another eight hundred million of the Sultan's funds (having promised him a quick, laundered, untraceable profit), I am about to complete a hostile take-over of Unigram. This is all predicated on the huge leap the share price will take when I unveil the third act of the Lucius Du Pre story. The third act I obviously no longer have. Those clowns over at Murphy, Murphy and Hinckley actually believe they'll soon be signing contracts that guarantee them an in perpetuity piece of Du Pre's back-end action. They're expecting the carefully stage-managed return of Du Pre to take place next week. Lucius Du Pre is in fact loose, out there somewhere in the world, liable to pop up at any moment and start giving his own unique take on recent events. I am finished. Game over. See you later, Sooty.

Suddenly, I can see it all ending. All gone. No more Learjets. No more chartering yachts at a million quid a week.

No more Bentleys and Aston Martins. No more houses in Holland Park and Beverly Hills. I'm living in, what, Queen's Park and Glendale? Worse? Harlesden and Pasadena? I'm flying premium economy. Going on package holidays. Driving a fucking Prius. Oh God. Oh sweet Jesus no. Not now. Not like this. *What the fuck have I done?* For a moment, on my knees on the floor in the back of the limo, a bottle of vodka in one hand and a handful of cocaine in the other, I actually think I am going to burst into tears. And then, thankfully, the familiar warm embrace of pure rage overtakes the grief . . .

That fucking piece of shit Trellick, dragging me into this nightmare. Cocksucker Du Pre and his fucking manager cunt Schitzbaul and bastard Dr Ali couldn't fucking organise a gang bang in a whorehouse, useless fucks. Bitch whore Ruth couldn't have seen this all coming on her fucking massive retainer. Fucking Murphys letting some paedo rapist lowlife animal use their own fucking kid as a human spunk bucket for a few quid. Chrissy, the useless cow, letting me fucking blow my load up her woefully fertile fucking fanny. They will all fucking pay. Every cunt is going to pay.

Energised by all of this anger, and, let's not lie, by the heroic belt of cocaine I have just stuffed up my hooter, I see that we are passing a strip of sleazy bars in Little Armenia. My throat desiccated by the cocaine, my stomach burning from the raw spirits, I am suddenly overcome with the desire for a simple glass of cold draught beer. 'Pull over,' I shout to Mike. I change my shirt (at some point I ordered one of the drivers to go into Barneys and pick me up a load of fresh shirts) and spritz some Evian on my face and figure I can just about pass muster to get a drink in one of these gaffs. I pick my way carefully across the parking lot. It has been a very long time since I stayed up for three days straight and I find I am really having to concentrate quite hard on just putting one foot in front of the other. 'Daywalking', we used to call it. The sign in the window says 'HAPPY HOUR 5–7. DOUBLES 5 DOLLARS!' I push the door open.

Thankfully the place is dark and loud, the clientele a mixture of old alkies who look worse than me and young hipsters who probably think this toilet is 'authentic'.

'Hi, what'll it be?' the barmaid (young, decent rack) says.

'Miller, draught,' I croak, pointing to the nearest pump.

She gives me a sideways eye as she pours. 'You OK?' she says.

I nod. 'Just tired.' I flatten a fifty on the bar and this – and probably the Rolex, the quality of my clothes – seems to ease her fears that I am a bum or a lunatic. She sets the frothing, beaded glass down and moves off along the long bar. This place is not filled with silicone-jugged models in tiny dresses. No actors or producers or pop stars. You need no membership to get in. There is no waiting list for tables. There is no designer furniture, no menus offering small sharing plates at twenty bucks a throw. Very much not my natural environment. A TV noiselessly shows some basketball game. *How? How the fuck did the drug-addled paedo cunt get away?* The last time I saw him he could barely lift a fucking teacup. Again I indulge the fantasy of pulling up a comfortable chair and watching while Terry really goes to town on Dr Ali: pliers, scissors, car batteries, starving rodents, the lot.

Up behind the bar the TV screen changes abruptly as the channel is switched – Trump's face filling it. He's talking to some interviewer with the sound down while the rolling chryo across the bottom of the screen says '*TRUMP ANNOUNCES UNITED STATES WILL LEAVE THE 2015 PARIS CLIMATE AGREEMENT*'. Of course, this being California, the hipsters in the bar are already booing the TV, shaking their heads. Muttering in disgust. One of the guys playing pool throws a cube of chalk at the screen.

As well as a picture of my impending financial ruin the other thing constantly looping through my gak-addled mind is this: the tiny madman in his padded cell. Growing. Three months she said. She'd not been sure because she has very light periods anyway and then the second time it happened she did know but she was terrified to think about it and then she finally went to the doctor and the test was positive and – oh who gives a fuck, I'd stopped listening at that point.

The fucker, I know from the stack of open Google searches on my phone, will weigh about twenty-three grams now – ironically about the same as the amount of cocaine I've got through in the last three (four now?) days – and will be three inches long from crown to rump, around the length of a pea pod. No doubt about it – it's growing fast in there, tucked in among the warm piping and tubing of Chrissy's organs. In a couple of weeks' time it'll be the size of an avocado. Then a melon, then … oh Jesus. I feel an icy trail of fear creep up my back and neck. The cells doubling, multiplying, unstoppable, like the chain reaction entrained by a nuclear device. The atomic power of my spunk, devastating, like the hydrogen bomb, with no theoretical upper limit. All of his organs and muscles will be in place, microscopic kidneys, heart, liver and spleen. '*Your baby's facial muscles,'* one of the articles says, *'are getting a workout as their features form one expression after another, squinting and grimacing, and they may even have hiccups now and then as they practise the movements necessary for breathing.'* The body will be starting to develop a fine coating of hair ('lanugo') to help keep the baby warm. The brain will be developing, too, particularly the part that's responsible for memory and problem-solving. For a brief second I almost manage a smile at this, at the thought of my child trying to solve a problem, perhaps one as thorny as its father is currently grappling with. The baby's father signals for another drink as he thinks how many of the tiny madman's brothers and sisters he's had aborted over the years. The enormous bills at private clinics. The red-eyed and broken former assistants and aspiring pop stars, comforted only by the eye-watering cheques. The entire football team of his would-be predecessors who've been unceremoniously hoovered, sucked and flushed to oblivion over the years. Funnily enough it's always more grief getting it done over here, as well as, naturally, far more expensive. It's a weird one, something the Shermans are mentally touchy about. You'd have thought – here in the land of the free, where market forces are king – that as long as you were able to smack the dough down then you'd be entitled to have some cunt who came bottom of their class in med school up to his fucking elbows in your unwanted foetus quick as you like. But, no, not the case. And it's probably only going to get tougher, given the way things are headed. (Like the man said, *'There has to be some form of punishment.'*) Then again, let's face it, it's only going to get tougher if you're poor. As ever, if you're minted, you'll be able to recline on scented pillows in what is basically a Four Seasons with saline drips and blood transfusions, sedate and stately under the woollen anaesthetic while the unwanted growth is deftly removed. If you're broke you can go on throwing yourself downstairs or into hot baths. Or taking yourself off to some former midwife with a pail and a bag full of twenty-year-old surgical instruments in her spare room.

I become aware that some diesel – tattoos, buzz cut, all the usual – is at the bar next to me, talking to me as she gets a round in. 'Sorry?' I say.

'This fucking guy, huh?' she says, nodding towards the news, where the Donald is still talking soundlessly, the captions still telling us that he is wiping his arse with the Paris Agreement.

'Yeahhh,' I slur. 'S'great, isn't it?'

Her eyes narrow. 'How's that?'

'Getting your country out of all that ... that fucking shit.'

'Hey, that affects the whole planet.'

'What does?'

'Climate change.'

'How?'

'Excuse me?'

'How does it affect you?'

'The ... the ice caps, man. The sea levels.'

'Fuck all that. No one gives a shit about that.'

Behind her one of the more bearish guys has appeared to help carry the beers. He's black, about six foot, and he senses something is afoot. 'Everything OK, Jane?' he says.

'Why?' I ask her, speaking kindly now, as you would to a child or an idiot. 'Why do you think Trump's undoing all of this, uh, Jane?'

'Hello? For, like, profit? To benefit coal and fracking?'

'Because,' the black guy chips in, lifting bottles off the bar, 'he doesn't give a shit about the environment.'

'No no no,' I say, shaking my head. This pair, the black fella and the dyke, have already noticed that I am much older than them. They are now clocking my shoes, the Rolex, the fine cut of my shirt and, undoubtedly, the fact that what questionable sanity I have has been fried by cocaine. But I am way past caring. 'That's not why he's undoing it,' I say. 'Think, kids.' I lift my refilled glass and take a long draught of beer. 'Think.'

'Why don't you just tell us, buddy?' the guy says. 'You seem pretty confident about American politics for a Brit.'

'Just leave it, Carl,' the girl, Jane, says.

I set my glass down. 'He's undoing it for the same reason he's going to throw millions of you off health care. He's undoing it *because a Negro did it*.' She flinches, like she's been slapped, but the black guy takes it. 'Don't you get it, you fucking clowns? He's standing up there and half of your country is cheering him on while he says "fuck all niggers".'

Carl drops the beer bottles onto the floor and makes a fist while behind him a barman is already vaulting the bar with a baseball bat clutched in his fist. I am ready for this. I am fucking *begging* for it. I leap off the bar stool and onto my feet, into a fighting stance. Weirdly this manoeuvre results in me lying on my back on the floor, looking up into the faces of Carl, Jane and the barman. 'You fucking asshole,' the barman growls as he brings the baseball bat up, over his head. *This is really going to fucking hurt*, I find I have time to think as the bat reaches the apogee of its backswing.

And then something happens behind me, a blur of motion, something moving over me, towards my attackers. There's crashing and banging while I scramble backwards, propping myself up against the bar. It takes a moment or two before my smashed, blurred vision allows me to comprehend what I am looking at: a man is standing with his back to me in a kind of karate stance. The barman and Carl are both unconscious on the floor and a mob of three or four of their friends, armed with pool cues and beer bottles, are facing the karate man.

I can hear girls screaming and sobbing. One of the guys lunges forward, swinging the cue. The karate man easily sidesteps the blow and, with apparently no effort whatsoever, deftly rabbit-punches the guy in the throat. He goes down choking and spluttering. 'Any more for any more?' the guy says, kind of cheerfully. The last couple of would-be brawlers drop bottles and cues and back away, hands up.

The man turns and extends a hand down towards me. 'Let's get you home, shall we, boss?' Terry says.

I pass out.

FORTY-THREE

So *this* is a hangover, I think, waking up. All those other things, they were just practice. Limbering up. Training for the big one. I prop myself up on the pillows enough to establish that I am in bed in my apartment – the effort of this sending sparks shooting through my vision, making my limbs ache as though I've just climbed a mountain – and see in the darkness that a tumbler of water has been placed beside my bed. I try to pick it up. It's like trying to lift a gold bar. A housebrick. I cannot remember the last time I felt like this and it is difficult to imagine that, back in the nineties, I woke up feeling like this three or four days out of every week. I cough, which feels like someone setting a pound of plastic explosive off inside my head. A moment later a wedge of light falls across the room and I see Terry standing in the doorway. 'Look who's up ...' he says.

'Jesus Christ. How long have I been ... ?'

'About twenty-four hours. We gave you a fair old load of Valium.'

'Fuck me ...'

'Take your time, boss, but throw some clothes on and come next door and I'll bring you up to speed. I've got some coffee on.'

Half an hour later I am in a dressing gown, gingerly sipping cappuccino while Terry lays it down.

'So, after a while, Ali admits a couple of things. It seems that Lucius had been off his meds for a few weeks ...'

'Why the fuck didn't he tell us?'

'Scared, I should imagine. I don't think he wanted to rock the boat. He's a pig in shit out there. Anyway, it gets better. It turns out your old pal Schitzbaul had given him a new credit card in the same name as his false passport. Just in case the bugger fancied a shopping spree or something. Somehow the new and improved Lucius got hold of passport and credit card, hid himself in a bloody laundry van, got to the city, jumped a cab to the airport and – boom. Bought himself a first-class American Airlines ticket to New York City. He's at the Plaza under the name Fergal McCann. Don't worry – I've got a guy in the lobby. We'll know if he moves. Apparently he hasn't left the room since he checked in two days ago.'

'How, I mean ... we got him into Qualam on a private jet straight into the Sultan's gaff. How the fuck is Lucius fucking Du Pre managing to walk about airports and hotels and New York fucking City without it being all over the news?'

'God knows,' Terry says. 'Must be in disguise.'

Terry is a total fucking pro. 'Terry? I owe you one.'

'Not a problem. Nice to get paid for actually doing something once in a while. On that note, I have to say, if you want my professional opinion, Dr Ali, Schitzbaul, the Murphys ... the old loose ends are fairly stacking up on this one ...'

He's not wrong. I think about all this for a moment, through my screeching hangover. 'OK. Bring Trellick up to speed and tell him we'll need the jet to go to New York. I'm going back to bed for a bit. Anything else?'

'Bunch of messages from that Chrissy. Want me to get back to her for you?'

Get back to her. I think of all the things that could mean in the formidable context of Terry Rawlings. Where there is a man there is a problem. No man, no problem. 'Nah,' I say. 'Leave it just now.'

The following morning Terry and I are sitting in a limo idling on West 59th Street, Central Park South, just across from the Plaza. We drove the short walk here from my apartment on Fifth Avenue, where I dropped my bag off. My hangover has moved from 'critical' into simply 'unpleasant', further soothed by a Xanax and a Bloody Mary on the flight from LA. On the jet, in the bedroom with the door closed, I finally spoke to Chrissy. 'Well,' she said after a bit, 'what do you want to do, Steven?'

What did I want to do? Normally of course she'd have been flat on her back with her feet in stirrups faster than you could say '*Roe v. Wade*'. But, for some reason, some unholy unfathomable reason, I couldn't pull the trigger. 'Look,' I said, 'it's crazy at the moment, with the takeover? There's problems with some other stuff that I can't even begin to go into right now. I should be back from New York tomorrow. We'll sit down. Talk. Figure it out.' (Talk?

Figure it out? What's wrong with me? I'm *riddled* with goodness.)

'OK,' Chrissy said. 'But, you know. There's kind of a ticking-clock element to this …'

'I understand. I'll see you tomorrow.'

I hung up and watched the billion-dollar battlements of Manhattan glittering in the sunshine on our left as the G5 banked over the East River, turning towards La Guardia.

Terry's phone chirrups into life and he picks it up. 'Righto. Got you. Thanks.' He hangs up. 'We're up. 1411.'

And we're out of the limo, across the lanes of busy traffic, through the lobby and into the elevator, Terry pressing the button for the fourteenth floor. Terry's boy on the inside said the only thing that brings Mr McCann in 1411 to the door of his suite is the clatter of the room-service trolley. We sat in the limo and waited until we got the call that Mr McCann was expecting delivery of an order. (Three pizzas and, apparently, the entire dessert menu. Who the fuck is the mad bastard entertaining in there?)

Terry knocks on the door. A muffled 'Who is it?'

'Room service,' Terry says in his best New York accent. A muffled 'Just a minute', the door swings open and –

Some fat cunt in a robe is standing there, the robe barely managing to tether around his waist. He has a Post-it note stuck to his forehead with the word 'JESU' written on it. Terry's hand goes instantly towards the swelling under his left shoulder, but I grab him, stopping him, recognising something, something about the eyes set in that jowelled mass of a face.

'Lucius?' I say, scarcely able to believe I'm saying it.

He squints and asks, 'Are you Jesu? PTOWW!'

It ... it's unbelievable. How come no one recognised Lucius Du Pre fruiting around airports and hotels? Around the streets of New York? Because they weren't looking for fucking *three* of him. He has to weigh sixteen stone. He has toilet paper stuffed in his ears and little bits of Plaza notepaper stuck all over himself, with something written on them in pencil. The single word 'JESU'. We hear the *ping* of the elevator from down the hall and Terry pushes past him into the suite – ignoring his squeaked 'HEY' – and I follow, closing the door behind me. The suite is quite the scene – plates, glasses, dishes, endless Coke cans. I turn to Du Pre as he sits down heavily in a low armchair. His robe falls open and I inadvertently catch sight of his penis. It is small and mottled, like much of the rest of his skin. (However, at least it looks to be intact. Considering all the surgery he's had done to the rest of himself it wouldn't have surprised me to see he'd got up to something truly crazy down there, like an extension job, or having it removed and replaced with something more mental. A fanny. An anteater's proboscis, the liquorice strip of the tongue darting out, flicking away at his balls.)

'What ... what the fuck happened to you?' I manage, sitting down opposite him while he rearranges the folds of the robe. I take the toilet paper out of the cunt's ears as he stares at me blankly. 'It's Steven, Lucius. From Unigram. Steven Stelfox?'

'Oh, Mr Fox. Oh good. You can help me. We can do a different kind of show. BRROOGHHH!' he says.

'What? What fucking show?'

There's a knock at the door. Terry goes down the hallway and I hear voices and then the door closes and Terry is wheeling a trolley laden with food into the room. Lucius's eyes brighten and he goes to stand up. I hold his wrist. His wrist is like a kneecap. His arms are like legs. His legs are like torsos and so on. 'Just start,' I say, '. . . start at the beginning.'

'I will be onstage, with a thousand children. And we will all be in white. And they will come unto me and be healed,' he begins.

Half an hour later I'm just staring at him. I have never really understood the meaning of the phrase 'off your meds' until this moment. Clearly the heart-stopping amount of pharmaceutical uppers and downers Lucius has been on for years had been performing the function of some kind of restraining bolt, some inhibitor circuit. Unleashed from them, free and unfettered, the cunt has gone crazier than a tower block of shithouse rats. I steal the odd glance at Terry while I listen to Lucius outline his plans for renewed world domination. It goes on for a very long time . . .

'You see, Mr Stalefix, I have had my forty days and my forty nights. I have wandered in the wilderness of the barren desert. MNNNGG! Praise Jesus. Frrt. And now I am ready to come back to my people and to bring forth the word of what I have learned. And there will be no shame. No shame for what I have done. No, sir. For it was a beautiful thing and together we can tell the world that.'

'Tell them what, exactly, Lucius?'

'That what I did was an act of *love*. Listen, I have my new single. "I LOVE JESU! HE LOVES ME! ME AND JESU ARE SO HAPPY!"'

From what I can gather the cunt is proposing that he not only confesses to buggering kids but that we present it as some sort of *holy act*. That the world simply hasn't caught up with his level of enlightenment yet. Like he's a fucking iron in 1966 or something, just waiting for it all to become legal. From the sounds of it he's proposing to launch some new religion that sounds like a cross between Scientology and NAMBLA, while looking like Jocky Wilson who fell asleep on a sunbed for three weeks. And then, to cap it all off, he's proposing a stage show where he touches up thousands of kids.

I mean, I've heard some crazed balls in my time, I've worked with fucking Rage, but this, this is something of a different order. More than anything else, it's myself I'm angry at. How could I have thought we could possibly work with this cunt? Control him?

'. . . and I will come out onto the stage, the stage covered in white rose petals, and I will kiss the boy, an act of love, yes, Mr Stalfax, and the world will see that there is no shame. BNNOOOO! No shame at all, sir. And . . . I LOVE JESU! HE LOVES ME! ME AND JESU ARE –'

I nod to Terry. Terry reaches into his jacket and comes silently up behind Du Pre.

'SO HAPP— OW!' He turns and looks at Terry, who has withdrawn the needle as quickly as it went in. 'What did –'

'Lucius?' I say. 'You need to get some rest.'

'Oh, but my time of rest is over. He says in Corinthians, verse sev—' Lucius keels forward onto the floor midsentence, out cold.

'Thank you, Terry,' I say.

'Pleasure.'

With great effort, Terry drags Du Pre off across the carpet and into the bedroom. He returns to find me looking out the window, into the New York night. 'So what now?' Terry asks. 'He'll be out for a while.'

'Get yourself a room,' I say. 'I need to think.'

FORTY-FOUR

I remember the first time I made more than a hundred grand in a year. That was kind of a milestone, twenty years ago, way back in 1997. Back then that kind of income would get you a mortgage for half a million quid. You could buy a house in Notting Hill for that kind of money in 1997. So I did. Then another. And another. By the time I turned thirty, I was a millionaire. And that's another milestone, a million quid. You briefly feel like a player. Until you start hanging out with people with *real* money. Then your sights logically shift onto making ten million. I hit that in 2007, after five years and five seasons of *American Pop Star*, when the show was firmly established in the number-one slot and the network offered me five million a year for another five years plus a ten-million-dollar signing bonus. And then you start to do some fun stuff – buying a proper house. Indulging yourself in a few bits of Warhol and Damien Hirsts and the Aston Martins and flying first class on your own dime and all that shit. The problem is, once you're worth ten million, you're hanging out with some genuine made men. The guys who own the networks, who own the multinationals who advertise on your show, the bankers who advise these guys. True. Fucking. Players. You're standing there with fuck all to say while they compare interior finishes on their new 727s. You might as well have the fucking *Big Issue* in your hand. So you think, right. A hundred million. A hundred million fucking dollars. Then every cunt can fuck off. You get there and you start doing all the stuff you've been reading about – the private jets and the yachts and the rest of it. And then what? At the point where you have enough money never to have to think about money again, you have to deal with something pretty interesting. It's called *you*. Astonishingly, and contrary to what I believed when I was younger, all the pumping and sucking and grinding and larging it in the world does not seem to fill this thing called 'you'. You start looking at the very top of the mountain – eyeing up that tiny plinth crammed with Zuckerbergs and Murdochs and Geffens and mad fucking oligarchs. Billionaires. And I am close. I am so close. *There's a ticking clock on this.* You're fucking right there is. Go big or go home.

My attention drifts back to the TV playing softly in the corner of Du Pre's suite, a reporter, talking to camera. He's standing next to what looks like the Thames. Then I notice the headline – 'TERROR ATTACK IN LONDON'. I thumb the sound up and watch for a few minutes. The guys jumping out of their van and going crackers with machetes. It's about as low rent as you get – basically the aftermath of a Millwall game in the seventies. They're still speculating as to the racial identity of the attackers – all shot dead of course – but we know. Everyone watching knows ...

As night falls over Central Park I gather my thoughts and make a few notes. I call room service and order coffee. I drink two cups and then I call Terry and run him through my thinking. He sits back and then does that low whistle through gritted teeth thing.

'Impossible?' I ask.

'Difficult,' he says. 'Not impossible.'

'How long would prep take?'

'I'll need to get my hands on a few bits and pieces and we'll need to take care of a few backstory elements. Two days minimum, going flat out. Gonna cost you too, I'm afraid.'

'Ballpark.'

Terry names an amount in the mid seven figures. I think for a moment. 'OK then,' I say. 'Let's rock.'

'Gonna be a fair amount of collateral on this, boss ...'

'Yeah, well. Omelette and eggs and all that, Terry.'

He nods and stands up. 'I'll need the jet.'

'I'll tell Trellick. I'll stay here with laughing boy.' I nod towards the bedroom next door. I pat my pocket, locating the brown tub of Demerol Terry brought, about enough to keep the crazed molester docile for a couple of days. 'Right, get to it.' Terry heads for the door. I start making a to-do list ...

Trellick

Dr Ali

Schitzbaul and Fred

Art Hinckley

Glen, Bridget & Connor Murphy

Ruth Blane, Les and Jenny
The Sultan and family
Brandon Krell
Chrissy?

FORTY-FIVE

'For the last time, Brandon, just tell them that as far as I know everyone's jobs are secure and the new management team have no plans for redundancies.' James Trellick slammed the phone down. Jesus Christ. The last few days had been brutal. When the news had broken there were dozens of phone calls like the one he had just hung up on: an entire company freaking out about the rumours that they were about to be out on their arse. Then, on top of all of this, there was the small matter of their golden goose going AWOL. He looked at the drinks cabinet in the corner of his office. Then at the clock – just after eleven. Fuck it. Sun's over the yardarm. It's five o'clock somewhere and all that. He was in the process of pouring himself a stiff belt of Grey Goose when the phone started ringing again. He hit the speaker. 'Yes, Sam?'

'Steven from New York on two.'

Hitting the button. 'What the fuck's going on up there?'

'I've got him.'

'Oh, thank fuck.'

'Listen, plan A is out of the window.'

'What? What the fuck? Listen, we —'

'No time to go into it right now. We're going another way.'

'What other way?'

'James, you really don't want to know.'

'But Lucius, what's happening with Lucius?'

'Lucius is gone.'

'How do you mean "gone"?'

'He answered the door covered in Post-it notes saying "JESUS" with bog roll stuffed in his ears. He's literally howling at the moon. He wants to do a fucking stage show where he touches up a bunch of kids and sings about Jesus.'

'Oh fuck me.'

'Listen, I need you to get someone in A&R to book some time at a decent studio here in New York – for tonight and tomorrow – and get me a good engineer.'

'What? What the fuck am I? A&R coordinator?'

'Just get it done. Then courier all the Du Pre out-takes from LA to the New York studio. Especially the reel marked "acappella stuff". OK? Then   are you getting all this?' Trellick scribbled something down – 'then get your marked-up copies of the Hinckley/Murphy contracts in order and bring them with you to New York.'

'I'm coming to New York?'

'Day after tomorrow.'

'Is there any point in asking what the fuck the plan is?'

'Not really. Later.' The line went dead.

'SAM!' Trellick shouted through the open door.

He had that drink.

FORTY-SIX

Dr Ali Hussain hadn't been to the golf course so much in the last week. He was drinking far too much for that, as well as taking frequent hits from his own supply of goodies. He'd fucked up. His one responsibility – keep him happy and keep him here – and he'd fucked it up. Relations with the Sultan and his heartbroken son had been frosty at best.

Where on earth had Lucius gone? All day, every day, he kept watching the news expecting to see the breaking story: found dead. All he wanted now was to go home. Back to his beach house in Malibu. Would he even get paid now? He almost had enough money not to need to work any more. He should have had more put away. All those wives. Fucking bitches. 'Stay put,' that guy Terry had told him. Who the fuck was he anyway? Ali worked for Lucius and, to a certain extent, Lance. This Stelfox guy who was calling the shots, who the fuck was he? Ali looked forlornly into his closet, at the bag he'd packed days ago, expecting to be summoned home. But no, here he languished, in limbo. In exile. His supply of girls had been cut off by the Sultan too. Without the golf and the fucking what was there here? MMFD. Maybe he could ... just get on a plane. Go anywhere. Start over. But there had been something in that guy Terry's voice. An edge. Something you didn't want to fuck with. It took him a moment to realise that the buzz cutting through CNN (the London terror attack – his 'brothers', ones who claimed to worship the same God as him. How could they ...) was his cellphone, marooned somewhere in the middle of the enormous bed. He found it. An overseas number. 'Hello?' Ali said.

'Ali?' the voice said, calm, gentle.

'Yes?'

'Steven Stelfox.'

'Mr Stelfox, Steven, I ... I'm so sorry about what happened. He, Lucius, he deceived me. I had no idea he was planning to do wh—'

'Hey, enough of that. Pack your bags, old friend, and get yourself on a plane. You're needed in New York, right away. There's a room reserved for you at the Plaza. Ask for Mr McCann after you've checked in.'

'But ... Lucius, do you know –'

'We found him. No harm done. See you in a couple of days.'

Click. And that was it. No censure. No abuse.

Ali did a little dance.

He was going home.

FORTY-SEVEN

Lance Schitzbaul was coping with the current situation better than most. Given the pressure of the last few months he'd developed a stress-busting routine: he began drinking a double bourbon on the hour, every hour, from the moment he woke up. Somewhere around lunchtime he stepped this up to one every half-hour. By the early evening he was just necking the Wild Turkey or Four Roses straight from the bottle. Combining this with regular handfuls of Xanax, he found he could contrive to pass out somewhere around 10 p.m. every night. When the phone rang it was late afternoon in Pacific Palisades and Lance was just the right side of total oblivion.

'Herrro?' he said.

'Lance? Steven. How are you?'

'Schteeven! Ah'mgreatbuddyhowsyou?'

'Sorry?'

Lance tried again. And again.

'OK, Lance? All you have to do is listen, OK? We've got Lucius. Keep this very quiet but you're coming to New

York day after tomorrow, on the Unigram jet. Fred has all the details. Just, he's coming with you. OK?'

'Fred?'

'Your guy Fred? Your bodyguard?'

'Oh! Fred! Thasssgreat. I love Fred.'

'Sure you do, Lance. Look, don't worry. It's all going to work out. Just take it easy, OK? Everything's going to be fine.'

'SchureSchteeeven. No pobbem. I ... I'll see you in ... in ...' Where had he said? What city? 'NEW YOIK! I'll see you in New Yoik, motherfucka! I ... thankshhh. Thankshh fo taking care o all the shit, this fn, fugging shit. I   I love you, man.'

But the line was already dead. Lance flopped back in the lounger on his deck, the western deck of the house, looking stupefied towards the ocean, a warm glow in his loins, content that something good had just taken place, disquieted only by the growing realisation that the warmth he was feeling was due to the fact that he had, once again, pissed himself. Oh well. He reached for the bottle.

FORTY-EIGHT

Art Hinckley hung up, laced his fingers behind his head, and looked around his office, at the fake wood panelling, the hissing fluorescent tubes, the nail salon across the parking lot. The Thai massage place where he sometimes availed himself of a happier ending than he was used to in his business dealings. He smiled. New York. They would be signing the contracts day after tomorrow. Goodbye, fake panelling. Goodbye, nail salon. Hello, happy endings. *Real* happy endings. Cash. Prestige. Power. Back end. Art had played the long game. Had doled his hand out slowly and precisely and had won. He looked at the stack of Unigram contracts on his desk, offering Behemoth Inc. (equal partners: A. Hinckley, B. and G. Murphy) a 5 per cent share in all of the company's future net profits on all of Lucius Du Pre's recorded output. There were similar contracts to be signed between them and Schitzbaul's company Platinum Talent, guaranteeing them the same split on all of Du Pre's non-record-company income:

touring, advertising revenue, merchandise and so forth. The contracts all had dozens of yellow Post-it notes sticking out of them – designating pages where amends and annotations had been made in Art's crabbed hand. Where he had thunderously struck out clauses that offended him, where he had countered some of his proposals Unigram had rejected with a furious 'STET!' He had used a lifetime of legal skills in this work and it had felt so good, knowing that upon completion he would receive something of a different order to his usual fee, his 50 per cent of some guy's four-thousand-dollar damages for twisting his ankle on an Orange County sidewalk. Upon signature of these agreements Art would receive his share of *twenty million dollars.* And that was just an advance. Like Stelfox said, if they got this back-from-the-dead record right, they all stood to make hundreds of millions. A true player. Go big or go home. He dialled the number. Bridget answered.

'It's done. We're there. Pack your bags – we're going to New York to sign the contracts.'

'Shit, really? Fuck. That's great.'

'We're going on the Unigram jet. Staying at the Plaza.' Art tossed this off casually, as though he were saying 'we're going to Domino's, getting a pizza'.

'Wow,' Bridget said, then yelling, 'Glen! HEY, GLEN! We –'

'Bridget, wait!' Art said. 'Listen, there's a condition.'

'What?'

He told her.

'No way. *No fucking way!* I don't want them in the same fucking room,' Bridget said.

Christ, Art thought, now you play the perfect mother. 'It's just for a few minutes,' Art said. 'Apparently he just wants to say goodbye.'

'I don't know,' Bridget said.

'Bridget, think for Christ's sake. We've been working on this deal for *months* now. Just one meeting and then we're done.'

'I don't like it . . .' Mother Perfect said.

'Well, you don't have to like it. We just have to get it done. OK?'

Finally, reluctantly, she said, 'OK.'

'Right. I'll email you the address of where we're getting the jet. Nine a.m. day after tomorrow. Tell Glen I said hi.' Art hung up. A couple more days and these jerks would be out of his life forever. Maybe out of everyone's lives if he went down the route Stelfox was suggesting. He'd need to look into this properly. Maybe have a few lunches and dinners with Stelfox. Get to know him better, now they were sort of partners.

Art was looking forward to that.

FORTY-NINE

Bridget walked up the hallway and found Glen amid the forest of packing crates, busy with the tape gun and the Sharpie. She didn't know where half of this shit had come from, or understand why he wanted to take it. As far as Bridget was concerned they could just buy new shit when they moved next week. She was enjoying looking around their house now that they were leaving it. Every patch of damp, every crack in the plaster, every worn patch of carpeting, reminding her of how far they had come, how well they had done. 'That was Art,' she said

'What? Problem?'

'Nope. It's all done. We're signing day after tomorrow. In New York.'

'Huh? Why there?'

'We're going on the Unigram jet. They're putting us up at the Plaza.'

'No shit?' Glen grinned, reached for a beer. 'See what I told you?' he said. 'That's some actual *respect* for you.

Fucking playas, playas ...' He did the little *Tropic Thunder* dance.

'Yeah yeah,' Bridget said. 'But listen, Du Pre is going to be there. We've got to bring Connor. He wants to say goodbye.'

'What?'

'Yup.'

'That sick, twisted, goddamned –'

'Art says we need to just suck it up. It's one meeting.'

Glen thought about making a scene. About telling them all to go fuck themselves. Telling them 'what kind of a fucking father do you think I am?' That he wasn't about to have his son in the same room as that paedophile freak for five minutes. Then Glen thought about something else – the image of millions of dollars coming into his mind. Boxes and boxes of crisp banknotes as far as the eye could see, *Raiders of the Lost Ark*-style warehouses of them.

'Ah fuck it,' he said. 'It's one meeting, right?' He popped that beer and chugged it down. Burping, he said, 'Hey, private jet, right? You know what that means?'

'What?'

'No security. Take a couple of grams, get high in the sky!'

'Jesus, Glen ...'

She walked back off down the hall towards Connor's room, to tell him about the trip, to tell him his special friend was still alive, and that he'd be seeing him one last time. Behind her she could hear Glen, doing his stupid dance, rhythmically chanting 'PLAYA, PLAYA, PLAYA ...'

FIFTY

'Steven? It's Ruth.'

'Ruth. Panic over. We've got him.'

'Oh, thank Christ for that. Where?'

'New York. The Plaza.'

'How did he get –'

'It's a long and mental fucking story. I'll tell you when you get here.'

'When's that?'

'Day after tomorrow. Nine a.m. You're getting the Unigram jet out of Burbank. We've got a lot of work to do so bring Les and Jenny.'

'Gotcha.' Ruth scribbling it all down. 'But tell me this – how the fuck did he get himself to NYC from fucking camel-fucker land without getting recognised?'

'Well, let's just say he's gained a little weight . . .'

'Oh man. How much?'

Stelfox laughed. 'Somewhere between Boss Hogg and Brando in *Apocalypse Now*.'

'Jesus Christ. You ... how come you're laughing?' She started laughing too. He had one of those laughs, a laugh you jump in with gratefully, a laugh that you would do anything to inspire.

'It's just too fucking good. You couldn't make it up. Wait until you hear his plans for the next phase of his career. But don't worry. I've got it all figured out. We're all going to make a ton of money. I'll see you soon.' He hung up.

'Les! Jenny!' Ruth shouted out of her ever-open office door. 'Get the fuck in here.'

FIFTY-ONE

'I mean, I've been thinking about it,' Chrissy said. 'I'm only twenty-nine. I've got my whole career happening right now ...'

'I'll come with you. You won't be alone in this, Chrissy.'

'I'd just ... I'd really like to see you right now.'

'Me too. Listen, I'm going to be stuck here for a bit. Trellick's coming to New York day after tomorrow, to tie this Unigram sale up. There's a few loose ends about the Du Pre estate too. I'll get the office to book you a flight, OK?'

'What? I just blow off work?'

'Exactly.'

'Oh, about work. Danny Rent called. He's willing to accept two hundred thousand for Norwegian Dance Crew.'

'Nazi Dance Crew? Fuck that. Wait another week and we'll counter.'

'OK.'

'About the other thing. I've got an excellent doctor here. I could book it in –'

'"It", Christ ...' said Chrissy.

'Sorry, sorry. Not "it". You. Us. Book us in.'

'Yeah, I guess so. Why wait?'

'Look, we'll talk more when you get here, OK?' The line was as clear as water, even though they were looking at different bodies of it as they spoke. 'Look, I have to run, Chrissy. I'm in the studio all day tomorrow.'

'Does Trellick, James ... does he know about ... ?'

'No. Of course not.

'OK,' she said. 'See you day after tomorrow.'

Chrissy hung up and put the phone down on the little metal table in the little garden of her little house in Silver Lake. She patted her belly, where the little thing grew. She had been anxious the last few days, more on the edge of her mind than she cared to admit. She was twenty-nine. Still young. She could have another baby. Steven was right. It was the right decision. She went into the kitchen and rooted in the drawer until she found them – a pack of Marlboro Lights, hidden under some tea towels. She'd stopped smoking when she found out. Oh well, it didn't matter much now. She went back into the garden and lit one.

She started crying.

FIFTY-TWO

Terry Rawlings was *slick*.

He'd parked high up in the Malibu hills and hiked in the dark through scrubland before gaining access to the rear of the property through the garden. The yards were large, the neighbouring houses far away, no one to notice Terry's lithe form in black night camo, moving low and fast through the trees and bushes. The basic alarm system had taken him less than thirty seconds to disable. And now here he stood in the kitchen, breathing softly, his ears cocked for anything, his pulse only very slightly elevated.

Terry moved through the rooms, noticing some of the things on the walls – framed photographs of the owner of the house with celebrities, framed professional certificates and degrees – as he moved towards the study, its location known to him from a study of the architectural plans of the house. He pushed the door open and there it was, switched off, inert. He set his heavy backpack down and turned the machine on, the Apple logo coming up obligingly in the middle of the screen. It was an older machine, a godsend. In less than a minute Terry had bypassed the computer's minimal security checks and was inserting his memory stick into the port. The program started uploading.

Terry sat there in the dark, his face blued by the light of the screen, the only sound the noise of cars, far below on the PCH1, roaring south towards LA, or north out of LA, through here and on towards Trancas and Big Sur. Now Terry didn't really understand tech stuff, he couldn't have explained to you how the Timelord program worked, he only knew that it did. What it did, when he'd used it on a few black ops jumps back in the day, was to load documents onto your hard drive in a manner that convinced the computer they had been there for some time. What it did was establish a non-paper paper trail. Satisfied the computer was doing its thing, Terry left it to it, picked his backpack up, and headed upstairs, moving low, below the windows.

He secreted several of the items in his backpack in the closet in the master bedroom. In the bathroom he worked hard, imprinting a fine residue of powder all around the large marble tub. As a final touch he placed a copy of the Quran and a few choice pieces of literature in the right-hand bedside drawer.

Back downstairs he saw Timelord had finished uploading the tranche of documents, the plans and schematics and instruction manuals. He unplugged the memory stick, turned the computer off, and wiped down every surface he'd touched. In the kitchen, by the sliding door to the backyard, he tapped at the alarm keypad, resetting it. He slid the door closed and locked it before before retracing his steps through the garden, over the fence and back into the scrubland. Twenty minutes later – a tougher hike than on the way down, the going all uphill, although his pack was lighter now – he regained his rented Dodge. He snapped the rubber gloves off and checked the timer on his watch – the whole thing had taken just less than an hour. Not bad.

The tyres kicked dust behind the car as he steered it down through the trees, back towards the coast, which he'd be following south, all the way to LAX, where he'd be catching a night flight back to New York, where the toughest part lay ahead. But first there was one more quick errand to take care of, conveniently in Santa Monica. Terry checked the address again and then looked at the place on Google Maps. Nice big house. Quiet street. Ideal.

He was tired. He'd sleep on the plane.

FIFTY-THREE

'For fuck's sake, no. More hypnotic. Trancey.'

'OK, OK,' Tim the engineer says, sliding his mouse, scrolling again through a library of beats. 'Hang on ...'

We're in a windowless basement, somewhere below the streets of Greenwich Village. It's been a while since I've done this and I'd forgotten that after a certain amount of time in a recording studio it becomes unreal. The recycled air, the low, artificial light, the sonar honks of bass and pings of treble, your peripheral vision studded with the red, white and yellow lights of innumerable instrument panels. You are on a submarine, desperately wanting to come out of the depths, to come up for air, but in this case, the surface is still some distance above us.

'How about this?' Tim clicks the mouse and a slow, churning drum loop purrs from the wall of speakers. It's nice. Nice, but ...

'Nah,' I say. 'Too slow ...' He works the mouse and speeds the loop up a few bpm. I give it a few seconds. 'Nah. Next.'

'Okaayyyy ...' he says. To be fair, the exasperation of his tone is understandable, forgivable even. We've been working on this one track for ten hours straight now and by rights I should have changed engineers, but I insisted on keeping him on at double his usual rate – because I am a genuinely nice guy and I want to minimise the pain and suffering that will be caused later on, in clean-up.

The first seven or so hours of the session were spent compiling a master vocal from the many different takes available. Some of these takes were separated by years rather than months and were recorded in a variety of different studios using different mikes and different miking techniques, as Tim the engineer never tired of pointing out until I told him to shut the fuck up about all the technical stuff and just make them all blend together so the average punter wouldn't know the difference. Gradually, it started coming together and we finally had a complete, acappella vocal track lasting just over two and a half minutes, though by the end of the process I thought I might actually go insane if I heard one more second of the fucker's voice.

'Stop,' I say, tuning into some beats Tim's just flipped through. 'Go back ...' He scrolls back up the screen of his computer, clicks on a highlighted bar. A warm, rolling groove begins. 'Turn it up,' I say. Tim slides the fader up and we both listen for a moment. The beat sounds simple, almost a straight 4/4, but as you listen you hear the delicate complexity within it, little accents – bells and woodblocks – tinkling away in the mix, working off the hi-hat and snare. It's nice and slow, but not too slow, with something uplifting to it. I check the counter on the screen – 62 bpm: right in the sweet spot for the human heart rate.

At this rate of beats per minute your brainwaves and your heartbeat begin to synchronise with the rhythm. Entrainment. It has been proven – scientifically proven, by actual fucking scientists – that music at this tempo calms human beings down. That it can be used on trauma sufferers and accident survivors to significantly improve their mental state. 'Tim, Tim,' I say, excited now, not wanting to jinx it. 'Stick a little bass in. The thing you had earlier.' He pushes a fader up and a low, underlying bass tone comes in, along with a whooshing sound, accentuating the trance-like quality of the whole thing, taking you into an even deeper state of tranquillity, of weightlessness. This ... this could be it.

'Put ... put the fucking vocal up,' I say.

He slides another fader up and Du Pre's voice comes in, midway through the take, ghostly, swathed in reverb, as he sings '*On the shore, dimly seen through the mists of the deep, where the foe's haughty host in dread silence reposes ...*' It's brilliant. Simple, minimal, eloquent. Music that would soothe and balm the most broken of hearts. It has an almost time-less quality, something outside and beyond pop music: a Gregorian chant feel, somewhere between Enigma and fucking Enya. 'That's it,' I say. 'That's fucking it.' Tim closes his eyes and we both listen along, joined together in the fact that we are the only two human beings in the world who have heard this music being created, who know what has been happening in this room.

'You want to add much to it?' Tim asks.

'Nope. Just make sure we can hear all the words, sweeten it up for mastering and we are done, buddy.'

'Woah. Thank God. I just gotta take a piss break ...'

Tim leaves. I reach into his jacket and find his wallet. His driver's licence tells me that Tim Montgomerie lives in apartment 4a, 18 Bennington Avenue, Queens, NY. I quickly photograph it with my phone and replace it.

He comes back and we spend another couple of hours getting the opening just right, starting very minimal, gradually introducing a little bass, then the drum loop. I yawn, exhausted, and look at my watch – 7.15 a.m. I realise that outside of the submarine of the studio New York City has gone from day to night and back to day again. I stretch out on the sofa at the back of the room and quickly fall into a deep sleep. I dream that I am at the Grammys, onstage accepting an award, one of many that I am clutching. In the audience Clive Davis and Ahmet Ertegun are both smiling and applauding. Ertegun winks at me and does gun-fingers.

FIFTY-FOUR

Ten passengers on the eighteen-seat Gulfstream out of
Burbank to La Guardia: Ruth Blane and her assistants
Les and Jenny, Lance Schitzbaul and his bodyguard
Freddy, Glen, Bridget and young Connor Murphy, their
lawyer, Arthur Hinckley, and James Trellick of Unigram.
There had been an awkward few moments between the
Hinckley/Murphy axis and Schitzbaul when they all
boarded, with Glen Murphy unable to help himself from
saying 'Hey, Lance, I guess we're partners now?' and
Schitzbaul having to be held back by Freddy, but, now
that the jet had reached cruising altitude and the champagne and cocktails were flowing freely, everyone had
loosened up a bit and the atmosphere was closer to a
school outing, or the weekend retreat of a group of
successful executives. These ten souls were, after all,
bonded by a unique shared experience: outside of Steven
Stelfox, Dr Ali and Terry Rawlings, they were the only
people in America who knew Lucius Du Pre was alive

and well. On her third Bloody Mary, Bridget Murphy came and sat in the empty back seat beside Schitzbaul, towards the rear of the cabin. 'Lance, look, I'm sorry about Glen. You know how he gets ...'

Schitzbaul looked along the aisle, to where Bridget's husband and son sat. Tough as he was, the manager found it hard to maintain anger at Bridget when the image of his client ... doing his thing with her son came into his mind.

'Ah hell, Bridget,' he said magnanimously, 'I'm fucken sorry. Sorry things got so fucken fucked up ...' He held his flute out, accepting a generous refill from the passing stewardess. Two more refills and another double Bloody Mary (as well as a trip to the bathroom for a bump of blow for Bridget) and the conversation had moved on, Bridget saying in a low whisper ...

'It's not as simple as people think, you know? I mean, my son, I ... I've known he is the way he is since he was small. As a mother, I, you ...'

'You know? Right?' Lance said.

'Right.'

'You know he's gay?'

'Oh, sure. And I mean, he was in love with Lucius. In love. He'd have, I mean, in history, the ancient Greeks,' Bridget wanted to try this line out again, 'they ...'

'It was no crime?'

'Exactly. That sort of thing, between an older man and a boy, it ... it was ...'

'It was accepted.'

'But, if you were in our position ...'

'Honey, I understand.' Lance looked at her. 'Listen, we're going to try and make it right. OK?'

'I'm glad we can talk this out, Lance. Like adults. Stay friends.'

'Sure.'

The manager and the blackmailer clinked glasses, Bridget savouring the strong liquor, the tingle of the cocaine, the smooth speed of the Gulfstream, all the touchstones of her new life as a rich woman. She turned the magical words 'make it right' over in her head as she looked to one of the front tables, to the tower of contracts stacked between Art and the label boss, Trellick, the documents, the legal instrumentation of 'making it right'.

'And you still need to lose clause 14, page 23 of the appendix …' Art was saying to Trellick.

Trellick looked at the offending text, a subclause designed to screw profit participants out of their back end, the kind of standard legalese he'd spent a lifetime engineering into deals. 'Listen, you fu—' he heard himself begin to say. Trellick fought back all his natural instincts, a lawyer's instincts, honed over many negotiations, instincts that told him to fight tooth and nail for every piece of real estate in a contract, and said 'Sure, Art …' as he took his Montblanc and struck out the offending paragraph. Art Hinckley sat back in the soft cream leather and ticked an item off his list of final deal points. He smiled to himself as he reached for the Pol Roger. Negotiating, with leverage and a glass of cold champagne, on a private jet: it was everything he'd dreamt about since law school.

Across the aisle from the two lawyers and their paperwork Ruth Blane was busy crafting draft after draft of the new press release while her assistants worked the bot accounts. Now, in addition to explaining how Du Pre had survived the plane crash and remained hidden for nearly five months, Ruth also had to account for the fact that his body mass had nearly doubled. 'Give me options,' Stelfox had said. Like a great film director, like Kubrick, Stelfox didn't always know what he wanted, but he knew when he saw it. When they'd done *American Pop Star* together Ruth had always been impressed with his instinct, very early on, for which contestants would play best with the public. For the kinds of backstories that had the right combination of factors: illness, unbelievable poverty, familial abuse, a hidden, overpowering talent that could not be denied. And, above all, a happy ending, a little piece of the American dream that everyone could buy into.

'Yep, this is going ...' Les said, sitting opposite her, wired into his laptop, 'two and a half thousand retweets and climbing.' He turned the screen around to show Ruth the tweet, sent from an account somewhere in Ukraine: 'Guys! Lucius is alive! Am hearing rumours he's gained a lot of weight! #LUCIUSLIVES.' Below it the replies feed was already crammed with exactly the responses you'd expect: 'I knew it!' 'Poor Lucius!' 'He's out there! Don't believe the FAKE NEWS!' and so forth. When they unveiled Du Pre many of these tweets would be trotted out again by the lunatics as proof positive that they had been right all along.

'OK, good,' Ruth said. 'Now, what do we think about a feeder? He got captured by a fan who was also a feeder?'

'Mmmm, interesting,' Les said.

'That's interesting,' Glen Murphy was also saying, up at the front of the plane, to Jenny, Ruth's assistant, Connor Murphy sleeping beside his father as he came on to a woman he had just met. 'I mean, I'm a Pisces, right? So the whole thing, we're sensitive, intuitive, we get easily overloaded by crowds or overstimulating environments. It's, like, hard to pin us down, because we're so, so, uh, keen on just getting away to a place where we can experience some downtime and meditative R&R, you know? People think we're flaky because of the way we, like, swim in and out of people's lives? But when we *do* surface, man, when we do surface we are magical friends. Ahhhhh, ahhhh …' He sniffed loudly. 'Rose-coloured glasses kinda people. We are attentive and inspiring. You know, composing a photo, listening to music, meditation in my Zen den. Einstein, Rihanna, Steve Jobs … they're all Pisces. You know what I'm saying, Jenny?'

Did this jerk do all the coke in the world? Jenny wondered as she searched for a reply, before realising any kind of reply was superfluous to requirements: Glen was already off into another anecdote, something about falling off his bike when he was nine. Jenny burned her eyes into Ruth's back, praying, willing her boss to acknowledge her, to ask her a question, to throw her a lifeline and get her away from this maniac scumbag. But no, she was deep into it with Les. So Jenny sat there and tearfully took both barrels of the coke-monologue. She held out her glass for a refill. Down there, below the clouds and the sunshine, something like Wyoming passed miles beneath them.

FIFTY-FIVE

Around the time the Gulfstream was crossing the Rockies, up ahead of them, on the East Coast, Terry Rawlings blinked the sleep out of his eyes, fighting exhaustion as he forced himself to stay focused. He had slept for just four out of the last forty-eight hours, on the night-flight back from LA, and he was having to do some very complicated last-minute assembly in the confines of the hall closet – a space just some two metres by one metre. He was holding a circuit breaker in his right hand and a small screwdriver in his left while he screwed an earth wire tight into position. Most of the job had been done in the privacy of his room several floors below, but there were a few last-minute adjustments that had to be done *in situ*. His left leg was cramping, due to having been bent against the wall for so long. Earth wire screwed tight, Terry snapped the circuit breaker into place, wiped sweat from his brow, and felt in the darkness for the 'on' switch. He flicked it – lights coming up on the panel in front of him, a very low hum.

He breathed out and began punching in his settings. It was quality workmanship this thing, German-made, but routed out of the Middle East with a paperwork trail that would be easily followed back to the beach house in Malibu. Satisfied all was in place, Terry was pocketing the remote control when he felt his phone buzz gently in his inside pocket.

He took it out and looked at the screen. From Stelfox. Terry clicked on the message: '*Apartment 4a, 18 Bennington Avenue, Queens.*' Terry sighed.

He'd need some coffee.

FIFTY-SIX

Dr Ali was tired too. There'd been a screaming brat in the first-class cabin and he'd forgotten his noise-cancelling headphones in his haste to pack and get to the airport. Leaning wearily on the counter in the huge marble atrium he watched while the desk clerk did his thing, tapping and punching away at his terminal. This was what long journeys felt like after a while — a lot of waiting while someone tapped and punched at a computer.

He took his backpack off and sat it by his feet. That had been another time-consuming exercise he could have done without tonight, but there had been no way around it. Mr Stelfox had been very clear that his bag of goodies would be needed later. And, since there was no way to get his bag of goodies out of Quatain and through customs on a commercial flight, he'd had to pay a visit to a Manhattan pharmacy right after he'd landed. In fact, he'd had to visit several Manhattan pharmacies before he'd succeeded in getting all the basic ingredients for Lucius's favourite cocktails, writing the prescriptions himself on his script pad in the back of the limo. Still, it was all done now, the vast quantities of meds safely in the bag at his feet. 'And you're all set ...' the kid was saying to him now. 'Room 1423. It's on the fourteenth floor. Do you need some help with your luggage, Doctor?'

'No, thank you.'

'Not at all. Welcome to the Plaza.'

In his room Ali stretched out on the huge bed, listening to the thrum of water through the open bathroom door as the huge tub filled. A hot bath, a snack from room service, and then a nice long nap before presenting himself and resuming his duties. If all went well it would be a short, but very profitable, re-employment. Breaking a rule about getting high on his own supply, Ali dug around in his backpack of goodies and came out with a strip of Xanax. He bit one in half and chased it down with a sluice of mineral water from the complimentary bottle by the bed. By the time it kicked in he'd be done with his bath. A nice, long nap.

FIFTY-SEVEN

I am in the bedroom, giving Lucius a few last-minute coaching tips. Under instructions from Dr Ali, Terry and I have spent the last forty-eight hours gradually getting him back on his meds and he seems calmer, more docile. He's stopped punctuating sentences with mad 'PTOOs!' and 'GRRRRs!' at any rate. From next door, in the suite's vast living room, I can hear the Plaza staff putting the finishing touches to the catering arrangements. I have organised a buffet dinner – a side of poached salmon, rare roast beef, beluga and sevruga caviar, oysters on the half shell – and a full, open bar: a glittering tower of every conceivable spirit, mixers, ice, chilled champagne and white wine. The whole thing will be self-service of course. We'll need total privacy due to the sensitive nature of the topics under discussion. 'Lucius,' I say from my seat near the window overlooking the park. 'Remind me – what do you want to get from this meeting?'

He's on the bed, propped up on a raft on pillows, his incredible bulk hidden beneath one of the new range of white kaftans I've bought him. Apart from my stint in the studio, I've pretty much spent the last forty-eight hours straight with Lucius. No mean feat. He plays video games. He will watch TV if it's a kids' film or it's about him. I am not hugely overburdened with what you'd call an inner life, but Lucius? He's got nothing. He gazes sadly at the great fleshy paddles of his hands and thinks for a moment before saying, very softly, 'I just want things to be beautiful, like they were before.'

'And they can be. They really can. But you have to follow my lead. Do you understand?'

He nods.

'These people, the Murphys and their lawyer, we can make them be quiet, Lucius, but we need to give them quite a lot of money. Our money and your money.'

'I don't care about that,' he says.

'Good. Then you can leave everything to us.'

'Will ... Connor ... will he ever be my special friend again?'

'Well, that, you know ...' Unbelievably it seems that the monstrous Idi Amin-sized fucker is already thinking about ... 'That's kind of out of my hands, mate. You haven't seen each other in a while. Let's see how it goes, eh?'

'But I'm so disgusting ...' Lucius surveys his gargantuan body.

'So you slapped on a few pounds. Long holiday, who doesn't? We'll get you the best guys. Personal trainers, dieticians. Have it off by Christmas. No bother. It's just important that we remember the name of the game here tonight. Right? And what is the name of the game?' There's a soft knocking at the partially open door.

'Uh, sir? We're done.'

I walk over and open it fully. The head of Guest Services stands there, his staff behind him and, behind them, the transformed suite. Soft lighting, a few candles flickering, lots of fresh-cut flowers in urns and jars. On one side of the room the buffet table groans with expensive treats, the burnished silver domes on the hot food, catching the candle-light, flickering and glowing. On the other side of the room the dining table has been set up as a kind of work area: multiple copies of the Behemoth Inc./Du Pre/Unigram contracts.

'Excellent,' I tell the guy as I press of wad of hundred-dollar bills into his hand. 'Thank you.'

'Thank *you*, sir,' he says. They leave.

'Lucius,' I say again, 'what's the name of the game tonight?'

'Make a deal,' Idi says finally.

'You're a prodigy,' I say. 'OK. Now just relax and leave the talking to us, OK?'

I walk across the suite to the bar and pour myself a slug of chilled Grey Goose. I take out my phone and dial her number. 'Hi there,' Chrissy says.

'Hey,' I say. 'Did you get in OK?'

'Sure, your housekeeper let me in.' Chrissy laughs. 'I still can't believe you have a place here ...'

'Where are you?'

'At the living-room window.'

'You can probably see me from where you're standing.' I move over to the windows and look down the darkness of Fifth Avenue, red tail lights, white headlights, Chrissy just a five-minute walk away at my New York apartment.

'I mean, it's so ridiculous.'

I know what she means. I know the room she is currently standing in: two thousand square feet, floor-to-ceiling windows, sunken conversation pit, wet bar, walls lined with hardback first editions. All, obviously, the work of the decorator.

'You know what's ridiculous?' I say. 'The amount of money I've made on that place. So, look, make yourself at home, but don't wait up. I'll probably be late.'

'Long negotiation?'

'With these fucks? Undoubtedly. I'll see you later, OK?'

I hang up. *Don't wait up.* When did I last ... ?

I sip my drink at the window, enjoying the warm rush as the neat spirit hits my empty stomach. Lost in thought, it takes me a moment to realise the doorbell is ringing. I cross the thick carpet and open it: the Murphys and Hinckley — obviously the first to arrive, the kid tagging shyly behind them.

'Guys!' I say, pumping hands, air-kissing. 'Art, Bridget ... and you must be Connor.' I extend my hand. The kid just looks at it until Mom nudges him.

'Shake hands, Connor, like a grown-up.' The little freak gives me a weak, wet shake. Man, if I had a kid ...

'Come on in ...' I say. 'Let me get you all a drink. Lucius!' I call out as I lead them into the living room. 'Lucius!'

For a moment it's like Lucius and I are an old married couple, entertaining guests in a sitcom. And then Lucius appears in the doorway from the bedroom. I savour their reactions: Bridget and Glen's open mouths, Art's shock. I mean, they almost flinch as this massive dark beast starts coming towards them. As for the kid, he just says, 'That's not Lucius,' as the doorbell rings again and I'm opening the door to Trellick and Schitzbaul. 'Hey, guys,' I say. 'Good timing. Lemme get you all a drink ...'

I busy myself with ice, bottles and mixers, my back to the room, enjoying the sound of a roomful of people trying not to say 'What the fuck happened to you?'

Terry Rawlings waits in the car. He's found a good spot, one of the street lamps is broken, affording him a nice, dark area to park in. There are lights on in many of the homes on this quiet street, but the curtains and blinds are mostly drawn at this hour, the blued flicker of TVs visible behind them. Only one real concern – the second floor of the building directly opposite him. Lights blazing, windows open, shadows passing on the ceiling as the occupants go about their business. He checks his watch, a little after 11 p.m. A few more minutes pass before Terry sees him, recognising him from the driver's licence photo on his phone, coming along the sidewalk on the other side of the street, walking from the direction of the subway, carrying a large pizza in its cardboard tray. He goes into the building. Terry gives it five minutes and gets out of the car.

A couple of rings on the doorbell. It opens on the guy standing there, a slice of pizza already in his hand.

'Tim Montgomerie?' Terry asks.

'Yeah?' the guy says, trying to place Terry. A salesman?

Terry brings up the silenced Ruger .22 and shoots him three times in the forehead, the only sound the metallic click of the slide of the automatic, ratcheting softly back and forward. Terry steps over the dead engineer and into the apartment, closing the door behind him, stepping around the spreading pool of blood on the hardwood floor, cocked and alert as he scans the small apartment for any other occupants. Satisfied there are none, he leaves, closing the door behind him.

Terry walks away from the building, back towards his car, the dark street still empty, that dangerous window opposite empty too. The key goes in the ignition and the car moves off. The gun and his gloves go into the East River, down near Hunters Point. Then Terry takes the tunnel back to Manhattan, coming out on FDR Drive, near the UN building, heading north and then west through the night-time neon of Midtown, towards the Plaza.

Now you'd think this meeting would be awkward, wouldn't you? All these people in one room? The blackmailers and the blackmailees. People with competing agendas. Sworn enemies. But no. This is show business, baby. Geffen would sit down with Azoff. Cowell with Fuller. The lion will regularly lie down with the other lion and they'll agree not to eat each other for a bit. For where there is a mountain of cash to be made, there is always the possibility of rapprochement. Granted it was a bit awkward at first, what with the paedo and his victim and the victim's parents and whatnot. But now, after a few hours, with a deal tantalisingly close, I look around and see only harmony – Glen and Bridget Murphy, coked off their nuts, pretending they understand what is going on. Dr Ali, over by the windows, smashing the buffet, having given Lucius a small but calming shot of his milk. Lucius and Connor, reconciled, playing video games on the TV over in the corner. Ruth, Les and Jenny, as ever hunched over their laptops, fingers trilling on the keyboards. Lance Schitzbaul, drunk and belligerent while he huddles with Trellick and Hinckley at the dining table, where our good friend Art is working hard on his 360-degree deal.

Have you heard about such deals? It's a good one. Way back in the day, in my day, in the nineties, record sales were so massive that we record companies were happy to just have that piece of the pie – the same huge piece we'd been taking since recorded sound was invented, since the first field hand crawled out of a Delta swamp and croaked his miserable blues onto a shellac disc. Then, shortly after the year 2000, after Sean Parker said to us 'Hey, cunts, check this out', as CD sales started to decline sharply year after year, we said, 'Hang on a fucking minute. Our piece of the pie appears to be getting tiny.' So we came up with the idea of the 360-degree deal. Another term for it might be 'give us the fucking lot, you tools'. We'd continue to do what record companies have always done – bung you a huge advance and interfere – but now, in return, we get a piece of *everything*. Recording, publishing, touring revenue, merchandise, sync fees, sponsorship and advertising deals. Our piece of the pie was no longer doing it for us so we helped ourselves to a whole bunch of smaller pieces.

'But, Art,' Trellick is saying, patiently trying to explain the distinction between what a label and what a manager does to Mr Pasadena-Have-You-Had-an-Accident-at-Work-I'm-New-to-the-Music-Business, 'that's not our decision. You'll have to broker a separate agreement with Lance to cover that . . .'

'Over my dead fucken body . . .' Schitzbaul says.

'Lance . . .' Trellick says. 'We've already given a lot here.'

'Five fucken per cent of touring and merchandise and Christ knows what else?' Schitzbaul says. 'This *pischer* ...'

Hinckley clicks his pen, smiles, and says, 'At this point I have to make the assumption that your client might never tour again.' He nods towards the bloated form of Du Pre, playing *Tetris* in the corner, oblivious to his financial fate being carved up.

'Look, we'll get the weight off,' I say. 'Right, Ruth?'

'Oh, for sure,' Ruth shouts over from the sofas, not looking up from her laptop. 'I know *the* guy. He does Hanks, DiCaprio.'

'Two per cent,' Lance says.

'Five.' Art.

'Hey, are we out of bagels?' Dr Ali, wandering in the background, useless.

'Guys, come on,' I say. 'Let's make a deal. Art, be a mensch. Take three per cent.'

'How about,' Art says, leaning in, 'Lance gives us three points on all the ancillary stuff – that's a point each for me, Glen and Bridget – and you guys –' meaning me and Trellick, Unigram – 'up our end of the recording revenue from five per cent to six? That's two per cent for each us.' He indicates himself and the Murphys.

Now it is Trellick's turn to colour and splutter. 'Are you fucking kidding me?' he says. 'We are cut to the absolute bone on this bloody deal as it is. I mean –'

'James,' I say, laying a calming hand on his arm.

'*Six points for doing fuck all?*' Trellick continues.

Art leans back in his chair. 'Yes, but it's not "fuck all", is it, James? It's us not sending *this* –' he strokes his brief-case, the one containing the hard drives, the memory sticks, everything – 'to every major news outlet in the USA. I mean, it's great we're all getting along and everything, but let's not forget why we're here ...'

'You lowlife, blackmailing, cocksu—' Trellick begins. I look at him, negotiating as though his life depends on it, and am filled with an unexpected tenderness for him. Something approaching genuine affection. It helps me to finally make a decision I have, frankly, been struggling with.

'OK!' I say, clapping my hands sharply together. 'Listen, everyone, it's late. We're all tired. But no one is leaving this room until we have a deal. So here's what's going to happen. Help yourselves to coffee and Danish and whatnot. Me and James are going to go out and have a huddle and come back in and give you our absolute best position on what Unigram can offer. OK? James? Trellick? Come on. Calm down. Let's take a walk around the block. We'll be back in ten, fifteen minutes.'

Trellick rants and raves about how we are getting fucked on this all the way down in the elevator.

Outside it is a warm, early-June night, just after 2 a.m. by the clock in the lobby, as we cross 59th Street and stroll slowly into Central Park, towards the boating lake. I am dialling a number on my phone while Trellick continues to talk his hardman lawyer stuff to/at me. 'I mean, we're giving the fucking shop away here! What's the point in going through all of this if we're not going to make any fucking cash, Steven? What's the matter with you? I've never seen you this ... this fucking *soft* on a deal before! I mean, you're the fucking owner now! Don't you want to –'

I bring my finger to my lips, shushing him, as my call is answered. 'Terry?' I say. '*Allahu Akbar.*'

I hang up and throw my phone into the lake. Trellick looks at me, thoroughly confused now.

'What the fuck are you —' is as far as he gets.

There is a flash of light. And then the gigantic explosion, bigger than I was anticipating, the shock wave from the blast knocking us both back on our heels, even from here, Trellick actually falling over onto the grass. He looks up, to the fourteenth floor of the Plaza, to the brick dust and mortar spraying into the night sky, great chunks of it crashing to the street, hitting cars, setting off alarms, flames rushing upwards from the windows, glass smashing and tinkling down. There is screaming and crying, people running away from the grand hotel. Trellick is going into shock, 'Oh Jesus, Jesus Christ, what ... what ... ?'

'It was all getting too fucking complicated ...' I say.

Trellick is staring up at me, his pupils massive, still not comprehending, as a shape comes towards us out of the darkness of the park. 'James.' I lean down, putting my hand on his shoulder. He's shaking. 'Pull yourself together. There's a car over there to take you to La Guardia. The jet's ready. Get back to LA. We've got work to do.' He looks over my shoulder, into the face of Terry, who I know is standing behind me now. *This could go either way*, I think. But Trellick starts to laugh.

'Holy. Fucking. Shit,' he says.

FIFTY-EIGHT

Fittingly, given his Christianity, his frequent ponderings on the Bible, God smiled upon Lucius Du Pre. Inside the suite, he was the last person left alive.

Old habits die hard and Lucius had taken advantage of the heated arguments raging between the grown-ups to take Connor into the bathroom, to show him some of the new toys he'd had delivered from FAO Schwarz across the street. They'd done a couple of minutes of foreplay, racing the little electronic fish and ducks up and down the huge tub, and had just been getting going properly when the room came apart, disintegrating around them as the sixty pounds of C4 went off in the hall closet.

Connor Murphy, there on his knees, had died instantly as a heavy marble sink exploded out of the wall behind him, smashing into the back of his skull with all the force of an automobile collision. This impact had the unfortunate effect of forcing young Connor's jaws to shut viciously ...

Lucius had instinctively gone to clutch his groin with both hands, but had found he was unable to do so as his left arm had been sheared off at the shoulder by a piece of flying masonry – blood gouting in a thick stream from the ragged hole at the socket. So it was that Lucius had stumbled screaming (screams Lucius himself could no longer hear of course, his eardrums gone, shredded) from the ruined bathroom and into the hellscape of the lounge, clutching his groin with his one remaining hand, blood spurting from the stump where his penis had formerly been (his penis, the cause of so much torment), as he took in the vista that awaited him through streaming eyes: the walls smeared with gore, the wind in his face, cool night air blowing in along the entire north wall of the suite, all gone now, just a jagged hole and the blackness of Central Park clearly visible beyond. Something had passed Lucius – a ball of flames he did not recognise as his former doctor, who had been at the bar when the wall of spirits was instantly transformed into an inferno. Lucius's feet had knocked into something else and he'd looked down and seen the head of Glen Murphy. Another shape, Glen's wife, Bridget, had been feebly trying to crawl towards her husband's head, but she'd stopped moving, a chunk of brickwork the size of an encyclopedia sticking out of her back. There were people Lucius would not see – Arthur Hinckley, attorney-at-law, Lance Schitzbaul, Freddy, industry legend Ruth Blane, PR extraordinaire, and her team. They were the lucky ones – the ones who had been sitting nearest the closet where the device went off, the ones who had simply become blood and viscera at the speed of light. Lucius collapsed onto the floor and looked up at the blackened ceiling, gratefully losing consciousness as the last of his life ebbed away between the fingers clamped around his groin, from the great wound where his arm had been. God's last favour to Lucius — this oblivion came just before the fireball engulfed the suite, the primary explosion now triggering the secondary devices, the incendiaries hidden around the room, flames consuming everything within it, reducing every corpse to ash, the ash sucked out into the night sky.

About a quarter of a mile away, just a five-minute walk, Chrissy Price was jolted from a deep sleep by the huge explosion that shook the thick windows of Stelfox's apartment. She hurried to the window and saw it to the north — orange flames, torching up into the darkness above the Plaza. *Steven*, she just had time to think as her phone started ringing. Shaking, she slid the bar across. 'It's me.'

'What ... what's happening?'

'I'm OK. Take it easy. I'll be home in five.'

FIFTY-NINE

We spend the next week at my apartment, the TV in the living room tuned to CNN, the one in the bedroom to Fox. Having anticipated the insane security lockdown that would be taking place in the city – especially in my building – and knowing that the housekeeper or any delivery services would not be allowed access for a while, I took the precaution of making sure the fridges and freezers were heavily stocked with food and drink. There are boxes and boxes of stuff from Dean & Deluca: quiches, chilli, lasagnes, sandwiches, cold cuts.

On the rolling news channels the story of the worst terror attack on New York City since 9/11 gradually unfolds. Thirty-two people killed. Two floors of the hotel destroyed. The huge device, placed in a closet in a suite on the fourteenth floor, the suite being rented by one Mr McCann, who has no backstory anyone can track down. Then the CCTV footage emerges of the man in the Plaza lobby ...

The mysterious Dr Ali, his grainy, pixelated, Arabic face appearing constantly on all the news channels, the time-sequenced shots of him walking across the foyer, carrying a heavy backpack, his form slowly becoming as familiar as the smirking features of Mohamed Atta, slinking through Logan in his dark blue shirt.

He checked into the hotel the day before the attack.

He had just returned from an unexplained trip to Quatain: a known terrorist proving ground.

He had a history of drinking and failed marriages. He was once physician to celebrities including the late Lucius Du Pre.

He was a sand negro. A dune coon. A fucking Muzzer.

The raid on his coastal home in Malibu turns up the inevitable materials: casings, timers and the like. The film of C4 explosive in his bathtub. His hard drive is a treasure trove of jihad, of crash courses in bombmaking, of extremist thinking: the well-worn copy of the Quran in his bedside drawer, some of the fierier, juicier, kill-all-unbelievers passages heavily underlined. (Internet rumours immediately begin that this Dr Ali was innocent. That he was a patsy for a darker conspiracy. People on message boards and chat rooms point out that Lucius Du Pre's ex-manager and a high-profile Hollywood PR woman died in the attack. These accusations are treated like the left-wing conspiracy theories they are. Like the accusations of Russian involvement in the election they are shouted down, drowned out in the nationwide roar of *fuck all Muslims*.)

The president, of course, *goes fucking bananas.*

He is most obviously outraged that a 'beautiful' building — a building that he routinely points out he once owned, that, contrary to the fake news media, he made a 'tremendous profit' on – has been destroyed. But more than this he is gleeful, gloating. Saying how he could have prevented all of this if only the weak, liberal courts had respected his travel ban, a ban which is now back, new and improved, with Quatain added to the list. It is not a good time to worship Allah in America. Attacks on his people skyrocket in the days after the attack. Mosques are smashed. Hijabs are ripped off faces in the street. Last night an angry mob, head to toe in chinos, polo shirts and red MAGA caps and waving flaming torches, marched from Central Park up into Harlem, provoking a full-scale riot in which four people were shot and killed, the violence swelling, engulfing the country, Chrissy weeping in the blue light of the TV while we lie wrapped in Frette sheets, drinking whiskey. The whole country is placed on Defcon 2, cocked like a pistol. Ready for war. I do my bit to help all of this of course, posting like mad on the old sock puppet accounts: 'MUSLIMS GO HOME.' 'MAGA'. I post Pepe the Frogs all over the show. Trump is never off the TV – his yard-long necktie swinging, his face red, flecks of spittle flying from his mouth, both of his hands constantly wanking tiny invisible men as he talks about what is going to be done to the worshippers of the ideology that fostered this egregious attack on America, about the warm work that will be done at Guantánamo and in other, secret, locations. From the way Trump is talking it seems like the treatment suspected Islamic terrorists were getting prior to the Plaza Hotel bombing was on a par with a spa weekend at one of his hotels. I mean, fuck waterboarding, he's talking car batteries and hacksaws. Racks, Judas cradles and iron maidens. He's talking about nuking Quatain. (Less reported in the Western media, understandably, they've had their hands full, has been the attack – suspected to be the work of Israeli extremists, in actual fact a crack squad of mercenaries subcontracted by Terry – on the home of the Sultan of Quatain. An attack that left the Sultan, his son and all of his staff dead. Also on the news, but far less reported, has been the murder of a Mr Brandon Krell, CFO of Unigram, who was shot and killed on the doorstep of his home in Santa Monica, California, the night before the Plaza bombing. Oh, another thing. Not in the news at all, reported nowhere, is the fact that Norwegian Dance Crew quietly signed to Unigram for 90,000 dollars.)

And there has been warm work for me too.

The day after the attack, via an intermediary, we slip the track to a junior producer at Fox and they use it on the evening news the following night, the ghostly voice of Lucius Du Pre soundtracking the heartbreaking footage from New York City – the ruined facade of the hotel, the body bags being brought out, the grieving wives, husbands and children – as he sings, '*Oh say can you see, by the dawn's early light, what so proudly we hailed at the twilight's last glooming?*' The slow, hypnotic backbeat unfurling at 60-odd bpm, the perfect tempo for soothing, for healing. The track goes nuclear. Within a few days you are hearing it everywhere you go. In diners. In taxis. In shops. At football games. It is streamed over a *billion* times on Spotify alone within a single week, pissing all over the Sheerans, the Biebers and the Drakes. Needless to say *The Resurrection* – the 'new' Du Pre album I have cobbled together from out-takes and odds and sods – will be ready to go by the end of the month. We are expecting record business.

Unigram's share price rockets.

One morning towards the end of that hot week of enforced captivity I wake very early, around 4 a.m. Still dark outside. Chrissy comes out to find me sitting by the huge picture window in the living room, looking over to the Plaza, drinking coffee.

She wraps her arms around me from behind. Down below us, in the blackness, is the small gaggle of protesters who have been there all week, in their cheap clothes, clutching their handmade signs. ('Love Trumps Hate' etc.) The New York night – as it always is, but even more so right now – is rent by the whoop and gulp of sirens, the red and blue circles strobing up from the canyon depths far below. The corner at Central Park South is still a major crime scene, the phalanx of police and ambulance vehicles ringed by the (fake) news trucks, CNN, ABC, MSNBC and all the rest of it. 'I can't believe you have an apartment in this fucking building,' she says again, still scandalised.

I bought the place ten years ago, when I first started making what I thought was real money, for 3.5 million dollars. It's one of the very rare 'J' apartments in Trump Tower, occupying the building's premier corner with spectacular views of Central Park and the George Washington Bridge to the north, grand sweeps west and south capturing panoramic views of the city. Of course, needless to say, I've hardly been here in the last year or so, given all the protesters and the Secret Service and the constant media presence and the tourists clogging the lobby and all the rest of the nonsense that's happened since the big man

descended the escalator down in the lobby and said '*have
some of this, cunts*'. I was actually thinking about selling it,
but, given recent events, I've developed a sentimental,
almost talismanic fondness for the place. More sirens erupt
below, heading along West 57th Street towards the site of
the atrocity.

'You know what?' Chrissy says, off those sirens, sighing,
pressing her already swelling belly into my back. 'I think
we're doing the right thing. I mean, is this any kind of
world to bring a child into?' The abortion – all booked for
tomorrow.

What kind of world is it?

It is, I think to myself, a wonderful world. A place where
ambition still outstrips talent. Where common decency is
about as common as Minotaur eggs. Where the kind and
the weak are ripped apart like loaves of bread, like
Cambodian babies in the streets of Phnom Penh in April
'75 (top lad Pol Pot). Where lefties and snowflakes –
increasingly as rare as Minotaur eggs themselves, as rare as
young Chrissy here, even now snuggling herself into my
armpit for the warmth – gather in huddles in corners of
the Internet and tell themselves that, although things are
bad right now, although hatred and intolerance seem to be
on the rise, this is a blip. That people are fundamentally
decent and honest and kind and that good will out. They
do not know, or refuse to understand, that the blip is the
size of several continents now and is going to go on for a
long, long time, a tiki-torch parade of screaming white
faces stretching into infinity. A world where might is not
only right, it is all. Where money doesn't just talk, or swear,
it *nukes*. It daisy-cuts. It levels all before it. The work is

done – even the poor think the poor are fucking cunts nowadays. It is a world whose richest, most powerful inhabitant cuts about stripped to the waist fighting tigers and shit while he burns families out of their homes to make way for pipelines and has his enemies killed. (*So what? You don't think we're killers too?*) I am thinking of the tax breaks – both corporate and personal – that, with a little luck, I will be getting in the Trump administration's first full budget. I am thinking of the BBC news report I caught from back home the other morning, the graph that showed the areas in the north-east of England who are going to be worst hit economically by Brexit. I'm thinking about all of the *Untermensch*, the no-marks, the zero-net-worth tolers who will be kicked off Medicare, who will lose their homes, who will see the pittance in their miserable pay packets shrivel to nothing, who will soon be living in a global Caymans – paying eight quid for a packet of fish fingers – and who fucking *voted* for it, and I find I am getting an erection.

I am wondering how all of this will mesh with my sale of Unigram. The unknown unknowns. Trellick does not know that he is about to have the shortest career as chairman of a major conglomerate in music industry history. He does not know about the fire sale that will soon be happening over at the company: our back catalogue sold off to Universal or Warners, our many prime parcels of real estate all across the globe turned into apartments and shopping centres. The boys over at Stern, Hammler & Gersh have got it all nailed down to the last telephone, computer terminal and company car. Turn it and burn it. Pop and chop. Break it up into tiny pieces and sell it all off to the highest bidder. SH&G are estimating that, with the currently enhanced share price, my piece of the sale should, at the very least, quadruple my 200-million-pound investment. Eight hundred sterling. Even at the current spot rate of 1.31 USD to the quid (I'm checking it half-hourly and know my broker can do better than this) that's exactly 1,054,683,009 and fifteen cents. It's there. Done. A billion dollars.

I am looking online into the kind of yachts that will cause Geffen to crane his neck upwards in astonishment, a shadow falling over his deck as my boat (the *Lebensraum*) comes in to dock next to him in the Tobago Quays this winter. The look on his face as he sees me - spitting down at him, shouting, telling him to get in the fucking oven. And, yes, with all of this comes the chilling thought – what then? What next? And, it occurs to me, I now know the answer to that one too.

About the size of my pinkie now. By the end of this week, week fourteen, he'll be three inches in length. He'd fit cosily into the cupped palm of your hand. Although Chrissy is unable to feel his movements yet, he's all over the place at this point, arms and legs waving, body wriggling. A proper hooligan. Feeling his oats, testing his new powers, his external sexual organs beginning to emerge, penis and scrotum, I contemplate for a moment the grief these could cause, the untold pain, misery and damage he might inflict with them. The tears and the suffering and the rows and the fights and the balled hankies clenched in trembling fists. *That's my boy. Go on, my son. Where's your tool?* His brain is forming, waiting for the input only I can provide. Because it turns out that in the end, even I, the

Übermensch, am not immune to it. To the primal, the oldest, impulse. An heir to the empire. Someone to be moulded in my own, fine image. Someone who understands what the world is, how and why men do the things they do. Someone who ...

'Chrissy,' I say softly, turning, 'let's have the baby.'

Her lip starts to go as she collapses into my chest, sobbing, the warm tears of gratitude soaking my shirt, her whole what-about-my-career-I'm-too-young-what-a-world-we-live-in spiel blown apart in an instant. Because her decision-making, her true desires, are not being driven by career logic, or age considerations, or political concerns about the state of the world in the early twenty-first century. They are being driven by the lunacy nature has packed into her stomach – the demented piping of the fallopian tubes, the ovaries, the womb. *You're carrying a bag around inside you whose sole purpose is to create another human.* That'd pretty much do it for you on the logical thought front, wouldn't it? That alone would drive you fucking insane. 'Are ... are you sure?' she says finally.

'Yeah,' I say. 'It'll all be fine.'

She takes a deep breath, then reaches for the words.

'I love you, Steven.'

I take Chrissy's face in my hands, up there by the window, high over Fifth Avenue. I look into her brown eyes, hot and trusting, like a puppy's, as I say the only thing to be said – 'I love you too.'

I fold her into my arms while, behind me, out past Queens, past Long Island, out over the Atlantic, a beautiful June dawn is beginning to break ('*Oh say can you see ...*'), pink summer light starting to fall across

Manhattan, spreading slowly from east to west, like spilled blood, flooding the dark trenches between the skyscrapers.

Morning in America.

Epilogue

Cedars-Sinai Hospital, Los Angeles. Monday 4 December 2017

It's a little after 7 a.m. I'm stretched out on the sofa, tired, shoes off, with coffee and iPad, as I shuffle between the trades – *Variety*, *Billboard*, *Deadline* – and the newspapers, *LA Times*, *New York Times*. The big story this morning is '*HOUSE OF CARDS* WILL RESUME PRODUCTION WITHOUT SPACEY'. I mean, he's finished, isn't he? Went full Du Pre. Tried to smash some fourteen-year-old actor kid's back door in. You can't help but feel sorry for the poor cunt, can you? Here he is just doing what every vaguely famous toerag has done for generations – openly using his celebrity to whip his cock out on some starry-eyed teenager and suddenly he's in fucking hiding? Largely, let's face it, because he's an iron. I mean, Elvis was all over Priscilla when she was fourteen and it was all good. Or here's old Bill Wyman back in the day, walking about free as a bird with the fourteen-year-old Mandy Smith, the bloody great

335

smirk on his face telling everyone, 'I'm right up this skank and there's fuck all anyone is going to do about it.' Or Jimmy Page in 1973, falling out of some LA nightclub with the fourteen-year-old Lori Maddox on his arm, dragging her back to the Hyatt for a proper beasting while the whole world looks on and says, 'Go on, my son, give her one from me.' But when you're a bender pummelling some teenager you're not one of the lads, are you? You're automatically just a straight-up fucking paedo.

I look at my watch and wonder how it can be taking so fucking long. It's been three hours since they wheeled Chrissy off to the delivery room around 4 a.m. We are, naturally – or rather, unnaturally – having an elective Caesarean. (I mean, come on. Throwing a sausage down a hall? Waving a flag in space? Fuck that.) I also made it very clear from the outset that while she would obviously have the best care money can shoulder others aside to give you, I would emphatically *not* be in attendance while the kid was born. I do not need to be looking at that atrocity, some unholy cross between an abattoir and a butcher's shop on fire.

Mind you, fuck Spacey, it's dark times for the lads too. Weinstein a couple of months back. I've had my moments, don't get me wrong, we all get a bit lively now and then, but it looks like Harvey was basically trying to rape anything that fucking moved. As they say, he'd come to your house and the fish would stop swimming. You've got to kind of admire it, haven't you? The sheer work ethic. In addition to making tons of films and winning Oscars and all that shit, Harvey was also up at the crack of dawn getting his cock out at every given opportunity. As well as reading all

those scripts and dealing with financing and budgeting and
hiring and firing, he was having to plot and scheme to find
ways to drag some young chick back to his lair and wander
out of his bathroom naked, or with his robe hanging open.
Then all the time and energy needed to meet with the
lawyers and deal with all the NDAs and the pay-offs, to
meet with the PR people and the private detectives to work
out your counter-attacks and dig dirt up on your accusers.
As I said, I like pumping and sucking and grinding as much
as the next man. Maybe not as much as I did in the crazy
days of my twenties and thirties, when, let's face it, guys,
most of us are running around like a cross between Ron
Jeremy and Peter Sutcliffe, but to like it to a Harvey degree?
And he was doing all this in the nineties and noughties,
when he was in his forties, his *fifties*. The commitment. The
passion.

The Donald, of course, has had a bunch of slags trying
to say for ages that he had a pop. Even his own ex-wife
reckoned he raped her but then (obviously) saw it slightly
differently when a massive fucking cheque appeared. Then,
just last month, it was Brett Ratner, Louis CK. It turned
out that what a lot of these dudes liked to do was to get
their cocks out and pull the head off it in front of some
sobbing cow. I've seen a few people arguing that this was
all about humiliating the women. I don't know. I'm not
sure. I mean, granted, I am not the world's leading expert
on feminist theories of sexuality and power, but I reckon
if you're standing there, softening cock in hand as a few
drops of your own rapidly cooling spunk patter onto your
bare foot, then there's an argument to be had about exactly
who is getting humiliated here. Whatever, it seems like

the boilers have finally had enough. Time's up. It's them too. This will not stand any more. The grand traditions by which men have lived for centuries – that if you have enough cash and/or fame you can basically use whoever you like as a human toilet whenever it takes your fancy – are on their way out. Well, you read this stuff – in the *Guardian*, in the *Washington Post*, in the glossy monthlies – and then you go out. Like the other night. Trellick (we're all good by the way, tighter than ever. His small block of shares cleared him somewhere in the region of sixty million dollars) and some of the lads took me out for a drink to celebrate the closing of the Unigram sale and we wound up attending the opening night of some new club in West Hollywood.

It was the usual – through the velvet ropes, through the crowded bar and dance floor, and then into the cool peace of the VIP lounge. Huge white sofas, table service and an ice bucket full of magnums of Grey Goose and Dom Perignon at five hundred bucks a pop. Soon enough, it began: the bouncers, parading a steady stream of girls from the main club past our table. They'd smile coyly. The hotter ones got asked to join us. The girls started hitting the booze. The bar sales went up. The bouncers got tipped. The bar staff got tipped. The girls got free drinks and we got ... well. Everyone gets paid. It is the American dream in microcosm and it is beautiful.

And these girls, the young girls who're fruiting about West Hollywood nightclubs at 2 a.m. on a Tuesday night, the ones getting off the bus from Omaha, or Boise, Idaho, getting off the plane from Latvia or Ukraine, let me tell you, I don't think they've been getting the message. I don't think they're reading the *Guardian* or the *Washington Post*. Because, in return for a few double vodkas and the promise of a reading for a non-existent pilot, they would literally suck your balls out through your urethra and store them in their cheeks like a crazed hard-gobbling squirrel getting ready for winter. Me too? *Fuck you.*

I put the paper down and look around the room: at the double bed, the wet bar, the fridge-freezer, stocked with food and drink, the rich carpeting and soft lighting. There's even a little Christmas tree in the corner. (Although the weather outside continues to do its LA thing: a soupy twenty-one degrees.) Indeed, the only clues that we are in a hospital are provided by the chart at the foot of the bed and the array of drips (saline, etc.) hanging in their translucent pouches by the headboard, in case they're needed later. This room is costing four thousand dollars a night. The birth of my son will end up costing me somewhere in the low six figures. Entry to the world, American-style.

But this is not a problem, I think, as I turn to look again at the huge flat-screen TV glowing with the sound down, showing Fox News. The coverage is still, as it has been for forty-eight hours straight, all about the new tax bill, which passed on Saturday. God bless Trump. 1.5 trillion dollars in cuts. It's early days, and it's complicated – we're currently moving the money from the sale of Uniggram around the world like it's Phineas Fogg on speed – but the boys at Stern, Hammler & Gersh reckon that, very conservatively, the new bill will save me a minimum of three hundred million dollars in taxes over the next two years. That's about half the cost of building the

Lebensraum right there. It's good news all round in fact – the average American family will be a thousand bucks a year better off. For a while. After that ... maybe not so much.

Laugh? I nearly bought a fucking round.

There's a soft knocking at the door and then it's opening and Dr Rosenstein, our obstetrician, is coming in. I sit up.

He's in a gown, with a surgical mask pulled down around his throat, and I am relieved to see there is no hint of blood or gore on his smocks. 'Mr Stelfox ...' he begins and I notice, with alarm, that his voice has a catch in it, fear, lodged somewhere in his throat. His hands are trembling as he sits down in the armchair by the bed, opposite me. He looks at me with pale grey eyes as I say, 'What?'

'I ... there's been a complication. This ... this very rarely happens ...'

I feel the floor sliding away, my stomach falling. What to hope for? *Who* to hope for? Who has died or is dying right now, somewhere along the corridor, surrounded by millions of dollars of technology and technicians? Chrissy or the baby? Who to root for? My mind is making calculations about full-time nannies and boarding schools alarmingly quickly. 'Is the baby all –' I begin.

'They're both fine. Perfectly healthy. Sorry, I didn't mean to alarm you. It's just, it's ...' He swallows. I've about had it with this cunt.

'*What?*' I say.

He begins talking.

Two or three minutes later I am being led along the corridor, shuffling, stunned, looking like someone who has survived an aeroplane crash, someone who cannot believe they are still here, still walking around. I am led through swinging doors into the delivery suite, the only coherent thoughts in my head to do with the 95 per cent accuracy small print he claims I would have been told, to do with lawyers and lawsuits, suing and countersuing. Chrissy is there on the bed, white as milk, as pale as an indie kid, as she cuddles the reddish-pink bundle. She looks up at me, shaking her head in astonishment at the turn of events, laughing a little now as she turns the bundle towards me, holding it out, offering it to me, the folds of bloody towelling falling aside, allowing me to see it briefly, the protuberant, lipped mound, bald, recognisable to me from pornography, from hookers.

'It's a girl,' she says.

Chrissy hands me my daughter and, taking in my astonished, utterly vacant face, adds, smiling, woozy, addled from the meds, 'Who knew? Five per cent chance the ultrasound was wrong. I'm still really happy, Steven.' I take a moment, breathing deeply, trying not to faint, feeling the sightless thing writhing and kicking in my arms, feeling the eyes of Chrissy, Rosenstein, the two nurses upon me as I clear my throat.

'Me too,' I say, numb.